THE
Evening News
COLLECTION

THE
Evening News
COLLECTION

With an Introduction by
Monica Dickens

Conceived by Mark Williams

CHAPMANS
1991

Chapmans Publishers Ltd
141–143 Drury Lane
London WC2B 5TB

BRITISH LIBRARY CATALOGUING IN PUBLICATION DATA
The Evening news collection 2
I. Williams, Mark
823.0108 [FS]

ISBN 1–85592–004–2

First published by Chapmans 1991

Phototypeset by Intype, London
Printed and bound in Great Britain by
Cox & Wyman Ltd, Reading

Introduction

MONICA DICKENS

The *Evening News* first hit the London streets and stations in 1894. From the start, the paper always gave its readers fiction; a short story weekly at first, then three times a week, and then daily for years, by popular demand.

This book is the second collection of these stories. Here are sixty of the best by an entertaining mixture of writers, some already well known when they wrote for the *News*, some unknowns who went on to become successful after this evening paper, which could sell a million copies in its heyday, gave them their chance.

Fifteen hundred words was the paper's strict limit (although I note that C. S. Forester and H. E. Bates got away with almost twice that length). The style is almost universally concise and crisply to the point, economical, with no self-indulgent superfluous conversations, or bypaths meandering off after minor characters. These are short shorts with a minimum of description, and 'fine writing' bravely resisted. None of the vignettes or mood pieces that can pass for short stories today, no danglers or open ends to put a large burden of work on the reader – to stimulate his creative imagination (euphemism for: author doesn't know how to tie up the plot). In the earlier pieces, short sentences and brief paragraphs reveal the enormous influence of Ernest Hemingway.

Dialogue follows the classic requirement: 'If it doesn't move the story along or tell you something necessary about the characters

– it doesn't belong.' There is almost always an unexpected and stimulating twist at the end. There are no clues missing or too diabolically disguised, so that you can enjoy guessing what the payoff will be, and have your enjoyment then doubled by a very cunning reverse twist in the tail that proves you wrong.

Nipping along, the stories don't always have the time to worry about getting all technical details absolutely correct and feasible. You may wonder: how would the robber's accomplice, planted as a workman in the target mansion, find out the combination of the safe that held the diamonds? If he did, why wouldn't he have grabbed them himself and scarpered? How did the destitute old man know so much about the violin? Would a young chemist in a laboratory be able to get her hands on deadly poison? Never mind; she did. Hence Herbert Harris's 'Dangerous Bend', which enthralled thousands of commuters on the train home from work.

Edward Campbell, literary editor of the *Evening News* for twenty-five years until it was assassinated in 1980 for reasons only understood by newspaper proprietors, had to defend his short stories almost daily from sports and features editors and others who were jealous of the fiction space, and its confounded popularity. At one point, John Gold, the editor, dropped the story in exasperation. The outcry was alarming. Sacks of vituperative mail clogged the passages. The switchboard was jammed. The *Evening News* short story was quietly reinstated within three weeks.

Edward Campbell knew what readers wanted, and where to get it for them. He was a meal ticket for dozens of struggling authors, and a secure repository for people who were between jobs, like comedians Spike Milligan and Peter Sellers. The weekly and monthly magazine market for fiction was certainly rosier than it is now, but Edward Campbell's newspaper was offering a story *every day*, and to a large readership. Many writers he never met blessed his name. For some, he remains the person an author never forgets, because he gave them their first chance, which perhaps changed their lives and condemned them to the seductive, solitary, secret world of their desks.

Margaret Webb, whose neat, surprising 'Postscript to a Betrayal' is the only supernatural entry here, sold her first story to the *Evening News*. So did Terry Tapp, although it did take

vi

another twenty rejected stories before he sold a second to touch Edward Campbell.

Even Campbell's scribbled rejection slips were worth having. Although he was a frantically busy man, daily swamped with unsolicited manuscripts, his 'The editor regrets . . .' usually contained a helpful nugget.

'Remember that a short story is not just a story that is short. There's more to it than that.' He perfectly understood its anatomy and energy, and his brisk editorial suggestions were partly responsible for the pith and polish of the stories he printed.

'You come up with really enterprising plots, but I still can't quite believe the ending.' If he found real merit in a story, he would work patiently with its author until it came right.

'Forget the purple writing . . .'

'You can't cheat the reader by saying it was "only a dream".'

'The average commuter doesn't have time for complex plots. He'll simply turn to the crossword.'

'The twist must derive logically from earlier elements which have been dropped so guilefully that the reader fails to notice their possible signalling of an alternative rationale.'

That might have frightened me off, but it was after my time. My story, 'The Tired Old Man', appeared in 1946.

During World War II when I was nursing in a London hospital, I sometimes used to take a bus to Kew in my off-duty and lie on the grass to eat a sandwich (butter eked out with soya bean flour) and read and sleep. I must have watched someone else sleeping on the restorative lawns and perhaps I daydreamed idly, 'What if he was not asleep, but dying?' Could I save his life and be a heroine? 'OFF-DUTY NURSE ON MERCY MISSION' – would even Matron be proud of me? If he was already dead, would I be called to give evidence at the inquest – brief bittersweet fame?

I don't remember. Actually, I don't even remember writing this story.

A very good Arthur C. Clarke has been chosen: 'The Trouble with Time', revealing in his laconic, take-it-or-leave-it way that there were tourists on Mars already in 1961, and all the irritating extra problems and risks that tourists create – although this was long before there were security checks at Heathrow.

Herbert Harris wrote one hundred and twelve stories for the *Evening News* and fifty-six for the *Evening Standard*, once gleefully appearing in both rival papers on the same day. He also got himself into *The Guinness Book of Records* as the most prolific story-teller in Britain. Not surprising that his entries here, 'Dangerous Bend' and 'Ratcatcher', are so smooth and accomplished. You think you know what he's up to, but at the last minute he derails you with a shocking surprise. A satisfying one though. Villainy is its own reward. Everyone likes a nice comeuppance.

Peter Sellers got his first stage job by phoning a producer and recommending himself for a part in the voices of two well-known actors. His story 'The Wastrel' is a bit of a spoof too, on the stiff-upper-lip Englishman with a ne'er-do-well son. He teases the reader and he's teased the editor too, by promising the necessary final twist and then backing off and washing his hands of the whole affair.

Sellers and Spike Milligan, who appears here with a pawnshop story from the sixties, were taking a break from writing radio scripts for *The Goon Show*, dodderingly believed to be titled *The Go On Show* by an exalted BBC pedant.

Leslie Thomas, who talked himself into a reporter's job on the *Evening News* while being handed a prize in one of its story competitions, wrote thirteen short stories for the paper before he hit fame and fortune with his 1966 book *The Virgin Soldiers*, which came out of his youthful stint in National Service. 'Short Measure', chosen for this collection, is touching, attractively simple, and woos your sympathy. Examining her humdrum life, a woman is dismayed to find herself so drearily on the shelf. Why does the vicar laugh at her?

The story by C. S. Forester, 'The Brand of Eve', was written in 1938, before he went into the Navy, or became well known. It's a funny, lovely, innocent story of a young girl's first kiss – and the consequences that imprint themselves upon her. But he never saw himself as a short story writer. He was to become famous for his books about the sea. After the Air Force won acclaim for the Battle of Britain, the Royal Navy wanted some good propaganda for itself to distribute to neutral countries like Sweden and Switzerland. They made enough rationed paper available to Forester and he obliged them by writing *The Ship*. They responded by complaining that the manuscript contained several technical mistakes. Forester unconcernedly suggested that they check them out, and was not surprised to receive an official letter: 'Their Lordships at The Admiralty regret that they ever queried anything that Mr Forester has written.'

The popular Hornblower novels were prompted by E. V. Lucas at Methuen, who wanted a book about Napoleon. Forester gave him *Brown on Resolution*, which they rejected as 'only a boys' book'. It remained unsold until J. B. Priestly spotted the manuscript and got it published. That book and all the subsequent Hornblower stories brought C. S. Forester tremendous success, but he remained always delightfully modest. Towards the end of his life, when asked what success meant to him, he said, 'It only means I can hail a taxi without feeling guilty and extravagant.'

'The Source of the World' is a splendid 1955 example of the genuine pastoral H. E. Bates. Since his death, he has been rediscovered by the television adaptation of his crudely comic Pop Larkin and his renegade family in *The Darling Buds of May*. Its popularity is somewhat ironic, since Bates was never beloved for the Larkin stories. They were a division that gained him some readers who wanted an easy laugh at the spiv culture of the sixties, but disappointed the thousands of faithful followers who wanted more of his evocative country stories. The one chosen here is a small boy's fantasy. It will take for ever to walk to the source of the river. Cloud masses become blue mountains, tiny brook fish are giant flat plaice, a one-eyed man a magical curiosity.

'Bartimeus' was the pseudonym of a captain in the Royal Navy. His story 'The Simple Sailor' appeared in 1949. Reading it on a page copied from the original *Evening News* of that year, I was sidetracked by a reminder of how long after the end of the war we were still lumbered with food shortages and rationing. Of course. Unemployment figures were bad enough without swamping them with all those clerks at the Ministry of Food.

In 1949 I note, we were glad to learn how to make Mock Cream, out of margarine, milk and hot water. Well, there is nothing ersatz about this second volume of *Evening News* short stories, selected with such obvious care by Mark Williams.

Contents

xi

xii

The Tired Old Man

MONICA DICKENS

In the dry flower-bed, not six feet away from where Winifred lay on the daisied grass, two sparrows were taking dust baths. Each had scrabbled a separate hole, and when it had fluttered there for a while, hopped over to sample the bath of the other. Winifred, lying on her side, lifted her gaze to the lawn beyond with its backcloth of rhododendrons, massed together like great coloured sponges.

The old man was still lying at the edge there, among the fallen petals. Poor old man; he must be tired. He had hardly stirred since they came by him an hour ago.

David had hardly stirred either. He was lying with his head fitted into the hollow of her waist above her hipbone, the solid blue glare of the sky quavering on his closed eyelids. It was many weeks since he had lain like this in the sun. He was a research chemist and for the last few months he had been working so intensively under his fanatical old chief that weekends did not exist, mealtimes were sandwiches snatched at the end of the bench, and a working day lasted for as long as you could keep your eyes open.

But now it was finished, the report written, and Winifred was showing him the kind of things he had been missing.

'I've been coming here nearly every evening,' she said. 'The peace after the crowds in town! That's what's so wonderful about

Kew. Thousands of people may have paid their money at the gate, yet you can get right away on your own under a hedge like this, and never see a soul. If it wasn't for hearing the buses in the distance you'd never know you were in London, would you? Let's come here a lot after we're married. We could bring our tea out. Isn't the grass fresh? And the leaves so crisp and light and green. You've missed the blossom though; it's never been so good as this year, one of the gardeners told me. And the smell! I used to sit under the trees where it had fallen. The May was like confetti.'

Winifred had been brought up to enjoy Nature vocally.

David was disconcertingly different. He would look at a view for a few minutes, then, while everyone else was still exclaiming and pointing things out, he would turn away without a word, so that you never knew whether he thought it had been worth that long pull up the hill or not.

All he did now was nuzzle his head deeper into her waist and grunt, 'Who did you come with?'

'Alone, of course,' she said, 'since I couldn't be with you. Oh look, now those sparrows have flown off together into that tree. I wonder if they're husband and wife. Darling couldn't we have twin baths in our flat, so that we could talk to each other? I never seem to get enough time to talk to you.'

'You can talk now,' he murmured, and fell asleep.

While he slept she looked at the bright green treetops against the bright blue sky and thought, if those two colours were together in a dress they wouldn't go at all, yet in a tree and the sky they're perfect. In fact, the colour of each is at its most beautiful just where it meets the other. She could tell David this; it seemed to be intelligent enough. He never wanted her to be clever, but she had noticed that when she did happen to make an original *or* intelligent remark, he was pleased with her, and it often inspired him to talk.

She loved it when he talked; on and on sometimes, with a wonderful flow of words. She did not always understand all of it, but she had to keep alert to make the right interpolations. If she said something which showed that she had missed the point, he would stop talking abruptly, as if he had been snubbed, and look at her with that expression which made her feel he was miles and miles away from her.

She would not wake him to tell him her thought about the trees and the sky. It upset him very much to be wakened when he had dozed off. He was so short on sleep, poor darling. She projected all her willpower at the gardener with the mowing machine, daring him to come any nearer.

David's head of soft, ungreased hair, to which he did not often spare the time for cutting, was pressing into where she thought her liver was, and giving her a stitch. Gently, she lifted his head between her two hands, shifted her body and sat upright, laying his head in her lap.

'Mm . . . mm . . .' he murmured, like a drowsy child, then gave a fretful little moan as he felt her stiffen.

'Oh, David, David!' she called in alarm. 'David, I'm sorry, but do wake up.'

He sat up, scowling and pushing back his hair, shaking his head like a man coming up from under water. 'What on earth – ? I had just got off to sleep.'

'I know, darling, but it's that old man over there by the rhododendrons, the one who was sleeping, I'm sure he's ill.'

He turned on one elbow and squinted across the lawn. 'Looks all right to me. He's still sleeping – lucky beggar.' He plunged his head back into her lap and closed his eyes.

'No, but just now he sort of raised himself up in the most horrible way with his back arched and coughed. I saw his eyes. He looked awful. Look, he's twitching now. Do go and see if he's all right.'

'Probably had a nightmare. Don't fuss. Win, I'm not a doctor, anyway.'

'But you know about ill people.'

'I'm not a St John Ambulance man, I'm a very tired chemist who's just perfected an important stage in the preparation of a drug. That old man will appreciate me in a few years' time, when he's cured of some revolting carbuncle.'

'A few years will be too late. Oh, darling, I'm serious; do go and see if you can do anything for him.'

'Why don't you go?'

3

'I wouldn't know what to do.'

'Go and ask him if he's all right.'

'I don't like to go,' she said doubtfully, wanting to go, yet not wanting to go without David's approval; afraid, half of the old man, half that David would think her silly.

'Well, neither do I like to,' said David, in the final tone of one who says goodnight for the last time. 'One doesn't butt in on people who've come to Kew for a quiet sleep. And since you won't let *me* sleep – come here!'

He pulled her down and began to kiss her. She tried to forget the old man. It would be dreadful if David thought she was thinking of something else while he was kissing her.

On their way to the gate, hand in hand across the long shadows, they had to pass the old man. He was dead. He looked as if he was sinking into the earth already. Everything about him was caved in, except the slate ridge of his nose. It was superfluous for David to drop on one knee beside him.

He said, 'Don't look darling,' with an attempt at gallantry.

Winifred had to look. After all, she had seen him die.

'While we were kissing, he was dying,' she whispered.

She had not meant David to hear, but he looked round and up at her quite irritably as if she had said something tactless.

She did not say: 'If only you had gone to him,' but he spoke as if she had, defensively. 'I couldn't have done anything for him.'

'No, no, of course not.'

'He must have been too far gone already,' he went on, pressing for the absolution which he desperately wished she could give him. She did not want him to be in the wrong. He was always the one who was right; she liked it so in everything.

'We must tell someone,' she said, looking round helplessly. 'What ought we to do?'

He stood up. 'We needn't say anything. They'll find him soon. We don't want to get involved; it would mean an inquest – all sorts of complications. And we couldn't help him now.'

He should not have said that, with the accent on the *now*, as if he admitted that he could have helped him before. They looked at each other for an instant. They were miles apart, strangers on distant peaks, divided by a desolate valley in which the old man,

4

accusingly, lay dead. David stopped with a half gesture, as if to tidy the outflung hand, bloodless as a chicken's claw. Then he stood up again without touching it and stepped back.

'Let's go,' he said, and walked away without looking to see if she were following.

On their way out every bird in the Gardens was singing; a brick wall glowed like an apricot in the setting sun which silhouetted the lawns into individual blades of grass. A flower-bed was like uncorked scent bottles, but they would never come to Kew again.

In the bus, they sat a little apart, as if the spectre of the old man sat between them, as indeed it did, triumphantly pushing them farther and farther apart in a crisis which should have brought them together. She tried to talk of other things, of anything, lest he should take her silence for reproach. But going over the bridge, instead of saying something about the barges, she burst out, 'Oh, David, he looked at us. He didn't want to die alone.'

'I couldn't have done anything,' he repeated stubbornly.

'I feel as if we'd killed him, David.'

What was she about? She was supposed to champion him, support him, comfort him, encourage him in everything he did. She was no use to him if she could not do that.

The bus reached the crest of the bridge and tilted downwards.

'Don't cry,' David said quite kindly, and put out a hand across the immense space between them. 'He's probably better off like this.'

She did not tell him that she was not crying for the old man but because she did not think, now, that they would ever be married.

The Cat with One Life

NIGEL MORLAND

The situation in the home of Monsieur Jean Bajouette was one of fascinating complexity. M Bajouette was deeply in love with his wife, Michelle, while she, with a sort of light-hearted Parisian insouciance, had a lover – less from inclination than from conformity with current fashion.

The maison Bajouette was a small house in the rue du Chat Qui Pêche, facing the Seine. The street was no more than a few yards long, the house being close to the rue Dante where M Bajouette managed a firm with a good business in commercial wax, run with the clerical methods of France in the 1920s.

Why the street should commemorate a fishing cat was a mystery. It was said by Courbet the taxidermist in the Place St Michel that during the annual flooding of local cellars by the Seine, an enterprising cat used to sit on the bottom step of the Bajouette cellar and hook up passing fish.

The Bajouettes also housed Madame Juillard, M Bajouette's mother-in-law, a formidable female of astonishing rotundity who ruled the house with an iron hand and worked little Charmaine, the skivvy, to death.

One September morning those long years ago, Madame Juillard was snapping at the wretched Charmaine with her usual '*Alors toi*!' which more or less meant what you wanted it to mean. The cowed M Bajouette crouched over his breakfast, forbearing, less out of pity for Charmaine than from fear of the dragon, to say that his coffee was cold.

Madame Juillard's brown chips of eyes considered him briefly and she said, with a sort of feral snarl, that he was due at his office. Coffee and half-eaten *brioche* were abandoned and M Bajouette fled, brooding on his way about his favourite dream – the demise of his mother-in-law.

This dream virtually sustained the poor man, for she was a tyrant who practically rationed his hours with his own wife. Further, like some French widows, she possessed a carefully guarded sum of money which was willed to her only child. And that, decided M Bajouette, meant to him (and sundry impatient creditors).

M Bajouette was short and stout, and was quite prepared to admit that he was no figure of romance, which perhaps explained why his wife spent time with Georges Mihailovic, her Serbian lover whose sole income was from the ladies he charmed with his good looks.

The practical demands of commercial wax left M Bajouette little time either for romantic thoughts about his wife or for lethal ones about his mother-in-law. But every midday at the Café of Two Nations in the rue Lagrange he undid the top buttons of his high-waisted trousers and began over coffee and *fine* to brood about the work he hoped to give to his friend in the rue Danton, M Ferrand, the undertaker.

But how, how? Contrary to dreams of popular novelists it is difficult to murder a large woman with an inbuilt suspicion of all men. He thought of many things, of robbers (could be), of riots (possible), of typhoid (feasible), even of heart failure (in a woman without one). It was all impossible, for Madame's virile person and scarifying tongue would defy death and all the legions of hell.

Winter arrived and M Bajouette, in a bowler hat and a bell-shaped overcoat, went one day to work, pausing a moment at the tiny police *poste* next to his home. He raised his eyes to the snow-filled sky and there, blue and age-dimmed, was the nameplate of his minute street: rue du Chat Qui Pêche. The Devil, no doubt tired of the formidable opposition of politicians, touched M

7

Bajouette lightly and solved his problem, maybe with a nose for a future recruit.

M Bajouette suddenly became a shrewd entrepreneur. He wanted a cat, but cats cost money, if not to acquire at least to maintain; worse, the local poor had a way with plump felines which was a short journey to the cooking-pot. Courbet the taxidermist solved the problem.

'You require a cat for your purposes, M Bajouette?' The pair were conferring in Courbet's evil-smelling shop.

'I have this idea to increase my income from the tourists, you understand?'

'Commendable, but how?' The mention of money had sobered Courbet.

'My home is part of a legend. I decided, a cat sitting on my bottom cellar step and an arrangement with the tourist guides to bring their cohorts to see the fishing pussy at, say, a franc a visit? I might even sell little postcards.'

'And,' breathed the awed taxidermist, 'sell miniature pussycats supplied by me at a fair price.'

Thus it happened. A moth-eaten moggy of unknown vintage now sat on the last step of M Bajouette's cellar. Madame Juillard's opinion was unprintable. For a long time she writhed and then, on the day of the great flood, she kicked the cat into the water-logged cellar, and must have slipped, banging her head on the steps.

At least, that was how M Bajouette explained it to a dubious *agent de police*, who considered the corpse when it had been gaffed from the flooded cellar, and considered it sympathetically – for who has not such a mother-in-law?

M Bajouette was in his own heaven. The household tyrant had died, an accidental death, with which the police seemed satisfied; his debts would be paid. And so it was until a little later, when Michelle did not come home. He probed into her possessions seeking a reason, and found the answer in his lovely wife's apron.

In the pocket were three things: a lottery ticket bearing his name, a handkerchief, and a letter. It was written in purple ink with a vile nib on unbelievable paper. It was to her husband, regretting the death of poor Mother, but now she has gone, thank

8

you, God, I am free and so are you, beloved Jean, for I have left Paris with my angel, Georges Mihailovic. *PS* Mother's money, the kind soul, she kept under her bed, so Georges and I will never want. Adieu, my heart.

M Bajouette's rage is still talked about in the quarter. He screamed and shouted; he threw things and spoke rudely to the Deity. He broke everything he could find, and was listened to politely by two policemen with the kindly tolerance of their kind.

But they bore him from the house, yelling obscenities, when he said the policemen were *cocu*. The insult was beyond bearing, and in his rage, he poured out the story about kicking his stunned mother-in-law into the cellar waters.

As he was being taken away a small man stood in his path, even when politely asked to step aside by the police. 'You are M Jean Bajouette?' he asked.

'Veritably,' said a policeman. 'On his way to spit in the basket one morning' – a none too courteous synonym for the guillotine.

'Oh dear,' said the little man. 'Now what to do? You hold a lottery ticket purchased on your behalf as a farewell gift from your wife who had inherited her poor mother's money, as she told the ticket vendor. And you have, my dear M Bajouette, won a prize of more francs than I thought existed.'

M Bajouette kicked the nearest policeman with superb precision – and was instantly laid out with the law's little white truncheon.

9

Trouble With Time

ARTHUR C. CLARKE

'We don't have much crime on Mars,' said Detective Inspector Rawlings, a little sadly. 'In fact, that's the chief reason I'm going back to the Yard. If I stayed her much longer, I'd get completely out of practice.'

We were sitting in the main observation lounge of the Phobos Spaceport, looking out across the jagged, sun-drenched crags of the tiny moon.

The ferry rocket that had brought us up from Mars had left ten minutes ago, and was now beginning the long fall back to the ochre-tinted globe hanging there against the stars.

In half an hour we should be boarding the liner for Earth.

'At the same time,' continued the Inspector, 'now and then there's a case that makes life interesting. You're an art-dealer, Mr Maccar, I'm sure you heard about that spot of bother at Meridian City a couple of months ago.'

'I don't think so,' replied the plump, olive-skinned little man I had taken for just another returning tourist. Presumably the Inspector had already checked through the passenger list.

I wondered how much he knew about me, and tried to reassure myself that my conscience was – well, reasonably clear. After all, everybody took *something* out through Martian Customs . . .

'It's been rather well hushed up,' said the Inspector, 'but you can't keep these things quiet for long. Anyway, a jewel-thief from

Earth tried to steal Meridian Museum's greatest treasure – the Siren Goddess.'

'But that's absurd!' I objected. 'It's priceless, of course – but it's only a lump of sandstone. You couldn't sell it to anyone – you might just as well steal the *Mona Lisa*.'

The Inspector grinned, rather mirthlessly. '*That's* happened once,' he said. 'Maybe the motive was the same. There are collectors who would give a fortune for such an object, even if they could only look at it themselves. Don't you agree, Mr Maccar?'

'That's perfectly true. In my business, you meet all sorts of crazy people.'

'Well, this chappie – name's Danny Weaver – had been well paid by one of them. And if it hadn't been for a piece of fantastically bad luck, he might have brought it off.'

Though I had never seen the Goddess, like most other departing tourists I had a replica in my baggage. It bore the certificate of the Mars Bureau of Antiquities, guaranteeing that 'this full-scale reproduction is an exact copy of the so-called Siren Goddess, discovered in the *Mare Sirenium* by the Third Expedition AD 2012 (AM 23).'

It was quite a tiny thing to have caused so much controversy. Only eight or nine inches high – you wouldn't look at it twice if you saw it in a museum on Earth. The head of a young woman, with slightly oriental features – that's all.

But it was an enigma so baffling that it had inspired a hundred religious sects, and drove quite a few archaeologists round the bend.

For a perfectly human head had no right whatsoever to be found on Mars, whose only intelligent inhabitants were crustaceans – 'educated lobsters,' as the newspapers were fond of calling them. The aboriginal Martians never came near to achieving space flight, and in any event their civilisation died before men existed on Earth.

No wonder the Goddess was the Solar System's number one mystery.

'Danny's plan was beautifully simple,' continued the Inspector. 'You know how absolutely dead a Martian city gets on Sunday, when everything closes down and the colonists stay home to watch the TV from Earth. Danny was counting on this, when he checked into the hotel in Meridian West, late Friday afternoon. He'd have Saturday for reconnoitring the Museum, an undisturbed Sunday for the job itself, and on Monday morning he'd be just another tourist leaving town . . .

'Early Saturday he strolled through the little park and crossed over into Meridian East, where the Museum stands. In case you don't know, the city gets its name because it's exactly on longitude one-eight-oh degrees; there's a big stone slab in the park with the Prime Meridian engraved on it.

'Danny spent the day going over the Museum, exactly like any other tourist determined to get his money's worth. But at closing-time he didn't leave; he had holed up in one of the galleries not open to the public. He stayed there until about midnight.'

'Just a minute,' I interrupted. 'What about the night watchman?'

The Inspector laughed.

'My dear chap! They don't have such luxuries on Mars. There weren't even any alarms, for who would bother to steal lumps of stone? True, the Goddess was sealed up neatly in a strong glass and metal cabinet, just in case some souvenir hunter took a fancy to her.'

That was true enough. I had been thinking in terms of Earth, forgetting that every city on Mars is a closed little world of its own beneath the force-field that protects it from the freezing near-vacuum. Beyond those electronic shields is the utterly hostile emp-tiness of the Martian Outback, where a man will die in seconds without protection. That makes law enforcement very easy. No wonder there was so little crime on Mars . . .

'Danny had a beautiful set of tools, as specialised as a watch-maker's. The main item was a microsaw no bigger than a soldering iron. It had a wafer-thin blade, driven at a million cycles a second by an ultrasonic power pack. It could go through glass or metal like butter – and left a cut only about as thick as a hair. Which was very important for Danny, as he had to leave no traces of his handiwork.

'I suppose you've guessed how he intended to operate. He was going to cut through the base of the cabinet, and substitute one of those souvenir replicas for the real Goddess. It might be a couple of years before some inquisitive expert discovered the awful truth. Long before then, the original would have travelled back to Earth, perfectly disguised as a copy of itself, with a genuine certificate of authenticity. Pretty neat, eh?

'It must have been a weird business, working in all that darkened gallery with all those million-year-old carvings and unexplainable artefacts around him. A museum on Earth is bad enough at night, but at least it's – well, *human*. And Gallery Three which houses the Goddess, is particularly unsettling. It's full of *bas-reliefs* showing quite incredible animals fighting each other; they look rather like giant beetles, and most palaeontologists flatly deny that they could ever have existed. But imaginary or not, they belonged to this world, and they didn't disturb Danny as much as the Goddess, staring at him across the ages and defying him to explain her presence here. She gave him the creeps. How do I know?' He told me.

'Danny set to work on that cabinet as carefully as any diamond-cutter preparing to cleave a gem. It took most of the night to slice out the trap door, and it was nearly dawn when he relaxed and put down the saw.

'There was still a lot of work to do, but the hardest part was over. Putting the replica into the case, checking its appearance against the photos he had thoughtfully brought with him, and covering up his traces might take most of Sunday, but that didn't worry him in the least. He had another twenty-four hours, and would positively welcome Monday's first visitors so that he could mingle with them and make his inconspicuous exit.

'It was a perfectly horrible shock to his system, therefore, when next morning the main doors were noisily unbarred at eight-thirty and the Museum staff – all six of them – started to open up for the day.

'Danny bolted for the emergency exit, leaving everything behind – tools, Goddess, the lot.

'He had another big surprise when he found himself in the street; it should have been completely deserted at this time of day, with everyone at home reading the Sunday papers. But here were the citizens of Meridian East, as large as life, heading for plant or office on what was obviously a normal working day.

'By the time Danny got back to his hotel, we were waiting for him. We couldn't claim much credit for deducing that only a visitor from Earth – and a very recent one at that – could have overlooked Meridian City's chief claim to fame. And I presume you know what *that* is.'

'Frankly, I don't,' I answered. 'You can't see much of Mars in six weeks, and I never went east of the Syrtis Major.'

'Well, it's absurdly simple, but we shouldn't be too hard on Danny; even the locals occasionally fall into the same trap. It's something that doesn't bother us on Earth, where we've been able to dump the problem in the Pacific Ocean. But Mars, of course, is all dry land; and that means that *somebody* has to live with the International Date Line . . .

'Danny, you see, had worked from Meridian West. It was Sunday over there all right – and it was still Sunday when we picked him up back at the hotel. But over in Meridian East, half a mile away, it was only Saturday. That little trip across the park had made all the difference; I told you it was rotten luck.'

There was a long moment of silent sympathy; then I asked, 'What did he get?'

'Three years,' said Inspector Rawlings.

'That doesn't seem very much.'

'*Mars* years; that makes it almost six of ours. And a whacking fine, which, by the odd coincidence, came to just the refund value of his return ticket to Earth. He isn't in jail, of course, Mars can't afford that kind of luxury. Danny has to work for a living, under discreet surveillance.

'I told you that the Meridian Museum couldn't afford a night watchman. Well, it has one now. Guess who?'

'All passengers prepare to board in ten minutes! Please collect your hand-baggage!' ordered the loudspeakers.

As we started to move towards the airlock, I couldn't help asking one more question.

'What about the people who put Danny up to it? There must have been a lot of money behind him. Did you get them?'

'Not yet; they had covered their tracks pretty thoroughly, and

I believe Danny was telling the truth when he said he couldn't give us any leads. Still, it's not my case; as I told you, I'm going back to my old job at the Yard.

'But a policeman always keeps his eyes open – like an art-dealer, eh, Mr Maccar? Why, you look a bit green about the gills. Have one of my space-sickness tablets.'

'No, thank you,' answered Mr Maccar. 'I'm *quite* all right.'

His tone was distinctly unfriendly; the social temperature seemed to have dropped below zero in the last few minutes. I looked at Mr Maccar, and I looked at the Inspector. And suddenly I realised that we were going to have a very interesting trip.

An Old Lady Sings the Blues

ROSEMARY TIMPERLEY

' I 'm going to wait here till my chance comes,' sang the blues singer, on the radio set with the fading battery.

She had turned it up full volume, extracting the last bit of life out of it, because she couldn't afford a new one this week.

But in spite of this the voice of the blues singer was becoming croaky, jerky – 'I-I'm g-g-going to wait right hhhh-ere till my ch . . .' and the battery finally died.

She switched off the set. It would recover a bit, enough to get the news later.

Not that she cared about the news any more. Why did she bother to listen?

Just to have a *voice* in the room really.

I'm going to wait right here till my chance comes . . .

But what am I waiting for, and what chance could possibly come? she asked herself.

For she didn't take chances. She lived within her means. Her means being her Old Age Pension. Enough to pay her rent and buy her food. It was adequate. It kept her alive.

She could still go for walks and save on her gas fire by sitting in the public library in the mornings, pretending to read the newspapers. And she wasn't the only one.

I'm going to wait right her till my chance comes.

Everything depended on the meaning of the word *here*. If she just waited here in her bedsit, the only chance likely to come would be the landlord asking for more rent – and as he was owner-occupier, he could do that.

He was outside the pathetic regulations. Professional landlords laugh at law.

Perhaps, she thought, I could wait somewhere else. But where?

Suppose I just stood in the street somewhere and waited for someone to take notice of me. What would happen?

It was an interesting thought.

What *did* happen if one just stood somewhere, out of doors, doing no harm, not being a nuisance to anyone, not begging or 'singing' or anything? Just stood. What would happen?

Suppose, she thought, I were young – one of these kids who take that non-subject called Sociology – then I might start on a thesis about 'What happens if you just stand in the street and do nothing?'

Would anyone bother? Or would you just die on your feet, passed by all those people? Mass equals inhumanity.

How about trying it then? *Now*? Instead of going to the public library.

And so she set out on the cold winter morning to stand somewhere and see what happened, to 'wait till her chance came'.

Her routine of plodding along to the library in the mornings was so fixed that she couldn't quite change it.

She walked halfway there, reached the corner of the shopping-street, then, instead of going down the side turning which led to the library, she stood on the corner. Just stood. Quite still.

No one took the slightest notice. She stood for an hour, two hours, three hours.

The first hour was the worst. It took so long. She felt the cold and longed to walk to warm herself up – or go along to the central heating of the library and the newspapers, waiting to be unread – but she didn't let herself give in.

No 'chance' came, but the second hour passed quite quickly. By the third hour, she was so accustomed to being there that she felt at home.

She had lost all self-consciousness. She watched everything and everyone, as an observer. And as she was ignored, she felt invisible.

It was rather like wearing dark glasses: you kid yourself that because you see only dimly, you can only dimly be *seen*.

As she stood through the fourth hour of her daytime vigil, she was positively enjoying herself. She felt a sense of achievement. It wasn't everyone who had the patience or the nerve to do this. She was exceptional. More hours passed.

Then, suddenly, as early winter dusk fell, a tall figure loomed over her. It was dressed in police uniform.

'Excuse me, madam,' it said, 'but are you all right?'

'Yes, thank you,' she said.

'Don't you think perhaps it's time you went home?'

'I feel at home here, thank you.'

'May I have your name?'

'No. It's mine. Why should you have it?'

The face on top of the uniformed figure grinned. 'Fair enough. How about first names then? I'm Bob.'

'I'm Ella,' she said.

'No fixed abode, Ella?'

'No, Bob, I have an abode, thank you, but I'd rather wait here than go back to it.'

'Waiting for anything special?'

'Yes. Till my chance comes!'

And instantly she was filled with life and warmth and a curious sensation which might almost have been happiness.

She spread out her arms, took an attitude as if she were on a lighted stage, or in a cabaret, and sang the blues number, 'I'm going to wait right her till my chance comes'.

A little crowd gathered, in spite of the cold and the increasing darkness. There was a scatter of applause and a cry of 'Good old girl. That's the stuff!' from a derelict passer-by.

Then suddenly the exhaustion and adventurousness of the day overcame her. The streetlamps began to dance round her in mad circles. She gasped for breath.

She was grateful for the strong, uniformed arm round her shoulders, and the voice. 'It's all right, old dear. Okay, Ella. Not to worry. I'm here. Old Bob's here. The arm of the law and all that.'

She fell into the arms of this friendly, respectable rescuer. A bit of a comedown, since in theory she'd always been 'agin' the law – but beggars can't be choosers . . .

She passed out completely.

When she came to, she was in a little room at the local police station. Bob was there.

'Hello,' he said. 'Wakey, wakey! You're all right now.' He added: 'I recognised you from the start, but I couldn't believe it. But you are, aren't you?'

'Perhaps,' she said.

'I heard one of your old records being played on the radio quite early this morning, before I came on duty,' he said. 'Then as I walked around, I saw you standing there. But I thought it was my imagination – because I'd just been listening to you. But now that I know you're *you* I'll see you're right. Where do you live? What's your landlord like? Can I do anything for you? You're the best blues singer I ever heard when I was a kid. You're not friendless any more, Ella.'

She answered his questions. He took her home. He fixed a dripping tap for her. He put in a new electric light bulb that she hadn't been able to reach. He said, 'I'll buy a new battery for your radio tomorrow.'

And that was how the song which had made her famous as a blues singer when she was young came true now that she was old.

She had waited right there. Her 'chance' had come.

He Couldn't Win this Waiting Game

JANE WALLACE

I am called Guiseppe Garibaldi. Every day my papa is telling me that I should live up to such a great and glorious name. On the day I leave school he says: 'Let us be men together. I do not think you will ever become the saviour of Italy, my son, but I will speak to a friend – in the Family you understand – and get you a job as a waiter in the Hotel Splendico.'

'*Si*, Papa,' I say, although the prospect does not delight me. I have only one love, the football. Two loves counting Rosa.

He raises his glass to me. 'Even if your papa pulls himself up the mountain by the tail of the *mulo*, you will be different. Work hard, my son, and one day you will get to the top.'

I work hard. I study English, French and German, so that I can translate the menu to the English, French and Germans. When they snap their fingers in the air I say, bowing low: 'What is your wish, sir?' in French or English. (My father has told me not to waste much effort on the Germans.)

I have one good customer with whom it is not necessary to make an impression, Signore Castelli. He is Italian, and instead of food we talk about the local football team in which I play every Thursday and Saturday. Sometimes I feel I am only happy when

I have the ball at my feet, and then I remember Rosa. That is another happiness.

For her I must get the big promotion and become a head waiter like Signore Mendosa. He is shaped like a pear and his eyes are buried in his head, like escargots which is French for snails.

The other waiter is Carlo, a thorn in the flesh. When you are close to him you can see the sweat on his upper lip, because all day long he dashes around on tiptoes for the English, French and Germans, saying, '*Prego, signore*,' in three different languages. If Signore Mendosa is like a pear, Carlo is like a banana.

'Work hard,' Papa says if I meet him on the steps with his *mulo*.

'Work hard,' Signore Mendosa says, 'I have been promoted to the Hotel Splendico in Naples. Twice as big as this joint.' (Lately we have had a coachload of American tourists.) 'So one of youse guys will get my job. Okay?'

I work hard. Carlo tells me I am clumsy. 'Get out of my way, footballer,' he says. 'Your brains are in your feet.'

I watch him with his banana-bow explaining the menu. 'We have Jambon Fume de Savoire, which is smoked ham, *otherwise* we have Filet de Porc, which is Filet Schweinelende, *otherwise* we have Paupiettes de Veau Clementine ... for you, Monsieur Dupont, there is no need to translate.' I am very envious of this big English word, 'otherwise'.

Signore Castelli is the only guest I can speak to like a man. 'I am working hard for the promotion, *signore*. But to tell you the truth, I am only happy when I am playing football, and, of course, afterwards with Rosa.'

Comes the big day. Signore Mendosa tells Carlo and me to report to him in the kitchen after the third breakfast. My knees knock together. I can see that Signore Mendosa is enjoying himself, a real Mussolini.

'I have given the matter of the promotion much thought,' he says. 'Even though you, Guiseppe, have learned the languages okay, you lack that *je ne sais quoi*.'

'Carlo now has this thing I speak of,' he says, seesawing on his little feet. He kisses his fingertips. 'So,' he smiles with joy, 'much as I am desolated, for you there is no promotion, Guiseppe. It is for Carlo.'

I am very sad. In the evening I present the menu to Signore Castelli. 'For you,' I say, 'there is no need of the explanation. You and I speak the only language in the world worth knowing.'

'Yes,' he says, 'there I agree with you. But it is not the menu I want to talk about tonight. It is the football.'

'Talk away,' I say, 'anything for a *divertimento*. I have received a bitter blow. I have missed my promotion.'

'There is promotion and promotion,' he says. 'Have you ever thought of turning professional? I am referring to The Game. I am scout for . . .' and he mentions a team almost as well known as AC Milano. 'Would you like to play football for money?'

I think I swoon, but it is of such short duration that no one notices. 'For that I would swim the Messina Straits keeping up with the hydrofoil.'

'Sign here,' he says, producing a contract already drawn up and a gold pen. 'And tell the chef with my compliments that I would be pleased if he would give me *soup* tonight instead of washing-up water.'

The crowd roars in my ears as I push the baize door into the kitchen. 'Guiseppe . . . *Prodigioso!*' I bump into Carlo who roars also.

'Watch where you're going, you clumsy oaf!'

'*Prego*,' I say 'but sometimes, banana one, it is good to have brains in your feet.'

The Real McCoy

LACHLAN McINTYRE

His personal dossier said he was Ian Muir of Ardnashiel. Thinking about it in the light of my present knowledge, I suppose that he could, just as believably, have been Ivan something or other from Archangel.

Not far from the meeting place of the waters, where the silent glens sprawl summer green at the feet of the great mountains, I sat on a bench against the wall of the old farmstead, waiting for him to come. The hum of wild bees among the bell-heather was the only sound to be heard in that remote place and I just sat there, savouring the loneliness and dreading the thing I had to do.

This aged building, a mere croft before renovation, had come to me from the ancient one, who had sensed, even then, that I would return. And each summer, all else permitting, return I did, to become refurbished physically and spiritually in the solitude.

But this was no vacation.

I'd been given some of the story before leaving London. Not all of it but enough. He was a 'double', they'd said; and they had proceeded to manipulate him so cleverly that in the end, I was the only one who he could turn to. He was expendable – and I was the instrument selected for his disposal. There was to be no fuss – nothing more than an unremarked disappearance. They could be just as bloody cunning down there by the Thames as they were on the other side of the Wall.

Well, for myself, I had to be sure. I needed to penetrate his alleged masquerade before committing myself.

There were two ways up here from civilisation: by boat or by walking over the moor. He walked. I saw him first, far off, moving along the track up from Fearna. Almost an hour later, he flopped down heavily beside me. For some moments he sat gasping for breath, then: 'God! Angus,' he panted, 'are ye the one to find? What wi' trains an' buses an' now this – this god-awful country – whew! I'm all in.'

Exchanging greetings, I looked him over as he got his wind back. He hadn't changed much. His hair was still worn *en brosse*; more sparse and streaked with grey now. I asked myself – was it possible that this man was either a Scots-born traitor or a foreign national who had infiltrated the service under a superb cover? The former possibility made me see red in more ways than one. My information was that he was a double agent.

Another thing bugged me – was he aware that his cover was broken? Anyway, if they were right about him – all I wanted was to get it over with.

'Ian, what's biting you? You haven't come all the way up here just to enquire after my health. What's the trouble?'

'That's just it, laddie – I'm no' sure. One thing's certain – I've been under surveillance. Damned if I know why.'

So he didn't know.

'Come off it,' I said, 'who on earth would – ?'

'I'm deadly serious,' he broke in, getting up and pacing to and fro, 'I don't know who, either, but I've been in this business long enough to recognise all the usual nonsense. I went straight to my rooms from Heathrow and began phoning around. I knew at once there was a tap on, so I had a quick shufti. Someone had been verra careful but I knew the place had had a going over.'

I lit a cigarette and blew out smoke thoughtfully.

'Why are you here, Ian?' I asked quietly. 'How did you know where to find me?'

'Look, Angus. They wouldn't see me. I had something for them but they weren't interested. I couldn't get to my own control let

24

alone the bloody chief of staff. I was knocked out – desperate – desperate to contact somebody who'd gie me an ear. Why, they even shied away when I asked about you. Then one o' them mini-skirted bitches in accounts let slip that you'd left – been slung out, was the way I got it.'

'That's right,' I agreed. 'A major difference of opinion over policy came up. Can't say I'm sorry.' I dismissed the lie briefly.

'Then I remembered the cottage in Hampshire and rang your father. He was a bit cagey at first, but eventually told me where to find you. I'm kinda sorry you're out of it, but mebbe it's all for the best.'

'All for the best – ?'

He hesitated.

'Why not come indoors an' tell me about it over a drink?'

'Aye, thanks.' He followed me in and sat down, gazing around curiously. I brought out glasses and one of my two bottles.

'Some paperknife, that,' he said, pointing to the wall. 'Antique.'

I poured two stiff ones and pushed one over to him. Then I reached for the 'antique'.

'Cheers!' he said.

'Cheers,' I acknowledged, toying with the weapon. I saw that he sank his drink in one. So I gave him another.

'Och, man!' he apologised, 'how I've missed the auld mountain dew – this is grand stuff – the real McCoy! Eh?'

I sipped my drink and thought about our first meeting in Berlin and how I had liked him on sight. That was the bitter thing. Just how stupid can one get?

Discounting his earlier disparagement of the rugged terrain, and even allowing for his unnatural failure to recognise that 'paper-knife' for the *skean-dhu* it really was – his last incredible utterance settled it for me.

Younger and fitter than he, I moved fast, putting the ancient Celtic dagger to its age-old use. It was over in seconds.

Helping myself to three fingers from my other bottle, I looked at the slumped figure and genuine regret – not for him – but for a marathon performance marred only by the final act. A pity! He'd been doing fine until then.

But, damn it, any crofter with a liking for a dram would have

25

known at once it wasn't Scotch in that first bottle – even if he
didn't know it was bourbon.

Hands

DOROTHY BENNETT

Those hands! Softly caressing, tender, teasing, tingling, tick-
ling; and so damnably cruel.

Long tapering fingers, possessive as the tentacles of an octopus.
Dominant hands, yet pleading, persuading, deceptive in their eter-
nal trickery – and so mysterious.

Max and Magic! Those hands! I looked at the ticket. 'Max
Brynder, Master of Magic.' So Max Brynder was top of the bill.
I might have guessed. He'd all the makings of a star even in the
old days when he was working clubs and pubs and private parties
and I was a male impersonator on the stage in the dying days of
the music hall.

His palming and sleight of hand were uncanny, out of this
world. I've stood beside him, watched wide-eyed as he placed a
lemon under a metal tankard and produced instead a coconut so
big as to be a tight fit.

I've sat beside him, watched him tear up a borrowed pound
note, scatter the scraps on the table before us, then produce it,
whole, same serial number, from an apple. Max, Master of
Miracles.

I've lain beside him and shared other mysteries. That's why I
hate him! That's why I shopped him. He'd looked elsewhere while
I was still with him.

I'd seen him borrow a fiver, do tricks with it on stage, and hand back a dud fiver. Dud for genuine. He did it dozens of times and was never spotted, never once. I shopped him at a small place in Wales and laughed like a drain when he got six months. Then I howled like a kid who's lost a favourite toy. Passing counterfeit money they called it. Passing me up, I called it.

I kept the cutting from local paper, a souvenir to gloat and cry over, for lack of those wonderful, wonderful, facile, fascinating hands, which spoke every emotion in the world. They did marvellous things beside producing coins, cards and doves from thin air. That was only minor magic. Those who only watched his stage magic knew a poor half of his legerdemain.

And now here he was on a one-night stand at the Helonerth Club. I *must* see him again, if only to relive those days, revive the pent-up hate. Or was it jealousy?

I'd given up my own act to become his assistant, his stooge. Actually, I hadn't sacrificed much. Music hall was on it's last legs. I'd no other gifts, and when I shopped Max I didn't feel like impersonating any male. So I became a travelling saleswoman in the rag trade; a van-load of dresses and a different town each day.

My path and Max's hadn't crossed again. One of my boutique customers was a member of the Helonerth Club and gave me her ticket. She'd bought it for her husband, to keep him out of the way whilst she would be otherwise and elsewhere engaged with a wealthy client. The husband was inconsiderately and inconveniently taken ill, so neither could go. Nobody would know me at the club. It was an 'Evening Dress preferred' do. I could hire a dress suit.

I was scared. I didn't know what my reactions would be when I saw him again. He'd been slender, elegant, smooth in the old days. Had he gone to seed? I hoped so. Nobody else should enjoy him as I had done. I took the faded cutting from my handbag. What wouldn't it do to his career if I publicised that affair from the past? It would finish him as an entertainer.

Thoughts still back in the yesteryears, I looked at myself, newly suited, in the mirror in the hotel bedroom. A man again! Still slender. Hair short, as is the modern female trend. Can't tell male from female nowadays. Yes, I was going as a man. If I disgraced myself I could get away without recognition – unless he recognised me. Doubtful. I was one of many; jealousy told me.

What should I do, throw an egg or a tomato? No, too vulgar. Keep it clean. Scream to the roof about his dud fivers? Ease my hurt by hurting him? Make him pay? Pay? Blackmail! On the strength of that cutting! He couldn't refute it. That was it. After the show he'd do some fraternising with the audience. I'd tackle him then. His old flame incognito.

I sat near the stage – and trembled as he came on. He was still very presentable. Tall, slender, suave; and oh, those wonderful, sensitive, wilful fingers, they squeezed my heart and it lost a beat. My fingers went into my jacket pocket, fingered the cutting that could wreck his life – as he had wrecked mine.

The show started. Doves, lovebirds appeared magically from his empty hands. Cards, coins, fivers fanned between his fingers and evaporated. A borrowed pound note, torn into confetti, vanished and appeared whole from the collar of a member of the band. Tricks, tricks, tricks and oh, Max, the tricks you played on me and the tricks I'll play on you tonight.

'May I have the assistance of two members of the audience please? You, sir, and you. You are placed so conveniently.'

So I appear on the stage again – and again in male attire. Strange touch of fate, that. Is that sparkle in his eyes recognition? Tricks, tricks and I tremble and vibrate as I feel his fingers upon me and he takes an ace from my shoulder. My volunteer companion grins sheepishly as his own watch is handed to him as we vacate the stage to a thunder of applause for Max.

I'll wait by the bar for him to come and mix with the crowd. I'll draw him aside, whisper my terms. I order a drink, pay with a note, accept my change, sip and wait. My terms? Monetary? Or take me back? A touch at my elbow.

'Excuse me, sir. Would you come with me?'

A summons to his presence? So he had recognised me! But I am led outside. 'Where are you taking me?'

'To the station sir, – or madam. The police doctor will be there. From information received we believe you to be female, and to be in possession of false fivers. Issuing counterfeit money, masquerading in male attire in public places.'

Max had got in first – again.

My last hope, the cutting in my pocket.

Which of course, it wasn't. Those roving hands and fingers.

The Führer's Last Farewell

PLICHTA HALL

Dark, ominous clouds hung low over Vienna. The clouds were pointing along the path of the Danube to Czechoslovakia. But they were too swollen and cumbersome; they dithered and hung where they were.

In a house in the Grellgasse two brothers stood close to a window and looked towards Der Ring where sluggish traffic drew the eye. A sudden snarl-up in the flow of vehicles caused a cacophony of forbidden hooting. One motorised clown took the opportunity to play the illegal horns he had bought in Italy and the first bars of Colonel Bogey blared through the concert.

'The Bridge over the River Kwai,' the elder brother said with a snort of disgust.

'What would you rather have?' said the other. 'Wagner maybe, to accompany the entry of a German Hero into Valhalla?'

A growl of anger caused them both to turn from the window. In the shadows near the door a bearded old man sat hunched on a straight-back chair. He stood up without gaining in height.

'The General is your father,' he shouted. 'Have you no respect? He sacrificed his life, his mind, his body to a great cause. He, too, wanted a world where true men could feel their roots, breathe their history, experience their chosen place in space and time. A place where men could reach back for the strength needed to gorge a future where ...'

'A future where the mentality of the anthill would reign,' the younger brother interrupted. 'Really, Albert ...'

He broke off as the door to the sitting-room opened. The man who entered had no hair on his head. He was small, grey, and dressed in grey.

'*Meine Herren*,' he said, 'the General is dying. Please go up to him. Ease his way.'

The two brothers left the room, the elder helping the younger. Albert scuttled behind them. Their progress up the marble staircase was slow, dictated by the speed of the younger brother who had the handicap of an artificial leg.

The bedroom was dark and smelled ill. The creature on the bed was snoring loudly.

'General,' said old Albert, who had manoeuvred himself to the fore, 'your two sons.'

'My sons?' The bandaged skull on the pillow moved. 'Why aren't they at the Front?'

'General, my dear,' Albert stroked the cropped, white head on the pillow, 'there are no hostilities. Your two officer-sons have leave of absence from their units, and have chosen to be with you.'

'But the Communist uprising in Russia?' the old General mewled. 'What of the uprising?'

'Ground back into the dirt from which it sprang, General. You remember? I read you the reports.'

'*Doch, doch*, Albert. Read me the news. What is our beloved Führer doing today?'

The old servant picked up a newspaper. A silence settled over the room as he began to chant, his eyes fixed vacantly above the newspaper that rustled in his trembling hands.

'The Führer today honoured the two astronauts who returned from the moon after claiming the Earth's satellite for Great Deutschland. While pinning the Iron Cross with Diamonds and Oak Leaves on the breasts of the two Luftwaffe majors, His Excellency, Adolph Hitler, said "Men, the step you took was a small one for mankind, but a great leap for the Aryan race." The ceremony, which took place on the lawn of the White House in Washington, was attended by a throng of over 400,000 spectators ...'

32

'You can stop now,' said the younger of the brothers. 'The General is dead.'

They descended the staircase in a silence, broken only by the creaking of the false leg. The doctor awaited them in the sitting-room.

'Passed?' he asked.

'Passed and over,' the elder brother replied. 'Has the undertaker been informed?'

'Three weeks ago,' said Albert. 'I will bring the death certificate tomorrow. *Meine Herren*, your most obedient servant.'

'I have the honour,' the two brothers replied in unison, and bowed to the departing doctor.

'Albert,' said the elder brother in the ensuing silence, 'we are aware of the debt we owe you. You were only a common soldier, but you risked your life to bring our father to his house, and you have cared for him these twenty-nine years. You were a true and faithful servant. You appeased his broken mind by telling him fairy tales of a German Empire. Surely it helped him.

'I offer you a pension for the rest of your days – may they be long – and I offer you the hospitality of this, our father's house.'

'No!' The younger brother turned quickly, and his leg creaked in protest. 'The pension you shall have. I will double whatever my brother offers, but remove yourself from this house. Albert Heider, I despise you!'

The servant seemed to grow smaller, and evil. His tiny eyes blazed between the grey of his hair and beard.

'You despise me? Perhaps because of your lost leg? That bit of bone and flesh that you left in Stalingrad. *Ach Gott*, are you so small?

'Be undisturbed. I go. I would not share a roof with such a small man. Your pension I do not need. Fools! My suitcase has been packed for nearly thirty years.'

The elder brother had turned away in embarrassment at the tirade of his younger brother and the reply of the old servant. He gazed, unseeing, out of the window. He heard a door close, heard a crackling as his brother came to stand at his side. Together they watched the old man hurry down the drive. He was swathed in a Hubertus greatcoat and carried a cheap suitcase.

'Did you really fail to guess? That is the man for whom you served so many years in American imprisonment. That is the man for whom I left a leg – and my soul – in Russia.'

'Really?' the elder man replied, surprised that he was not surprised. 'That is he?'

'That is he.'

It started to rain.

Dangerous Bend

HERBERT HARRIS

She stood by her car, waiting for him to drive up the quiet lane towards her. She knew that this was the time he always passed over this route. In a glove-pocket of her car was a flask of brandy. In the brandy was a little-known poison which had neither taste nor smell and left no trace.

The man who was keeping an appointment with death whistled a cheerful tune as he drove. He was soon to marry a girl he adored, a girl who had brightened his hopes for the future. He smiled in spite of the cold. A light fall of snow had frozen on the ground. His hands and ears were numb.

The girl who stood waiting by her car was glad when he came into view. She couldn't have stood the icy wind much longer. She was relieved also that the time had come for definite action.

When Mary Kane decided to kill the man she had once loved, but now hated, she followed the path of most women killers and chose poison. An obvious choice in her case, anyway. She had access to poisons as a chemist in a research laboratory.

It was at the laboratory she had met Frank Toomey, a man whose future as a research scientist had been menaced by his addiction to alcohol.

A sombre, brooding girl, almost afraid of her own sensuality, she had known a strange kind of loneliness until Toomey entered her life. He had never been in love with her. She was not his type really – not the type he would marry. But there was an animal magnetism about her and when she was near him the purely physical desire was irresistible.

During the several evenings they spent together, they drank a good deal, although her capacity for alcohol was well below his. She never objected to his drinking. It made him affectionate. She even took to carrying a flask of brandy, his pet drink, so that he could have a drink after the pubs shut.

Toomey was not blind to the danger of their relationship. She was plainly neurotic and he knew that a physical liaison with such a girl can end disastrously when the attachment is severed. His anxiety deepened when he became more and more deeply involved with a girl called Carol, a new secretary in the laboratory offices. Carol represented his ideal as a potential wife and mother – practical, good-humoured, uncomplicated, blonde. The attraction was mutual and grew stronger.

And so it became an embarrassment when Mary Kane persisted in plaguing him. There was no other word for it. She was so insanely in love with him that she had become a pest. One evening, in one of the pubs they had been wont to visit, fortified by brandy, he broke the brutal truth to her: 'Mary . . . I want this to be our last meeting. Carol and I are engaged . . .'

Her face was chalk-white and made ugly by venomous jealousy. 'I wish that bitch would die,' she said, her mouth a scar as she spat the words. Frank Toomey was suddenly frightened.

'It would make no difference if she died,' he said.

'You still wouldn't want to marry *me*?'

He shook his head. 'Sorry, Mary . . .'

'I loathe you . . . *loathe* you!' She spoke with quiet venom. Then she got up and walked out, leaving him there alone. That was all. All over. Or so he had thought . . .

Taking the corner carefully over the icy surface of the little-used lane, he spotted her car some time before reaching it. Mary's car had skidded partly off the road. One wheel had slid over into a shallow ditch. He didn't want to stop. It meant cool, polite conversation. But on humanitarian grounds he couldn't leave her here to freeze.

'You seem to be in trouble,' he said, pulling up.

'I've been hoping someone would come along, but I never expected it would be *you*,' she answered. 'I'm afraid I took the bend too fast. One wheel's in the ditch. I'll need towing out.'

She sounded more rational. He managed a smile. 'Then I'll have to rescue you, won't I? I've a towrope in the boot.'

'Thanks.' There was no warmth in the smile she returned, but at least she hadn't scowled at him.

The rescue operation was not easy on the icy surface, and took longer than he'd thought. When he had put the rope back in the boot of his car, he stood blowing on his fingers, banging his arms across his frozen body.

'God!' he exclaimed. 'I haven't felt so cold all winter!'

'I've got just the thing for that,' she told him. He eyed her curiously. She said. 'Wait . . .'

He was about to climb into his car, when she caught his sleeve.

'Here. Just like old times, don't you think, Frank?'

Invitingly she held out the flask containing the poisoned brandy. There was an evil smile on her lips. She felt no stirring of remorse, only a sense of excitement bubbling inside her.

'The old brandy flask. Have a good swig. It should warm you up.'

Toomey shook his head. 'No . . . not any longer.'

'How do you mean?'

He smiled. 'Never touch it now. Doc's orders. If I took just one sip of the stuff, it would start me off on the bottle again.'

Her face was black with fury. 'Doctor's orders . . . or Carol's?'

'That's none of your damned business!' he snapped at her. He got into the car and slammed the door.

Mary let out an agonised scream and in a wave of sick nausea he knew why. He leapt out and looked at her hand, wincing. He had shut the door on her fingers and he stared at the bruised and shattered flesh.

'Oh God!' he shouted. 'Oh God, you poor little devil!'

Her eyelids were fluttering, her body beginning to sag. Toomey supported her in his arms as she started to faint. He snatched up the brandy flask she had dropped and held it to her lips.

'Here,' he gasped out, 'drink this!'

Obediently, half-consciously, Mary Kane drank . . .

With a Song in Her Heart

MARTIN K. HOWARD

Out of the darkness the diminutive figure of the singer stepped into the pool of brilliant light splitting the blackness of the stage.

Her entrance started a thunderous applause from the audience packed like sardines. She bowed and held up her hands to the adulation. They had all played this theatre, from Piaf to Bassey. Now it was her turn.

From my seat in the second row I could see her every move and expression and feel every word as she coaxed her willing audience into a unique love affair which was to last for the rest of the evening. Even I, who had seen her many times and had loved her more than anyone there, felt it. It was a feeling which would last for days.

Halfway through her act she took a break. During this I remembered her before she became an international superstar, when she had been singing for peanuts in a dingy nightclub. I was the only one who clapped at the end of her turn. She came across to the bar and smiled – a smile that seemed to light up the joint.

'Thank you, kind sir,' she said, 'for your appreciation. Would you like to buy a working girl a drink?'

I did so and thought that it was an odd pick-up. Then I looked more closely. She had class and wasn't on the game. We chatted for a while. Then she said: 'Well, it's time for me to quit this hole and head for home.'

'Do you always leave so late?' I asked looking at my watch. It was 2.15 a.m.

She nodded. 'Sometimes later.'

'Don't you mind crossing London so late on your own?'

'I get a cab usually and sometimes a lift.'

'May I give you a lift tonight?'

She shrugged and said: 'Okay. I live out at Dulwich.'

I drove to her flat, as seedy and as depressing as the nightclub. She invited me in for coffee. She chatted as if she needed someone to talk to.

'With a voice like yours,' I said, 'I'm surprised you're not in a better place than the Blue Horn.'

She laughed. 'Brother, you've no idea how hard it is to break through. I've had auditions. Unless you're prepared to hop into someone's bed, no deal!'

I nodded. 'Have you tried the Dragon's Tooth?'

She stared at me across the top of her chipped coffee mug.

'Are you mad?' she asked. 'You don't just walk in there and ask for an audition. You have to be known and good. I'd give my lot to sing there.'

The next day I went to see my friend Bernie Goldheim, owner of the Dragon's Tooth and told him about her.

'My boy,' he said, chewing on his fat cigar, 'if you say she's good then I'll hear her. God help you if she isn't!'

She had the audition with Bernie. I can still remember the expression on her little face when I told her. If someone had given her a million she couldn't have been happier.

Bernie liked her and gave her a job at the Dragon's Tooth. He liked her so much that he became her agent and manager and built her a career beyond her wildest dreams.

At first we saw a lot of each other. I planned to marry her but she kept shying. Slowly her engagements mounted up. I saw less of her until eventually she went abroad and I didn't see her except on TV. I wrote a song for her but I never heard anything. She had forgotten me.

The break ended. She came back and went straight into a

number. The audience were right there with her. At the end of the show she stopped and held up her hands for silence.

'Ladies and gentlemen! You've been a fantastic audience and I've had a ball. For my last song I'd like to sing a number that is completely new. It was written by a close friend of mine some time ago. I've been saving it up until now. I know he's in the audience tonight. I'd like to sing it especially for him with all my love.'

The audience applauded at this touching piece of sentiment and I felt a lump in my throat.

She held up her hands again and said: 'And if he's not doing anything afterwards perhaps he'd like to buy a working girl a drink!'

Perchance to Dream

CARDEW ROBINSON

Foster Hemmingway was the stage-screen idol of millions, among whom there was no more devoted fan than Foster Hemmingway himself.

He was daydreaming about his latest rating when he saw George Goring collapse with a hollow groan into the deepest armchair in the Nomads' Club.

'What the devil's the matter with you, Goring?' demanded Hemmingway. Even when genuinely concerned, the actor's manner resembled the late Attila's when addressing a reluctant Hun.

George Goring, business executive, past fifty, and present physical wreck, raised his head. It seemed to need an effort that might have raised Tower Bridge on a windy day.

'I'm not getting my proper sleep,' said the wretched man.

'You mean you've got insomnia,' proclaimed Hemmingway.

The volume of the actor's voice was now having a catastrophic effect upon the mangled remains of George Goring, but he bravely faced the storm.

'Look Hemmingway, I haven't got insomnia. I sleep with no difficulty whatsoever. It's what happens *when* I sleep that is ruining my health.'

'Ah!' boomed Hemmingway, and Goring turned several shades paler. 'A psychological problem. Now I have some experience in these matters. Tell me the story.'

More to still the raging torment of Hemmingway's voice than for any hope of assistance, Goring complied.

'No sooner has my head touched the pillow, than, in my dream, I get up, dress and go out. Outside my house is a ten-ton lorry. I get in and drive it to Doncaster. All through the night I drive. The whole length of the A1; every mile; through every gear change – and the gears on those lorries are quite something – I have only one stop at some dreadful transport café. The rest of the night, I'm at the blasted steering wheel, staring ahead – and changing those blasted gears all the way to Doncaster, and of course it's daylight when I get there. As I drive into the town I wake up. And believe me, when I do wake up I'm really exhausted. I might just as well not have gone to bed at all.'

'Well, well, well,' Hemmingway's voice, under the influence both of concern, and the consulting-physician role which he was now playing to the hilt, had quietened down to a bellow.

'Lucky you told me. I'll recommend you to Rowlinson. First-class chap. He'll unscramble all this in no time. I'll phone him and you'll see him today.'

He was now so utterly dominating that the shattered Goring had no more freedom of choice than one of Attila's minions ordered by the warlord himself to get on with the looting and no more nonsense.

Goring was pleasantly surprised when he found that the psychiatrist was bluff, big, and business-like.

'Hum. Interesting,' said Rowlinson. 'Tell me, did you ever have a nasty experience involving a lorry or a lorry driver? You can be quite frank with me. In fact you must be.'

'Certainly not,' said Goring.

'No matter, the treatment is simple. I shall put you under hypnosis. During this I shall put a suggestion into your mind. This suggestion will at first considerably shorten, and then finally dispel your recurring dream.'

Moments later, with Goring under his influence he was saying, 'Tonight, in your dream, you will drive the lorry as usual. But this time, when you get as far as Mill Hill, I shall be waiting for you in my car at the roundabout. It is a Ford Capri HYD 707H. You will get out of your lorry and into my car. I will get into your lorry and drive it to Doncaster for you – in your dream of course. You will drive my car back to London, which should only take you half an hour or so.

'You'll go straight home, get into bed and go off into a dreamless sleep. The next night I'll be waiting for you at Hendon. Each night in your dream we will cut down the distance you drive, until quite soon you won't get up at all. You'll be cured.'

Sure enough, that night everything happened exactly as the psychiatrist had suggested. In the dream Goring made the exchange and drove Rowlinson's Capri back home. He then enjoyed a sound sleep. Within a week he was cured.

Goring's account of all this to Hemmingway left the actor with a warm glow of satisfaction and when, shortly afterwards, he saw another club member, Masters, the bank manager, displaying precisely the same symptoms as Goring – if anything more acutely – he was quick to demand details.

Masters had no more chance than Goring of keeping them to himself. The bank manager, sure enough, had the same trouble as Goring – but with interesting variations.

'In my dream,' he said, 'I wake up every night in the same strange house.

'The bedroom is exotically furnished in Eastern style. The bedroom door opens and in walk four gorgeous Oriental girls, very scantily clad. I am naturally entranced and soon find myself making passionate love to one of them. But what is *not* so natural, especially in my case, for I am not normally a demonstrative man, is that afterwards I make love to the other three, one after the other, all through the night. My prowess astonishes them, and it certainly amazes me. In the morning, not surprisingly, I am utterly exhausted.'

'No problem whatsoever,' roared Hemmingway. 'Job for Rowlinson. Just cured one member here. I'll phone now and get him to fit you in this afternoon.'

Rowlinson used the same system he had with Goring. Under hypnosis Masters was told: 'You will, in your dream tonight, make love to one of the girls. Then I will come in, take over, and make love to the other three. You can leave at once.'

Masters lived in a flat opposite the Nomads' Club and the next morning Hemmingway, dropping in to the club for a quick look at the Press reviews of a new show, saw the bank manager emerge and cros. the road towards him looking, if possible, worse than ever. The unhappy Masters had barely enough energy to recount his sad story.

'He put me under hypnosis,' he muttered, 'I don't know what he said to me. All I know is that I awoke, in my dream, in the usual exotic bedroom. The four lovely girls came in, also as usual, and I made passionate love to the first one. Then in came Rowlinson and immediately got cracking with the second. Straight away I left the place and what do you think? I find myself driving a damn great lorry all the way to Doncaster.'

A Friend in Greed

PHILIP ALLOTT

Edmund Jennings always used to say that he had been born free. An orphan, abandoned by his tormenting foster-parents when he was sixteen, he had lived on his wits for more than ten years.

The time had come to improve his station in life. He had considered a life of crime, becoming a monk or going into politics. But he didn't want to waste his talents. So there he was, on a plane to Paris, at someone else's expense, with most of his worldly goods in a small suitcase which fitted conveniently on the empty seat beside him.

In his advertisement he had said: 'Anything legal considered.' Not that he knew very much about the law. The reply from someone in Paris had been on very expensive writing paper and had contained an offer which was admittedly vague, was not obviously illegal, and was financially promising.

The taxi took him to an address in the Avenue Foch which fully lived up to the writing paper. It was a very grand house indeed.

'I take it that you are a completely amoral young man, Mr Jennings.'

'Why do you assume that?' Edmund had not expected quite such a direct opening move.

'Decent people don't advertise themselves in newspapers.'

'Do decent people reply to such advertisements?'

'Perhaps not.'

Edmund was puzzled by Mr Gray. He didn't look like the owner of such a house. He looked like a middle-aged, middle-rank civil servant, tired and impatient, in need of a good tailor and a long rest.

'Have you ever met a countess before?'

'Not knowingly, no.' Edmund was, once again, surprised by Mr Gray's dry directness.

On the following evening, he found himself sitting next to a countess at a dinner party of ten people in that same house, which had seemed dark and silent, but had now somehow been brought to bright and warm life.

Mr Gray, who was presiding at one end of the dining table, had been nothing if not economical in his instructions to Edmund.

'I'm not asking much,' he had said. 'The Countess has been in a mental hospital for the past twenty years, until last week. You will be her friend. That's all.'

Mr Gray would not say more and the Countess von Graben herself seemed to share his frugality in the matter of words. She was a dignified woman in her early sixties with pale blue eyes and a sad smile. Edmund could see no way in which his own morality, or lack of it, would be relevant to their relationship. He decided to treat her like the mother he had never known.

Over the next few weeks, he accompanied the Countess in the daily life of an average wealthy and solitary Parisian woman of a certain age. Each evening, after dinner, he left her at a very private and very expensive hotel in the rue Christine.

On one occasion Edmund explained to the Countess that he had been working as a foreign exchange broker in London.

'Then you know about gold? What is its value nowadays?'

Edmund described the working of the new relatively free market in gold. The Countess was pleased and even excited to hear about it.

'Very good,' said Mr Gray, when Edmund reported the conversation to him. 'You should encourage her to talk about such things. Sooner or later, she will have to take responsibility for her own affairs again.'

Edmund's encouragement of the Countess led to a surprising

result. She extracted a promise of secrecy and proposed a train journey. It took them to Bordeaux, then by hired car to a deserted farmhouse near Hourtin. There was ivy growing in and out of the window-frames and rusty farm machinery filled a farmyard jungle-deep in weeds.

'We were here during the war,' the Countess said, as if it were a sufficient explanation of their journey.

Edmund, following the directions of the Countess, had soon cleared the rubble and broken glass from a rotted wooden window-seat and had prised it open to reveal a flight of crumbling stone steps. He helped her down into a cellar which stretched the length and breadth of the farmhouse. It was cold and damp and empty except for the remains of three wooden packing-cases, almost decomposed into the mud of the floor.

The Countess said nothing until they were back in the car. 'It was the whole of my husband's fortune. You see, we came from Germany in 1937. Pictures and jewellery and . . .' Her voice trailed away '. . . and gold,' she said at last.

Two days after their return to Paris, Edmund learned that he would not be seeing the Countess again. 'She re-admitted herself to the hospital,' Mr Gray told him. He was giving Edmund a farewell dinner at *Le Procope*. He had clearly been preparing for the occasion with Scotch.

'I might as well tell you now. You've probably guessed. But perhaps not. She's my stepmother, the Countess. My father's name was Graben. Second wife. They left me in Germany in the thirties and came to France. They left me with an aunt. Took everything we possessed. And when my father died, she was the only person in the world who knew where they'd hidden it all. Millions. It was worth millions. Would be now, anyway. Then she went mad. She wouldn't speak to me for years.'

'So you hoped to use me to find out where it was hidden?'

'It was the only hope, the last chance. Now even that chance has gone. She is back in hospital, more withdrawn than ever.'

Edmund saw no reason to tell Mr Gray about the visit which he and the Countess had paid, not to Nice as they had told Mr Gray on their return, but to Bordeaux. There was no need to destroy Mr Gray's last hope of adding so much more wealth to

47

his present prosperity. And Edmund would be quite happy to act on some future occasion as a temporary son, if not heir, for the sad and gentle Countess.

Not long after his return to London, he had a telephone call from Mr Gray.

'The Countess is dead. Her last wish was that you should have the solid gold ring which she always wore.'

'That's very kind. I'd be honoured to have it.'

'Mr Jennings, one other thing. In her note to me, she said that the ring was to go to "my dear Edmund, heir to all my secrets." I shall be in London next week. I very much hope that we shall be able to meet and have a talk.'

'That would be very pleasant and could be very interesting,' Edmund said cheerfully.

An Egg in the Hand

P.W.R. FOOT

It was hot that midday and the sun drove me down Bolters Hill to the cool interior of a typical Dorset inn, nestling by the river. Outside a Jaguar was parked.

There was only one other customer; an untidy, middle-aged man, with a pair of binoculars slung over his shoulder.

'So you're a schoolmaster,' he said, after quizzing me with the ease with which one talks to strangers in the country.

'I specialise', I said, 'in what some call mentally retarded children.'

'Now, that's interesting. The Thickees, you mean, eh!' and before I could remonstrate about this appellation he went on: 'I suppose they pack 'em all off to town schools now, but when I was a lad every village had its idiot. You don't find 'em now.'

'Isn't that a good thing?'

He never replied but said again, 'Schoolmaster, eh!'

'And what do you do for a living?' I asked.

'A bit of this and that. Nothing at the moment – just a spot of bird-watching. Good area for birds. I know it well – grew up here, you know. Ever been bird-watching?'

'Not much chance in London.'

He lit a cigarette, coughed and spat in a spittoon which I was quite surprised to see near him on the floor. Then he became reflective.

'Years ago,' he said, 'this pub was run by a chap called Crabbe, and he employed a lad whom everybody knew as Luke – the village idiot, if you like.

'He couldn't read or write and the village schoolmaster had long given him up. He was an orphan and slept rough but Mr Crabbe discovered he was good with animals, so he let him sleep in the back of the inn and look after a few cows and the pigs down by the river. When Mr Crabbe began to take in the odd tourist he discovered something else about Luke. It happened like this.

'There was a boy staying here with his parents for a few days and he met Luke one afternoon while out for a walk. Luke was sitting on the gate that separates the pathway from Bolters Hill and the river.

'The boy was lonely and he wanted someone of his own age to talk to and there was Luke, more of a scarecrow than a human sitting there looking as though he was watching the river, equally lonely. Actually he was spitting at a worm wriggling on the tow-path. The boy said hello. Luke merely looked him up and down and said nothing.

' "Hello," the boy said again. "Look what I found this afternoon." And from his pocket he drew four twinkling bird's eggs. Luke poked his long nose at them, sniffed them and then suddenly began to laugh – a sneering kind of laugh.

'The boy was disappointed. "What's the matter?" he asked.

'Luke told him. "Why, they be robin's eggs!" And he laughed again.

'At this the boy got a bit annoyed. " I don't see anything to laugh at." He had wanted to tell how he had found the eggs high up in a thick, thorny hedge, and then he remembered that Mr Crabbe had mentioned Luke as being a bit soft in the head. "I don't suppose you know one egg from another," he added.

'Luke laughed again. "You traipse all over them hills to find eggs and find robin's eggs!"

' "Well, what if they are! What's wrong with them?"

' "They be cursed. That's what's wrong with them."

'Now it was the boy's turn to laugh. "What absolute rot!"

' "If you takes robin's eggs then the hand that takes them turns into a claw."

50

'He put out his own dirty paw and slowly bent his fingers to show what happened if you took robin's eggs. He told the boy how young Smithers up at Beckett's Farm had taken robin's eggs and how his hand had gone all scaly and bent.

'The boy laughed again. "Go on! You're having me on."

' "No I baint. His hands went just like that, I'm telling you." And the earnest look in Luke's eyes showed that he meant it.

'The boy was no fool. He had heard of country superstitions and how one had to humour those who believed them, so he pretended to be concerned. "Is there nothing I can do then?"

' "Oh yes, there be that," said Luke. "Them eggs has got to be back in the nest afore sundown."

' "Well, I'm not going all that way back," said the boy.

'Luke shrugged his shoulders and turned his attention to the worm. Then as the boy began to leave him he said: "I could put 'em back for you."

' "But you don't know the nest, and I don't think I could find it myself very easily."

'Luke gave an exaggerated wink. "A robin can't build a nest hereabouts without be known. I know 'un," he added waving his hand at the hill.

' "Are you sure?"

' "Yes, no one dare go near that nest for fear of the curse."

' "All right," said the boy. "See they go back safely." And he placed the eggs into Luke's waiting palm.

'He left Luke still sitting on the gate, but he had to look back when he heard that laugh again. He saw him place the eggs into a large red handkerchief, climb languidly over the gate and amble slowly up Bolters Hill, laughing as he went.

'It quite mystified the boy, but it confirmed the fact in his mind that Luke was barmy.'

The bird-watcher told this story with evident relish and then I said, 'Yes, but you said Mr Crabbe then discovered something new about Luke.'

'That's right. You see, the next day when the boy was leaving with his parents, he happened to tell Mr Crabbe that he had met Luke, and Mr Crabbe said, "Talking about Luke, he's a rare one for finding things. Why, last night he came in with four of the most beautiful bird's eggs you ever saw."

' "Robin's eggs?" asked the boy gently.

' "Bless you, no; much rarer than that! I made him show me what else he had in that chest of drawers in his room, and believe me had a collection of eggs that would make any collector green with envy."

'He broke off suddenly and looked at the boyo. "Did that Luke tell you they were robin's eggs? The rascal! I asked him what they were but he wouldn't tell me. Though he knew all right?" Just then Mr Crabbe discovered that Luke, who had positioned himself behind the door, had heard every word.

' "Come here, you rogue!" called Mr Crabbe, but Luke with that laugh of his scuffled out of the inn. "He's quite a simpleton, really," said Mr Crabbe.'

The stranger gulped down his beer, swung his binoculars to the rear and made to go. 'Incidentally, it had the effect of making that boy take an interest in birds.'

'May I hazard a guess that you were the boy who encountered Luke?' I asked him with what I thought admirable perspicacity.

He had his hand on the door handle. With great accuracy he spat into the spittoon across the other side of the bar.

'Have another guess,' he said and went out to his Jaguar.

The Farewell Gift that Just Wasn't Enough

JOY MARY HIGHAM

The servants departed singly as their tasks were completed, the cook after breakfast was served, the skivvy when she'd washed up.

Miranda, her ladyship's personal maid, had scuttled through most of her duties; now all that remained was to help her mistress finish dressing before she, too, was free to go.

'One moment, Miranda. Just one moment,' the old lady boomed, as the girl offered the mink wrap.

Meekly the girl watched as her mistress, poker-backed, turned from her own bare, discarded rooms, and opened the door which led into those so recently occupied by her late husband.

Here nothing had been touched for in her grief she had not tolerated any disturbance. Everything was – and would stay – as it had been on that fatal day when he had gone out never to return.

His study desk was strewn with pens, pencils, blotter; a sheet of paper scrawled with indecipherable notes; drooping flowers in a discoloured vase; photographs of laughing people. Herself when young; the children; brown-haired Fenella, to whom she was about to escape . . . South Africa! How he had looked forward to going some day.

In the dressing-room she fingered his garments, gazed again on her gifts to him: watches, signet rings, cuff links: each an occasion remembered now with sadness. She picked up the heavy hair brushes, silver backs so intricately ornamented. She'd bought them in Munich, just before the war.

But his bedroom brought the deepest hurt of all: for a moment she stared, breathing deeply; then walked to the window. How right he'd been to insist they made their private suite on the top floor of the house.

'But the view, my dear!' he'd enthused, overcoming objections. 'And we can always have a lift installed!'

Resolutely she closed the door behind her. 'Very well, Miranda,' she said holding herself poised for the wrap to be draped across her shoulders.

Her ladyship smiled wanly into the mirror, holding out a hand for gloves and bag.

'Thank you, child . . . Tell me, how long have you been in my employ?'

'Just over a year, m'lady.'

'And you have another position to go to?'

'Yes, thank you, m'lady.'

'Good.' She opened her handbag and took out a small envelope. 'Here,' she said imperiously, 'is my farewell gift.'

The girl took it eagerly.

'Oh, thank you very much, m'lady.'

'And now – goodbye, Miranda.'

She was like a queen, Miranda thought, trying not to giggle. 'Goodbye, m'lady.'

She waited until the lift door closed and she heard the cage start down, before tearing open the envelope.

Quickly she flicked through the notes. 'Ten ruddy quid!' she hissed in disgust. 'The mean old devil!'

Miranda glanced out of the window, saw the Daimler glide away, skipped out of the room and down the corridor to a door at the far end. 'Okay, Jess, you can come out now. The coast's clear!' she sang, flinging open the door. 'I'm the only one left!'

He came, a paunchy man in an old raincoat, with a bunch of canvas bags dangling from stubby hands.

'How much did she give you then?' he asked.

'A tenner.'

'That all?' He laughed, a fruity, unhealthy laugh. 'Never mind. Your cut'll be worth ten times that!'

'I should bloody hope so! Here – look – this is the study.'

Practised eyes scanned the scene and found it good.

'How long's she going to be away?' he demanded.

'Five – six months.'

He laughed again. 'Good. We'll take the lot. Plenty of time to shift it.'

Quickly one arm swept gold and jewelled paraphernalia from the desk while Miranda upended drawers.

'Look at this knife – all that carving!'

'Inlaid ivory,' he said. 'Worth something. Put it in.' And he turned his attention to the forest of photos in heavy silver frames. 'We'll have that inkstand,' he added. 'Solid, that is. And get the pictures down.'

'We don't want pictures.'

'Course we don't. But we want the frames.'

Antique ornaments, inlaid boxes, clocks with jewelled faces all were stuffed unceremoniously into capacious bags.

'Now the dressing-room.'

Everything went: jewelled pins, gold watches, platinum and ruby cuff links, engraved cigar cases, heavy gold rings. A fur coat, silk shirts, immaculate, handmade suits, a rack of tussore ties, binoculars, cameras, racquets, sticks.

'What's in the bedroom, then?'

Greedily he toured the sumptuous room, scooping the remaining trivia of his lordship's earthly life into the already bulging sacks.

Miranda, glancing out of the window, saw that the Daimler had returned. She watched with mounting horror as it pulled up at its accustomed spot by the kerb. She saw Phipps climb out, speak a few words to her unseen ladyship, then climb the steps to the front door. Panic tightened her throat as she shouted to Jess.

'Here – we must get out! Phipps is back. He must have forgotten something. Quick! Into the lift!'

'But won't he come that way?'

55

'He hates lifts. He'll be up the stairs. Come on! We'll be out through the back before he gets down again!'

Together they struggled with the heavy bags along the corridor. Piling them into the tiny cage left little room, but they squeezed in, slammed the door shut and jabbed the button.

The lift was poised between the fourth and third floors when Phipps threw the main switch he had forgotten to turn off.

'Here! What's happened?' Her voice was sharp with fear.

'How the hell do I know?' In the sudden blackness he was groping at the panel of buttons, pushing everything.

'I don't like it, Jess! I don't like it!'

'Oh, be quiet!' He was still working frantically.

But she couldn't. As the Daimler slid unseen away she started to blubber, weak little cries that rose to a full-bodied scream.

Jess hit her very hard across the face. 'Shut you mouth, you silly fool!' he hissed. 'Do you want someone to find us? Here? With this lot?'

But it never mattered if she did or did not. And when in the spring, the house was reopened, what was left of Miranda and her accomplice was very far beyond caring.

Getting McGinty's Goat

DILLON McCARTHY

You've all heard of Paddy McGinty's goat, the one that ate the stick of dynamite, and sat by the fire afterwards. That goat had nothing on Joe McGinty of Ballydammit, who came across a recipe for making guncotton.

Now I'm not going to tell you the secret – there's enough sorrow in the world. The only things I'll tell you is that it's safer than petrol if you carry it wet, but not too wet, and that all you need to get the mixture right is a twin-tub washing machine.

This is because you have to wash it and wash it to get all the impurities out of it. If there's a little wee bit of dirt anywhere in the mixture, you could set it off by sneezing, wet or dry. And when you've washed it, you have to spin the surplus water out of it, which is where the twin-tub comes in. I have to tell you, too, that anywhere in the washing or drying process the guncotton can go off without warning, which was something nobody told Joe McGinty.

Joe was a grand fella. He had nothing against the English except their income tax system, but as he had never joined it, it didn't embitter him personally. Though he wept for the sorrows of Ireland, the one that grieved him most was the Republic's ideas of social security, and since the Marx brothers, Chico, Harpo, Groucho and Karl, were all one to him, he wasn't a revolutionary. But when he came across the recipe for guncotton – I'm not telling

57

you where – Joe thought it would be a terrible pity to waste it, and besides he wanted to see if the recipe would really work.

He was against violence, especially since the only experience of violence he'd had came from his wife, when she hit him with the baby's bottle.

'But, sure, making a wee bit of guncotton isn't exactly violence,' he said, talking it out with his brother; it's more like fireworks: we couldn't be expected to be blamed if people didn't use it strictly according to the instructions.

'And, anyway,' he said, 'all that rebuilding is going to make work for a lot of good men: it's not for nothing so many Irish are self-employed builders and decorators.'

Joe had more sense than to make the guncotton in the house: he didn't want another bang with a bottle, or worse, and his wife's uncle was a sergeant in the constabulary. He took the fuse out of the plug of the washing machine, so that it wouldn't work, and then waited till his wife nagged him into doing something to get it mended. Then he got his brother to have a look at it, and his brother told Mrs McGinty it would have to go back to the shop.

McGinty and his brother got the washing machine away to a shed on McGinty's brother's allotment. They ran an extension cable from a handy streetlight for the washing machine, and they had a hose from a standpipe for the water, and they had various other things to mix up.

The only ingredient I'll tell you is cotton wool – and they did all the things they were supposed to do, and then they washed it, and then they put it in the spin-drier, and they started to spin it.

Now Joe McGinty knew nothing about spin-drying. He had twelve kids, so he ought to have had some idea, but he was never in when his wife was doing the washing. So he filled the spinner tub too full, and he didn't get the load even, and then when he put the lid down and the spinner started, the guncotton began to pile up over the edge of the drum, and the drum started to thump against the sides of the tub, and Joe and his brother just managed to get to cover before the whole thing went off.

The Provos complained to the Officials, and the Officials complained to the Provos, and the Chief of Staff called a Press conference in Dublin and claimed the credit, but this was all afterwards.

It all took a bit of sorting out but he will be discharged from hospital any day now, almost as good as ever. The doctors said it was a pity he was still wearing his hat when his wife hit him.

There remains, of course, the matter of the twin-tub. But Joe's wife doesn't even mind that now. She's got a new washing machine due any minute but Joe doesn't know that yet. The new washing machine is called Joe McGinty, and Mrs McGinty reckons that since Joe is fond of washing, he can get on with the washing for all fourteen of them, until such time as the troubles are over, and he can go back to work. She's even thinking of taking in washing from the neighbours, as it will give the ladies more time to get on with organising the peace movement.

The one who suffered most was Joe's brother. Somehow or other, he got the blame for the whole thing, and became the first man in Irish history to have the Provos, the Officials, the Ulster Defence Association, the constabulary and Mrs Joe McGinty after him at the same time. He had to go on the run, and had nowhere to run to.

In the end, the safest thing he thought he could do was to go to England and join the British Army, but they posted him to Belfast. He'd desert right enough, only he has nowhere to desert to.

I'm telling you, I know what he's talking about, because he's me, and I never disliked Britain at all till I got posted to Ulster.

The Judge's Dilemma

LOUIS ALLEGRI

Judge Calderon was peering down at him from a seemingly great height with his long, stern, Spanish-type face. He seemed unwilling to reveal his row of large bottom teeth that showed up like white tombstones during one of his rare smiles. The judge was as proud and unbending as some Old Testament prophet when it came to the letter of the law. Well, that was all to the good. Didn't want him to bend with the wind – or rather with the tempest that was to come.

Meyer shifted his feet in the dock of the steaming, Central American courtroom. He spoke Spanish, but with an accent, and that was the main reason he had been accused of the murder of his partner. They had fallen out over the proceeds of an earlier burglary and someone had heard his voice during the struggle. But his 'alibi' – and Calderon's pride – would save his neck. Meyer restrained his excitement as shadows fell across the crowded courtroom this second and probably final day.

'This fictitious woman you claim you were with at the time your partner was murdered,' the obese prosecutor sneered. 'You say she was tall, about thirty-three, with a pale, ethereal beauty, a cultured, opulent background and reddish hair. Strange, is it not, that she hasn't been found or come forward to save the life of her friend. There's been enough publicity.'

Meyer shook his dark head, looking sorrowful. 'Her husband,

from what I could glean from her, is as stern and unbending as . . . as that tree out there,' he said.

He felt like bursting into laughter as all eyes turned towards the gnarled, almost petrified oak tree that could be seen through the courtroom window.

'I feel her innate decency will eventually make her come forward, but she must be going through hell at the moment at the thought of her husband's reaction to the scandal.'

'Your imagination is over-reaching itself,' the perspiring prosecutor said.

'When I met her in the bar of that new hotel on the south side of the city,' Meyer continued hurriedly, they mustn't stop his flow yet, 'she was in a terribly depressed state. I was willing to listen and – and she agreed to come to my place. I'm sorry to say it, but – the poor woman was an alcoholic. Drank like a fish. She was filled with guilt.'

'She did open her heart to you, didn't she!' The prosecutor stood, arms akimbo. 'Is there any more?'

'Yes, yes, there is more!' Meyer turned towards Judge Calderon.

'Go on – Mr Meyer,' he detected a break in Calderon's voice, and trembled with a fearful excitement. His wits stood between him and the gallows.

He had been casing Calderon's luxurious villa for weeks before the incident with his partner. He knew a lot about the household. The judge, still only in his forties, was one of the wealthiest men in the country, and when Meyer escaped the probing donkeys of this inquisition, he was all set up to make his big haul, and then settle back in the States.

'She had – unusual earrings, sapphire, I think. Finely engraved with an astrological sign . . . the Gemini twins. She told me her birthday was May the – ' The prosecutor muttered something, but what made him shiver was the noise of Calderon's pencil snapping!

'Oh, and she loved music; Verdi's *Rigoletto* was one of her favourites.' He was stabbing at the very heart of his judge now. Well, here was the *coup de grâce*. 'And – she had a large mole on her upper left thigh . . .'

He heard Calderon suck in his breath and turned to see the

judge's thin lips were bloodless and quivering as if he had a violent tic . . .

It had been the only way he could escape the gallows. As Meyer lay in his cell that night, he savoured the image of his tormented judge. Calderon would give his verdict in the morning.

During the casing of Calderon's villa, meticulous as ever, he had noticed that mole through his binoculars. She was the only creature Calderon loved. And it had all fallen into place when a friend, who had been helping him, found she had been secretly drinking in some bar at the time of the murder.

Calderon was probably confronting her at this moment, charging her with infidelity. Meyer stretched himself on his bunk as he thought of her lying desperately; nothing worse to alcoholics than revealing their drinking vice. He heaved a sigh of satisfaction; he was dictating events, not his judge . . .

The following night Meyer sat on the edge of the bunk, trying to control the surging panic that threatened to overwhelm him as he struggled to interpret that morning's events.

Calderon, looking like death itself, had sentenced him to be hanged!

Had he misjudged the man? No! It was out of character! He must surely have convinced Calderon that woman was his wife!

Meyer jumped as the cell door opened and a tall, gaunt man entered . . .

'Look!' Meyer broke the silence. 'I now know who that woman is. She . . . well, she's – Judge Calderon's wife . . . !' He watched as the man raised his heavy, black brows, momentarily revealing small, sharp eyes. 'Do you understand? Judge Calderon is bloody harsh, but will always apply the law to the letter. Who are you?'

'I'm the public executioner.'

Meyer struggled to his feet and fell against the dank wall.

'A – man of Calderon's calibre would never allow such a miscarriage of justice,' he stammered. 'When it comes to the law he's as – as rigid as that tree in the courtyard. Even though I was involved with his wife, he could never – '

'Ah,' the visitor said softly, nodding his small head several times. 'Things are clearer now. Judge Calderon resigned his office after sentencing you because he is a man of principle.'

'What sort of principle is that which lets an innocent man hang for personal revenge?' Meyer clenched his fists, his head ringing with anger and fear.

'Even Judge Calderon had his breaking point,' the gaunt man's face darkened. 'Your axe bit too deep. I see now why I was asked to – make your end as unpleasant as possible. Señora Calderon committed suicide this morning.'

Bomb in the Bed

HARRY SECOMBE

'Hurry up, buddy,' came Johnny Owen's impatient voice from the outside.

'Can't find the blasted gaiters,' I panted, banging my head for the umpteenth time against the iron framework of the three-ton truck which had been our home all the way across North Africa and three-quarters of Sicily.

'Come on, mun, Lieutenant Cattermole's gone back to the Battery. There's gallons of lovely vino waiting for us, buddy,' Owen niggled, his false teeth jockeying for position on his gums.

He had been a cinema projectionist in civvy street and had watched so many American films that his normal Welsh accent was overlaid with a nasal Yankee drawl.

'Are you sure that the vino place was open?' I asked as we trudged dustily up the track towards the little village.

'Of course, boy. We've got at least three hours before the rest of the unit arrive, and by then, buddy . . .'

The signals officer had gone back in his jeep to report that the area was suitable as a camp site.

The village in front of us seemed deserted as we marched in ragged step towards it, the white dust filling our eyes and mouths. It was very obvious that it had been bombed from the air.

A few yards further on took us into a little square with a fountain, where a girl stood filling a can with water.

'That's the vino place – the door's open, anyway.' Owen pointed across the square to a low whitewashed building.

I turned my attention to the girl, who was regarding us with apprehension in her dark liquid eyes. What a cracker!

She smiled certainly as we stood appraising her.

'Leave this to me,' said Owen.

'Hello, nice dayo.' He firmly believed that loud English with an 'o' added on here and there was a good substitute for Italian.

'Us,' he said 'Englisho. Not harmo you. Where vino?'

She beckoned us to go with her across the street.

She stopped outside a shabby two-storeyed tenement house on the other side of the village.

We stood in a central hallway with passages leading off it and in front of us a worn stairway. The girl walked to the foot of the stairs, turned, and said again 'Come along' in Italian.

Owen joined her side as she walked up towards the next floor.

'This is better than the films, boy,' he whispered.

When we had reached the head of the stairs she turned left and stopped outside a door. She motioned us inside.

'Good heavens, look!' Owen gasped, his face drained of colour.

I peeped over his shoulder. It was an ordinary peasant type of living-room with onions and peperones hanging from a hook in the wall, a faded picture of the Virgin Mary, a crude dressing-table with a battered alarm clock on it, and in the middle of the room a huge brass bedstead.

From a hole in the ceiling a shaft of strong sunlight lit up the centrepiece of our little tableau – a large, unexploded five-hundred-pound bomb. It lay at an angle on the bed, its nose buried deep in the springs.

We stood rooted, the silence broken only by the loud ticking sound. The girl looked at us.

'She wants us to take it away, Johnny.' I stammered.

'That's ticking,' he shouted. 'It's alive! It's a time fuse, mun.' He made for the stairs. The girl ran after us pleading, 'Take it away.'

'We come backo,' shouted Owen from the security of the other side of the street. 'Get helpo.'

I stood uncertainly at his side, my mouth dry, watching the girl

65

who had come as far as the entrance and now stood with her hands on her hips shouting angrily. What she was saying needed no translation. We were cowards, all Englishmen were cowards, any one brave Italian soldier would have taken the bomb away by himself.

Blushing furiously we beat a hasty retreat back to the square. The vino shop door was still open.

Owen and I avoided each other's eyes as the big raffia-covered bottle of rough country wine and two chipped tumblers were placed before us.

We sat wordlessly, drinking glass after glass in quick succession, until the heat of the sun, and warmth of the wine began to work.

'It was much too big for us to handle,' Owen began. 'No point in getting ourselves blown up, buddy. After all, it's a specialist job, removing bombs.'

Owen's fifth glass rocked slowly in his hand. 'She was a corker, buddy. Imagine what would have happened if we *had* been able to take the bomb away. The village would be ours, pardner, we'd be heroes, boy.'

The wine fumes wreathed delicious shapes in my head.

'What fools we are!' Owen cried. 'That ticking – that wasn't the bomb, mun, that was the old alarm clock on the dressing-table.'

'That's right,' I said dimly remembering.

'Well then,' shouted Johnny, 'that ruddy bomb's harmless – there's no time-fuse. It's a dud, boy. All we have to do is push the bed out of the door, down the hill outside the house and we are heroes. The village will be ours, boy. Come on, we've still got another couple of hours before Cattermole gets back.'

Outside the house the occupants were gathered, gesticulating and arguing, the girl in the middle of them. They fell silent as we approached, and Owen bowing low before the girl, announced. 'We take it away.'

She flung her arms round his neck and kissed him soundly on the cheek.

Another girl not quite as good-looking as Maria seized me, and gave me a garlicky kiss.

'Me sister Maria,' she gurgled. 'Me Rosina.'

66

Johnny started for the stairs, the grateful Maria clinging to his arms. When he reached the door he turned round and motioned for silence.

'Mustn't make it look too easy,' he said behind his hand.

He ordered everybody to leave the building. The ticking seemed louder as we entered the room.

'Fancy us being scared of an old clock ticking,' Owen laughed giving the bomb a playful clout on the tin. 'You get the far end and I'll take the front – the bed's on casters so it'll move easily down the stairs.'

As I moved around it to position, I picked up the clock – then I sobered quickly. The clock had stopped, yet the ticking was still going on.

'Johnny,' I began, 'there's something you . . .'

'Come on, come on,' he shouted pulling the bed towards the perilous journey along the passage.

I could only hang on nervelessly, as the bed bumped its way through the door. The sharp left turn jerked the bomb sideways and the ticking noise stopped. I moaned softly.

Owen turned his head sideways and winked.

It was obviously useless to get the message across to him and as I was trapped behind the bed I would have to see the drama through.

By the time we had begun the descent of the stairs I was a limp, sweating, gibbering wreck.

After a thousand years we reached the bottom of the stairs and Owen turned around towards me for the first time since we began the job. Behind him the excited villagers were grouped in the doorway.

'That's it, boy.' He grinned. 'Make it look good now they can see us. That expression on your face would get you an Oscar.'

'For heaven's sake, Owen,' I said brokenly, 'get this thing outside.'

We pushed the bed into the street.

Outside, I shoved Owen aside and shouting like a lunatic got the crowd behind the building. Then I pushed the rickety bed to where the steep road led the way down from the village.

Owen, with his arms around Maria, was watching indulgently.

'That's it, boy,' he yelled.

With one last despairing effort I sent the bed careering down the hill.

'Get down, you fools,' I sobbed as I stumbled back towards Owen and Maria. I fell on my face pulling them down with me.

Ten seconds later the bang came. A black cloud of smoke rolled lazily skywards and the one remaining pane of glass in the vino shop window tinkled gaily as it hit the street.

I lay still, my face to the earth.

'Dear heaven,' said Owen's hoarse voice in my ear. 'It was alive all the time.'

I nodded wearily. 'That alarm clock wasn't working. I was trying to tell you but you wouldn't damn well listen.'

'You knew?' Owen couldn't believe it.

Before he could say any more the villagers were upon us. I was plucked from the floor by Rosina. Owen was clasped by a weeping Maria and the rest hugged each other laughing and crying. A table was dragged into the street, bottles of wine appeared from hiding places and in the look in our girlfriends' eyes there was a promise.

We had just sat down when we heard the jeep. I looked at Owen.

'Cattermole,' we said in unison.

'You're under arrest,' he shouted, red-faced. 'We're moving on in ten minutes and here you are swilling wine with the ruddy natives. Get in that Jeep before I shoot the whole damned lot of you.'

The silent villagers watched us climb sheepishly into the vehicle. Maria and Rosina waved their fingers in a pathetic gesture of farewell, the tears already starting in their eyes.

It Could Only Happen Once

SPIKE MILLIGAN

I t could only happen once in a lifetime. It happened to Joseph
Schilkraut. His pawnshop was the sole survivor in the district
of wholesale shutdowns during the 1930 depression.

'There ain't no more money left in the world,' he told his wife
at breakfast. 'Nobody *ever* redeems their pledges these days. Look
at the stuff I got in the shop! I can't get a penny for any of them,
ach! There just *ain't no more money.*'

A host of pawned clocks chimed ten from the shop. In the good
old days he would have been opened at eight-thirty sharp, but
now there was no point.

He finished his tea and pulled the shop blinds. It was cold. He
wiped condensation from the windows.

Across the road, outside the Labour Exchange groups of grey,
cold, unemployed men, stood talking. Some wore army medals –
'Poor fellers,' thought Joe.

Farther down the street some had started a fire with orange
boxes.

The day passed without a customer.

'I suppose,' thought Joe, 'people ain't got anything to pawn any
more!'

It was the shortest day. At four he lit the gas. The singing
mantle bathed the room in a sea of sepulchral green.

'Ach, might as well close,' Joe muttered. But what was this? Someone coming in! Yes. Yes, he was.

The shop door opened, an elderly man made a shuffling entrance.

'You still open, mate?'

Joe shrugged his shoulders. 'Well mmm, yes. What you got then?'

The old man held up an army sandbag. 'Do you give anything on musical instruments, mate?'

Joe winced. 'Instruments?' He pointed to a host of trumpets that festooned the walls. 'You can see how much I need instruments.'

The old man stood silent – his great shabby overcoat hung from his stooped shoulders like tired wings.

'Oh, all right!' There was a note of pity in Joe's voice. 'What you got?'

The old man laid the sandbag on the counter. 'It's a fiddle, mate,' he said sliding it from the bag.

At first glance Joe could see it was old. Very old. He took it behind the counter under the light and peered into the 'f' holes. The floor of the instrument was thick with dust.

All the while the old man stood silent.

'Won't keep you long,' said Joe removing the dust with a paint brush. *Niccolò Amati 1640*.

Joe polished his glasses and looked again *Niccolò Amati 1640*. That was what the label said.

Steady, Joe, there's a million fakes floating about. This could be another, except this didn't *feel* like a fake. The label was vellum, and the signature in faded brown ink. Joe had a strange feeling come over him. The old man stood waiting, Joe showed no outward emotion.

'Is it worth anything?' asked the old man.

Joe laid the violin on the sandbag, took off his glasses.

'I don't know, sir. Leave it here a day or two and I'll let you know!'

The old man took a pace forward. 'A *day* or two? I was hopin' I might get somethin' right away, mate. See I'm skint and hungry – bloomin' hungry. Couldn't you let me have a couple o' bob on account? I mean, it *must* be worth more than that!'

Joe put the violin into the sack.

'All right – two bob.'

The old man took the coin. 'Good luck,' he said spitting on it, and shuffled from the shop.

Heart beating heavily, Joe bolted the shop door. He took the stairs to the loft two at a time. He pulled down his lexicon of 'Violins – Viols and Cellos.'

For an hour he compared the violin against illustrations. Measurements, wood, scroll – all signs pointed in favour. There was one person who could tell him for sure – Uncle Alfred.

Eight minutes later, the phone rang in Uncle Alf's shop. The babbling voice of nephew Joe came racing over the phone. He told all.

'You got to come down now and verify it or I won't sleep.'

'Me come down now? I'm in Leeds remember?'

'Leeds, Schmeeds, this could mean a fortune – you can have your cut.'

'I'll be down on the night train.'

At six-fifty the following morning Uncle Alfred was in the shop. Without even letting him remove his hat or coat, Joe pushed the violin at him.

Screwing an inspection glass in his eye, Uncle Alfred started to shake.

'Joe – it's real,' he said. 'It's an Amati! Worth forty thousand pounds anywhere in the world.'

The two men stood silent in the room. Then Joe started to speak.

'Forty thousand pounds,' he kept repeating.

'And that's putting it at a minimum,' interjected Uncle Alf.

Joe fell back into the chair. This meant the start of a new life – no more penny-pinching, no more bargaining, bills, arguments, sleepless nights, rent. All over, all over. He started to cry.

Uncle Alf was speaking: 'You ain't told me where you got it.'

'An old feller came in – I give him two bob deposit.'

'Two bob,' Uncle Alf clapped his hands. 'Then he don't know the value. We're home and dry, ha ha!'

Joe held up his hand. 'Just a minute – he's entitled to a slice of the money – it's his violin.'

Uncle's face dropped. 'You mad, Joe? Who found out it was worth forty thousand? Him? No, it was *you* and *me*. No son, that's the luck of the game – offer him two quid – and later – send him an anonymous hundred. He'll be happy. Come on, now, wake up! Business is business! He'd do the same to you.'

A day went by, two, three, a week the old man never appeared. Joe and his wife were taking sleeping pills.

Late one January evening, the old man came.

'Sorry I been so long,' he coughed. 'I been ill wiv the flu. I lives on me own so I don't get much attention.'

There was a pause. Joe waited for the man to ask the question. He did.

'Er – did you make up yer mind about the fiddle?'

Joe drew a deep breath. 'Yes,' he exhaled. 'I have.'

'Thank God. I need a few bob – huh.'

'All I can give you is two quid.'

At the mention of money the old man swayed.

'Two quid?' he echoed.

'Yes.'

'Ah.' The old man stood blinking in the middle of the room. 'I fought it might be worth a bit more.'

Joe laughed. 'More? How much you reckon it's worth, then?'

The old man gave Joe a steady gaze. 'Forty thousand pounds,' he said.

The Wastrel

PETER SELLERS

O n a hot and rainy July afternoon in the year 1901 General
Sir Charles Hanley-Adamant sat brooding, the long thin
legs of a hunting man stretched out before him, in the long, oak-
pannelled dining-rooms of Coplands, the country home of the
Hanley-Adamants for nigh on four centuries.

In every angular line of him there was something significant of
one of England's country gentlemen, the pride of many closely
knit generations. But at this particular moment his physiognomy
was clouded.

With a heavy sigh he ran his hands through his rapidly thinning
hair and, as he did so, rose jerkily from his armchair until he was
very nearly erect. After a moment or two he lurched, his beautifully
shod splay feet making no perceptible sound on the thick pile of
carpets, to the window and gazed lackadaisically out. He seemed
to be on the point of coming to a momentous decision.

Outside the rain beat a ceaseless tattoo on the bent back of old
Chambers, the head gardener who, with the deceptive ease born
of long practice, was busily engaged in spraying both the roses
and himself with a secret preparation that had been handed down
to him from time immemorial.

Suddenly a kind of muffled sob burst involuntarily from the
General's lips and his wife, Lady Cicely who, until this moment
and for the past three hours had been industriously, but to little

practical purpose, plying her needle, looked up in concern from the music-stool on which she was sitting.

'Did you say something, Charles?' she queried, not without some solicitude.

'No, no, it was nothing – nothing at all, I assure you. I beg of you to dismiss the matter from your mind entirely. It is of no consequence whatsoever.'

With the awkward grace which invariably accompanied nearly all her movements, Lady Cicely Hanley-Adamant set down her embroidery and glided swiftly to her husband's side with a rustle of silk, chiffon and bombasine.

'Something is wrong, Charles,' she urged, grasping her spouse by the upper part of one of his skinny arms. 'I can sense it. Tell me if you will. Have I not always been the one to share your confidence, thereby, to however small a degree, lightening them?'

'It is your son,' he finally managed to ejaculate thickly.

'Lance?' faltered Lady Cicely.

'Who else?' returned the General mechanically.

'I merely wondered, that is all,' vouchsafed his better half somewhat timidly. 'Why, has he done something to distress you, Charles?'

The General made an impatient gesture which sent a small cut-glass bowl of antirrhinums whizzing through the French windows.

'It is no use,' he groaned aloud. 'I can stand it no longer. I will not have a wastrel and a milksop for a son. As the last of a great and proud line he has certain responsibilities – but what has he done since being sent down from Cambridge? Nothing! Nothing but skulk in his room scribbling poetry and slouch about the place like a pickpocket!'

Instantly Lady Cicely sprang to the defence of her only child. 'But surely, Charles,' she temporised desperately, in a wheedling tone, 'you are aware as well as anyone that Lance is – well – sensitive and not quite as other boys.'

A close observer would have seen a vein beginning to throb in the venerable warrior's left temple.

'My mind is quite made up,' was the curt rejoinder. 'As you know his uncle has recently been good enough to offer him gainful employment in the City, and I have decided that either he takes advantage of this opportunity or I renounce him entirely. This is your son's final chance!'

Lady Cicely gave a pathetic little cry and swayed slightly before slithering carefully to the floor in a swoon. Tried beyond endurance the General yanked savagely at the bell-sash and tottered from the room.

After tea that day, in the selfsame room, still half-stunned by the information which had only seconds before been imparted to him, Lance Hanley-Adamant, a comely, well-set youth with a loosely knit face which did little or nothing to belie the thirty-nine summers that rode so easily on his sloping shoulders, stood aghast in a loosely cut pepper-and-salt knickerbocker suit before the stern-visaged author of his being.

'I say, really, look here, dash it all, Pater, it's a bit bally thick on a fellow and all that sort of rot, I mean to say . . .' he blurted lamely.

'Silence, sir!' exploded the General. 'How dare you adopt that tone with me! You have heard the terms of my ultimatum. Either you will do what I have said, or I shall have nothing more to do with you and this house will be barred to you forever. There is no more to be said.'

For a second or two the young fellow stood like one transfixed. His pointed chin worked nervously and there was a look in his eyes that was not easy to understand.

'You really mean that, Pater?' he breathed.

'I am not in the habit, as far as I am aware, of saying what I don't mean,' was the sardonic reply.

There was a short, but pregnant, silence broken only by the sound of a muffled explosion from the wine cellar. Lance Hanley-Adamant seemed to be trying to realise the full significance of his father's words. He was evidently fighting an inward battle too.

Suddenly he reeled and turned the colour of whitewash.

'But what about Ethel?' he cried hoarsely. Pursing his lips, General Sir Charles Hanley-Adamant, his face assuming an even graver mien, leaned back in his chair and, having made one or two abortive attempts at placing the tips of his fingers judiciously together, decided in favour of abandoning the project.

'Ah,' he observed with as much crispness as he could muster

to cover his momentary confusion. 'I am glad that you have brought up the matter of your fiancée.'

There followed another short, albeit pregnant, silence, this time broken only by the sound of someone falling downstairs.

'You are no doubt doubtless aware,' continued the older man, 'that I was more than gratified when you first began to pay attention to Ethel Edgbaston. It was what both her father and I had long hoped for. But George Edgbaston naturally has to think for his daughter. I received a letter from him by this morning's post.'

A new light shone in the young fellow's eyes.

'What did he say?' he enquired hoarsely, eagerly, anxiously.

For a full minute, perhaps less, father and son eyed each other askance.

'He says,' returned the General icily, 'that he will have no idle, indolent, listless, useless, moon-struck, dawdling, loitering, footling, dabbling, fribbling, fiddle-faddling ninny as a husband for his daughter. Furthermore, he declares that, until you turn over a new leaf, his doors also will be closed against you.'

'He says that?'

'Yes.'

'But Ethel will stand by me. I know!' babbled the distracted youth. 'I must hasten to her at once!'

A curious smile played about the grim features of his sire.

'It is a trifle late for that,' asseverated that worthy drily. 'Ethel Edgbaston has already been dispatched to stay with relatives in the country for an indefinite period.'

Again Lance reeled, turning even whiter than before. Then, by a supreme effort of will, he regained some of his composure.

'I still cannot do what you ask.' The words appeared to be jerked out of him.

'You are aware of the alternative?' persisted the other.

'Yes, goodbye, Pater,' was the only reply.

With bowed head and leaden gait, Lance Hanley-Adamant somehow stumbled blindly through the door.

On the dramatic scene which took place at Coplands that night between the parents of Lance Hanley-Adamant there is no need to dwell at length. In fact, there is no need to dwell upon it at all.

Months dragged wearily by and nothing was heard of the prodigal.

Of course, during the whole of this unhappy time, there raged far away in South Africa, the South African War.

Then, suddenly, it was rumoured in Society circles that someone resembling Lance had been seen drilling in a private's uniform, with almost uncanny lack of precision, at Wellington Barracks.

And Lady Cicely, far too excited to keep the news to herself, rashly divulged it to her husband.

'I thought I had made it perfectly clear,' declared Sir Charles, 'that I did not wish to hear his name mentioned again.'

'Yes, yes, I know, Charles,' pleaded the mother, 'but I can't help it. Besides, if it is true, it is a noble thing he has done. He has offered his life for what he believes to be right.'

'As to that,' returned the father harshly, 'many of the greatest scapegoats in the country have gone into the army. Young fools, knowing nothing of what war means and posing as heroes. And consider it! A son of mine a private! A friend of every groom, bootblack, potboy, crossing-sweeper and shop-walker in his regiment. But it's just like him.'

As a matter of fact it turned out that it actually wasn't Lance Hanley-Adamant who had been seen drilling in a private's uniform at Wellington Barracks.

We shall, therefore, never know the identity of the unfortunate warrior who *was* seen drilling etc., etc., and even supposing that we did, it is extremely doubtful whether any of us would be a penny the wiser.

I suppose you will be wanting to know what happened to our hero in the end. But that is another story entirely, and, much as I should like to, I really don't feel quite strong enough to go into it just at the moment.

The Cat Burglar

VICTORIA EDEN

Alec left his van against the blackness of the hedge, and dodged stealthily through the side gate and into the walled garden. He was carrying a dark cloth bag containing his tools, and under one arm was a short folding aluminium ladder. The veiled moon gave sufficient light for him to see the path, although he had a torch in his pocket.

He followed the path until he was in the shadow of the house. Peering nervously about him, he surveyed the layout. The big window at the left was his target, and he crept towards it, pausing to glance up at the burglar alarm box fixed high on the wall. He smiled. He was confident that he could overcome it.

Things hadn't been going too well for him lately, but this time was going to be different. He had planned this job with military precision, taken account of the obstacles, and had devised ways round them. He had thought of everything.

He knew the geography of the place, and what he was looking for. Mind you, the information had cost him a packet. But he reckoned it was worth it. His informant had spent several weeks there as part of a team of decorators. He had kept his eyes and ears open, and the knowledge he had sold to Alec was very interesting.

Alec licked his lips. If this job was successful – and it would be – he would own a little bag of diamonds worth fifty thousand smackers. The owner, a Hatton Garden merchant, was taking them to Amsterdam early tomorrow. So it was tonight or never.

Alec looked at the window. He couldn't force the catch – it was connected to the alarm – but he knew how to get round that. From his bag he drew two large rubber suction pads and stuck them on to the glass at diagonally opposite corners. Then he carefully went to work all round the window with a glass cutter. It was a genuine diamond and it cut effortlessly. When he had finished he grasped the pads and lifted the entire pane out cleanly, leaving a hole large enough for him to enter. He stuck a reel of masking tape over the glass rim that protruded from the frame – he didn't want to be a casualty, especially if he had to make a quick getaway.

He knew that there was an alarm mat under the carpet, beneath the window. One foot on it would set the bell ringing . . . that was where the ladder came in. He carefully rested one end on the sill and lowered the other to the floor, where it rested some five feet in.

Now for the dodgy part! He started inching his way down the ladder, his nerves jangling. When at last he put his feet on the floor and straightened cautiously, the sweat was pouring down his face. He felt as though his stomach was tied in a knot. But he had done it! Only one more hurdle to clear.

Alec was in the diamond dealer's study. He knew that the safe was concealed behind an innocent-looking landscape on the wall. He put his ear to the safe door. He could scarcely hear the tumblers clicking above the thumping of his heart, and he forced himself to calm down. Carefully he turned the dial, listening intently, and gave a muffled cry of triumph as the last digit slid into place.

His throat was dry with a mixture of excitement and fear as, already poised for flight in case the bell went off, he slowly pushed the handle down. The door swung open without a sound, and he let out a shuddering sigh of relief.

Alec shone his torch into the aperture, and almost shouted with delight when he saw the little chamois bag resting on the shelf. With shaking hands he took it and, loosening the thong round the top, poured the contents into his hand. He whistled soundlessly as he surveyed the flashing stones that sparkled in his palm. He picked one up and examined it with awe. Flawless! And there must be at least thirty here! He stood motionless for a moment.

Then the alarm went off.

Alec jumped violently as the strident sound of the bell shattered the stillness, and his hand shot up involuntarily, scattering the gems all over the room. With a startled oath he groped for his torch, and knocked it flying.

He stared wildly, trying to penetrate the blackness around him, and plunged towards the window. With a yell of despair he tripped and fell headlong to the floor. He was still struggling to get up, panic-stricken and half-dazed, when the light snapped on. A man stood at the door brandishing a revolver.

'Don't move, or I'll shoot!' he threatened, levelling the gun at the cowering Alec.

'Well let me get up, guv!'

The man gestured with the revolver for Alec to rise, then motioned him over against the wall.

A woman burst into the room. She was clad in a bright pink dressing-gown. Her hair was in curlers, covered by a lacy boudoir cap. Her hand went up to her mouth.

'Oh Thomas!' she squealed. 'You've caught a burglar! What shall we do?'

'Do?' snorted her husband. 'Call the police of course.'

Looking scared, the woman picked up the telephone. The man turned to Alec: 'And don't you try any tricks, or I'll blast you to kingdom come!'

He looked at the ladder.

'Very ingenious,' he acknowledged. 'But you weren't quite clever enough, were you?'

'What do you mean?' said Alec. 'And what made the alarm go off?'

The diamond merchant said triumphantly. 'You used the ladder to avoid the alarm mat, didn't you?'

He pointed to a cat that lay on the armchair washing itself.

'You see him? I put him out last night before I went to bed. When he saw the open window, he obviously decided to come in. He jumped straight down on to the mat. He didn't know about the alarm, you see!'

Postscript to a Betrayal

MARGARET WEBB

I'm putting this on paper to try to clear my mind. To get the facts sorted out. I'm changing the names, just in case . . .

I've got a decision to make.

I was rather pleased with myself when after a few weeks of writing, telephoning and pleading I finally succeeded in persuading Robert Shenton to give me an interview. Yes, *the* Robert Shenton, the boffin who caused all the brouhaha twenty years ago by leaking classified information to the other side of the Curtain. He'd done his time and was living like a recluse. It was to be an exclusive interview and I reckoned I could make my own terms with one of the national papers if I pulled it off.

But my elation evaporated when my jalopy turned into the drive of Shenton House. There was an ambulance at the door. The driver told me the news.

Robert Shenton was old and frail and known to have a heart condition.

I rang the bell. At least I might be able to get some information on his illness that might make a national story. There was no answer and just as I was turning away I realised that the door was unlocked. I went inside but there was no one about.

I went into a room which seemed to be a study, book-lined and furnished with high-backed leather chairs and a desk. But what riveted my attention was the sight of a life-sized portrait of a woman on the wall above the desk. I recognised her from Press photographs taken at the trial. They hadn't done her justice. She was beautiful all right but it wasn't just that. It was rather the expression on her face, half hidden under a cascade of shining hair; diffident, but extraordinarily appealing.

Cressida Shenton. She had loved and married Robert Shenton. When the scandal blew up, it broke her heart. An overdose, they said, but everyone knew that Robert Shenton had killed her as surely as if he had stabbed her.

I had imagined I was alone in the room, but I was mistaken. There was a movement in one of the high-backed chairs in front of the fireplace, and a bearded face peered around at me. He might almost have been Robert Shenton himself – there was at any rate a strong family resemblance. His hair and beard were grey and he had that drawn, ascetic look characteristic of so many intellectuals. A brother, perhaps?

'Come in, come in,' he said. 'Forgive me for not getting up. I've had a bad day . . .'

'Yes. I'm sorry,' I said. 'My name is Grey – Betty Grey. I'm a reporter. I was going to interview Mr Shenton . . .'

'Ah, yes. Well, Miss Grey, I think I can help you. Robert has no secrets from me.'

'And you are, sir . . . ?' I opened my notebook and looked at him enquiringly. But his head was turned to the portrait above the desk. His look was quite calm – sort of considering, as if unable to make up his mind.

'She's very beautiful,' I said.

'*Was* beautiful. Yes indeed. Tell me,' he said, 'what do you think of her? Apart from her beauty, I mean. Her . . . character, shall we say?'

It seemed an odd question. Everybody knew about Cressida Shenton and her blind love for her husband, and her loyalty.

I said stiffly, 'I think the portrait says it all. She's . . . well, sort of unworldly. Innocent, if you like.'

As he lowered his gaze I added, 'Her death was a tragedy.'

'Yes. It's a sad story. But she had to die, you know. They would have no mercy.'

Defensively I said, '*They*? There was no Press persecution.'

He looked thoughtfully at me for a few moments, then said, 'I wonder, Miss Grey, if you would do something for me. There are some papers to be destroyed. It's important, or I wouldn't ask. I'm quite helpless at the moment . . .'

I realised he must be crippled in some way.

'Yes, of course,' I said.

'There's a sealed packet in a concealed drawer in the desk. It's marked "Private". I want you to take it into the other room – there's a fire in there – and burn it.'

'But does Mr Shenton . . . ?'

'It's his wish, I assure you,' he said.

I went over to the desk and following his instructions, found the packet and took it across to him. He looked at it, his expression unreadable. Then he waved me away.

'Burn it!' he said. His voice was suddenly urgent and his face was deathly pale. 'Promise me you'll burn it!'

I promised. I went into the other room. The fire was very low and the envelope was thick. I had to tear it open to burn the contents piece by piece.

They were letters, typewritten, on thin foreign paper. They had no heading and no date. I couldn't avoid reading the first few sentences, and then I read the whole letter, and the next, and the next. There was no doubt of their meaning or to whom they were written. They must have been at least twenty years old.

It was all there, the details of the information wanted, the instructions for delivery, even the amount to be paid.

I rushed into the study with the letters still intact in my hand.

'I can't . . .' I began. But the room was empty.

I tried all the rooms, calling as I went, but there was no result. I was alone in the house. I sat down by the fire and tried to think.

Eventually I came back to my flat and telephoned the hospital. Again, I had a presentiment of what they were going to say.

'Mr Robert Shenton? I'm very sorry. I'm afraid he died in the ambulance. A brother? No, we understand he lived alone. No relations . . . or friends . . .'

So now it's left to me. Do I burn those revealing letters? Or let the world know about Cressida. Sweet, innocent Cressida, the traitor, the spy, the destroyer.

Or do I keep faith with Robert Shenton who took her guilt upon himself and gave twenty years of his life expiation, even holding back death itself to protect her name? And I promised . . .

Jimmy Pawson Doesn't Care

HILTON AMBLER

This is a river bed. Once there was water in it to wash the stones, but it may be ten years before a river runs this course again. The wettest thing in the river bed is Jimmy Pawson.

He is dead. He lies under a deep lip of overhanging rock, which is perhaps why the vultures have not found him. Jackals and hyenas, too, have let the body lie.

When he died, he was crawling for cover. His last movement was a spasm, part effort and part inertia, that turned him like a beetle on his back, flinging him over a rock so that now his pelvis juts obscenely upwards, supported by the rock, while the rest of him is sagging into the earth.

Jimmy drank too much and his face was flabby, but the mummifying effect of dry warm air had taken up some of the slack in his death-mask, so his face has an ascetic look. It is not too bad. Beneath the clothing, the top side of the body has fared less well than the face. The under side, wherever Jimmy touches the ground is unpleasant – to say nothing of the hole the bullet made in him.

A little wind toys in its boredom with the shirt that was white, and with the soiled lightweight slacks. Jimmy's clothes are all stirring, except his shoes. This wind is too inconsequential to shift even the shoe that used to be on his left foot. It is much lighter than the right shoe because in its heel it has a big space for diamonds. This shoe is not on Jimmy's foot. It lies twenty yards away, near where his car was parked, but he doesn't care.

Rita Pawson doesn't care either. She sits in the trading store, naked under her thin dress and wishing she could take off even that. It is hot and though today there is an unexpected Kalahari wind, it is no more sweet than the breath of a drunkard. She knows about drunkards, being married to Jimmy.

When will he be back? Not that it matters. Even six months away is not unusual for him, and in the meantime Jager keeps her happy.

Perhaps he will come tonight – Jager. He will come through the back door, undressing on his way to the bedroom. In half an hour he will be in his big police car again, patrolling. One might think the middle of the bush a strange place for a police patrol at night, but this outpost is on the edge of the great diamond fields by the mouth of the Orange River. Night is the best time for diamond runners. Jager knows this because he works with them.

He calls at Rita Pawson's trading store on his rounds, and never once has he made the mistake of calling when Jimmy is at home, because he knows when Jimmy will be away on business.

Night in the iron bed. Jager has come.

'Did you hear from Jimmy?' he asks.

'Don't make me laugh.'

'I like you to laugh. Did he write to you?'

'Jimmy never wrote a letter in his life.'

Not to you, perhaps (but Jager doesn't say it). Jimmy is a month overdue, according to the last note Jager had from Windhoek.

'He didn't say when he's coming back?'

'Would he tell me? What's your hurry?'

'No hurry.'

There is some hurry. Jager knows that Jimmy had too many stones for one trip. Those he couldn't carry this last time are in the trading store, somewhere.

'Where does he go when he goes away?'

'Windhoek. Or Swakopmund, or Walvis Bay. He has women there, I know about them. He spends money on them while I stay in the stinking store.'

'Where does this money come from?'

86

'How do I know?'

'I think it comes from diamonds.'

'You're mad. Jimmy isn't clever enough for diamonds.'

'I think he is.' Not that Jager knows about the bullet hole and the river bed, but he can guess. 'And why does he stay so long?'

'Find out if you must, but you'll be sorry if you drive him away. I'll go too.'

'Perhaps.'

No more tonight, for Jager. He goes quickly, as he usually does.

When Jager has gone, a black man comes to rob the store. He comes inside, bringing with him the lump of concrete that keeps the back door open. By now Rita is asleep, replete and full of beer. She doesn't move as the concrete hits her head.

The bush and the desert go on, indifferent. There is a balance: hoof to rock, rock to thorn, tree to kudu-horn, an immutable algebra that overrides the private panic as each thing dies.

Eventually the black man dies, and the lump of concrete dyed with Rita's blood is in the little Black Museum at the police station. Although it is tagged as an official relic, Jager thinks of it as a private memento. Jager can now search the trading store for diamonds.

The man who shot Pawson is called Martens. He has never seen the outpost trading store, nor Rita, nor Jager. He travelled through the bush to meet Pawson, then went away. He is in London, but sometimes thinks of the Kalahari, and of the man crawling along the river bed like an injured crab. He thinks of crawling after him and taking the left shoe off, hacking the heel open. He wonders if Pawson is still under that rock.

Martens has money – Pawson's share and his own. He came by cheap ferry from Amsterdam, so as not to appear ostentatiously rich. Martens may go back to Windhoek, or he may stay in London where it is damp and there are no thorn trees snatching at life.

Here, there is a balance that overrides private panic as each thing lives. A taxi is bigger than a bullet and slower, but just as deadly for Martens. They torture him for a week in hospital, insisting that he must live. But he doesn't.

So we are left with the diamonds. They are in a polythene bag, fifty large octohedrons: and the bag is inside a lump of concrete pied with Rita's blood. Small chance that these stones will go to Amsterdam, then to sparkle in Hatton Garden and at the Ritz.

Perhaps it will rain and the river will flow for a few days. Then Jimmy Pawson might come floating out from under his rock. More likely he will stay there.

The small panic is over and Jimmy Pawson doesn't care.

Love Letter Straight from the Heart

TERRY TAPP

There were six letters on the doormat – four bills, one circular and one green envelope. It was, of course, the green envelope which caught Robert's eye.

He picked the bundle up and ambled through to the kitchen, systematically slitting the letters open with his thumb. Then he put the kettle on for a cup of tea, lit a cigarette and sat at the table.

Purposely teasing himself, he opened the accounts, read them and placed them to one side – envelopes in a neat pile ready for the waste bin. The circular came next and Robert spent a tantalising two minutes deciding that he did not require a set of 'see-as-you-cook' cards. Now for the green envelope.

At that moment the kettle whistled and, with a rueful grin, Robert went to the stove and poured the boiling water over the tea in the pot. His heart was pounding.

With not so much as a glance at the green envelope, he poured the milk into the cups, added sugar and waited for the tea to infuse. And all the while his stomach was knotted with a curious mixture of guilt and excitement.

'I'll write to you,' she had said.

'Do you think that wise?' he had asked anxiously.

'What is wise about love?' she had laughed.

Robert poured his tea and took the cup back to the table. After a sip or two, he could stand the tension no longer and he pulled the letter out.

My Darling, it started. *I promised you that I would write . . . but what can I say? I could say I love you, but the phrase is all used up nowadays: I adore you . . . I worship you. No, it means much more than that. To be terribly romantic, I think I would lay my life down for you if you asked it. I want, any way I can, to make you happy.*

Robert lit another cigarette, inhaling deeply.

Our stolen time together was an island in my life. I must see you again. God knows, it isn't often during a lifetime that two people meet and fall in love. For us to have met, like strangers lost in a big city, was a miracle and I cannot let it go at that.

I know you are married and I know you feel guilty about our affair, but I am helpless to stop myself pursuing you.

> *Ever yours,*
> *Your unsigned lover.*

Robert read it again and again. He drank his tea and smoked another cigarette and then read the letter through again, savouring each word like a fine, rare wine. Who would have guessed that he, a middle-aged executive would fall madly, crazily in love with a girl half his age?

It wasn't as if he was unhappily married either. Cynthia had been – still was – a good and loyal wife. He bit his lip, struggling against the guilt which surged through him.

Another cup of tea and another cigarette.

What would he do if she became too serious? Would he be prepared to give up everything for her?

Divorce? Oh, God, he thought. Not that.

Yes, he loved her, this gay slip of a girl, and she was obviously madly in love with him; but to give up everything, the home, the safe, stable marriage . . .

Yet again he read the letter, his thoughts clashing against his skull like steel pins until he could no longer think properly.

Did he love her? Did he love her more than he loved Cynthia? How can a man answer such a thing? They were separate loves, pigeon-holed, waterproof emotions which could not possibly be mixed. He would, no matter what, always love his wife. Yet, he could not deny it, he was like a schoolboy at the thought of spending more time with his new love.

As he placed another cigarette between his lips, Cynthia came into the kitchen to start the breakfast.

'Tea in the pot,' he said, as he always did.

She nodded, removed a cigarette from his pack and lit it.

'Just a boiled egg,' he told her in reply to her upraised eyebrows. Funny that Cynthia never had to speak. A look here, a nod there and that was all that was needed. He observed her anew.

Dressing gown, tatty slippers, hair not yet brushed. She stood over the stove, cigarette dangling from her lips, thoughts a million miles away. Yet, as soon as she had prepared his breakfast, it would take but ten or fifteen minutes to transform her. She would be washed, dressed in something smart and her make-up would be flawless. Robert grinned. It was a dilemma.

'What are you smiling at?' she asked suddenly.

'Nothing,' he said.

She shrugged. 'Did I hear the postman?'

'Yes,' he answered, suddenly realising that he was holding the green letter in his hands.

'Anything interesting?' she asked.

His heart went thump-thump-thump. 'Nothing much. Just a few bills and a circular.'

'Nothing else?'

'No.'

She placed the egg in the boiling water, noticed that the shell had cracked and said, 'Damn,' causing a cylinder of ash to fall from her cigarette into the boiling water.

Again she shrugged, then went over to the table and laid plates and knives and spoons. 'What's this?' she asked, picking up the green envelope. 'I thought you said it was only bills and things.'

'Nothing,' he replied, noting with some annoyance that his voice was trembling.

'It's a letter,' she said.

Robert pushed the corner of the green page deep into his pocket. 'Just business,' he told her. 'Anyway, you know we have this thing about reading each other's mail. This happens to be private.'

She held the envelope between forefinger and thumb as if it were infected. 'In that case,' she replied, 'perhaps you would be so kind as to tell me why you opened a letter which is addressed to me.'

It's a Dog's Life for a Greedy Tramp

ROY GRANVILLE

The tramp stopped in the dusty track, and squinted his eyes against the bright sun. He decided that the farmhouse at the top of the track was too far to go without a further rest. He sat down on a rock. Taking a stained red rag from a pocket of his wrinkled suit, he patted the sweat from his forehead. Being a fat man, not used to exercise, he perspired heavily in the warm weather.

Just then a mongrel dog came sniffing down the track, saw the tramp and looked curiously at him.

'C'mon, boy,' the tramp called, offering an outstretched hand. 'C'mon.'

The dog stopped and started in accordance with the urging of the man. Gaining confidence the dog came right up to the hand that beckoned it, whereupon the tramp imitated a ferocious bark right in the dog's face. It scampered away to a safe distance before barking back.

The tramp, his face creased with delight, laughed loud and long. The mongrel kept running further away still barking at the strange human he had just met.

After a short rest the tramp continued up the track to the farmhouse, still amused about the dog.

'Morning, ma'am,' he said to the woman who came to the door. 'Would yer be kind enough, ma'am, to give a meal to a poor ole tramp like meself? 'Tis almost a day since I had a bite.'

'I'm not fond of beggars,' she said coldly, 'but if you're willing to work I can give you a meal.'

'Surely, surely, ma'am, 'tis what I meant, to work for a meal. I always said a man should work for his supper while he's able. Even if he's like meself and not too robust.'

'I only want some logs cut. Leave your coat and – er – things here, I'll show you where they are.'

She was greying, about fifty and he guessed she was a widow. Her face was attractive but the tramp was uncertain about her. He thought he could see amusement in her blue eyes.

''Tis very kind of you, ma'am,' he said and followed her to the back of the house.

'If you'll cut up those logs and stack them with the other logs over there, I'll have a meal ready for you in an hour.' She strode off leaving him, axe-in-hand, looking at two massive logs about six feet long.

The tramp was furious. He couldn't remember when he had last had to work for a meal. Usually he could play on a woman's sympathy, but this one was a tartar. But tartar or not nobody was going to make Jackson work. He looked around for a way out of his dilemma – and found it. He dragged the two long logs out of sight behind a shed and began to rearrange the existing log pile to make it look as if more had been added. Satisfied that this would fool the widow, he chuckled to himself and sat down behind the pile of wood for a smoke.

Sitting peacefully in the sun, the tramp shut his eyes, and thought of the forthcoming meal. The peacefulness, the smell of the countryside and the farmyard noises intoxicated him with pleasant feelings.

Footsteps approached and the tramp jumped up to meet the woman. 'Just finished a moment ago, ma'am. Piled it up with the rest,' he said quickly.

'Did you cut up both of them?' she asked.

'I did, ma'am, and very hard work it was. As I said, I'm not a strong man.'

94

'I don't see any fresh chippings and you were very quiet.' She was definitely suspicious. The tramp spotted a broom in the yard.

'No, ma'am, I swept them up. I wasn't wanting to leave you any mess to clear up.'

'If you come to the kitchen you can have your meal.' She walked away and the tramp followed. In the kitchen a large plate of eggs, bacon and beans was placed before him. For personal reasons he had hoped for something different, but it was well-cooked and he enjoyed the meal.

'Very nice, ma'am,' he said as he collected his coat and haversack. 'Thanks and goodbye.'

'That's all right,' she said, 'and thank you for cutting the logs.'

The last remark tickled his sense of humour. 'Thank you for cutting the logs,' he repeated to himself all the way down from the farm. He thought this was so funny that finally he couldn't keep a straight face and burst into roars of laughter. He laughed and laughed till tears came to his eyes, still thinking of the woman's words, 'Thank you for cutting the logs.'

Eight miles further on and dusk beginning to fall, he stopped behind a hedge and began to light a fire. Then he noticed the mongrel dog standing looking at him a few yards away.

'Hello, boy,' he called, smiling. 'If you've been following me you must be hungry too. Fancy a bit of grub with Lazy Jackson?'

The dog eyed the tramp nervously as he knelt down to his haversack and drew out a small frying pan. He then stared into the haversack and his actions became jerky. He threw out all sorts of things except what he was looking for which was a can of beans, an egg and a lump of bacon.

Realisation hit him. The woman hadn't been fooled. She had fooled him. Knowing he was tricking her she had played a trick on him, she had fed him his own rations.

He fell on his back and began howling, a mixture of laughter and anger.

The dog feeling that the situation, whatever it was, called for some contribution ran round and round him barking.

The Sea Serpent

W.W. JACOBS

That unforgettable character The Night Watchman is spinning yarns about his sea-going days to his waterfront cronies. He tells them about the time he sailed on the George Washington, *bound for New York from Liverpool. In mid-Atlantic they sighted a sea serpent.*

'Like a flagpole stuck out of the water, it was, and making straight for the ship. It was about a hundred yards long and every now and then it opened its mouth and let us see down its throat.'

'I wonder whether it eats men,' ses the skipper. 'Perhaps it'll come for some of us.'

'There ain't many on deck for it to choose from,' ses the mate, looking at 'im significant like.

'That's true,' ses the skipper, very thoughtful; 'I'll go an' send all hands on deck. As captain, it's my duty not to leave the ship till the last if I can anyways help it.'

How he got the hands on deck has always been a wonder to me, but he did it. He was a brutal sort o' man at the best o' times, an' he carried on so much that I s'pose they thought even the sarpint couldn't be worse. Anyway, up they came, an' we all stood in a crowd watching the sarpint as it came close and closer.

We reckoned it to be about a hundred yards long, an' it was about the most awful-looking creetur you could ever imagine. If you took all the ugliest things in the earth and mixed 'em up –

gorillas an' the like – you'd only make a hangel compared to what that was.

'It seems peaceable,' whispers the fust mate, arter a while.

'P'raps it ain't hungry,' ses the skipper. 'We'd better not let it get peckish. Try it with a loaf o' bread.'

The cook went below and fetched up half a dozen, an' one o' the chaps, plucking up courage, slung it over the side, an' afore you could say 'Jack Robinson' the sarpint had waffled it up an' was looking for more. It stuck its head up and came close to the side just like the swans in Victoria Park, an' it kept that game up until it had 'ad ten loaves an' a hunk o' pork.

'I'm afraid we're encouraging it,' ses the skipper, looking at it as it swam alongside with an eye as big as a saucer cocked on the ship.

'P'raps it'll go away soon if we don't take no more notice of it,' ses the mate. 'Just pretend it isn't here.'

Well, we did pretend as well as we could; but everybody hugged the port side o' the ship and was ready to bolt down below at the shortest notice; and at last, when the beast got craning its neck up over the side as though it was looking for something, we gave it some more grub. We thought if we didn't give it he might take it, and take it off the wrong shelf, so to speak.

But, as the mate said, it was encouraging it, and long arter it was dark we could hear it snorting and splashing behind us, until at last it 'ad such an effect on us the mate sent one o' the chaps down to rouse the skipper.

'I don't think it'll do no 'arm,' ses the skipper, peering over the side and speaking as though he knew all about sea sarpints and their ways.

'Suppose it puts its 'ead over the side and takes one of the men?' ses the mate.

'Let me know at once,' ses the skipper firmly; an' he went below again and left us.

Well, I was jolly glad when eight bells struck, an' I went below; an' if ever I hoped anything I hoped that when I go up that ugly brute would have gone, but, instead o' that, when I went on deck it was playing like a kitten a'most, an' one o' the chaps told me as the skipper had been feeding it again.

'It's a wonderful animal,' ses the skipper, 'an' there's none of you now but has seen the sea sarpint; but I forbid any man here to say a word about it when we get ashore.'

'Why not, sir?' ses the second mate.

'Becos you wouldn't be believed,' ses the skipper sternly. 'You might all go ashore and kiss the Book an' make affidavits an' not a soul 'ud believe you. The comic papers 'ud make fun of it, and the respectable papers 'ud say it was seaweed or gulls.'

'Why not take it to New York with us?' said the fust mate suddenly.

'What?' ses the skipper.

'Feed it every day,' ses the mate, getting excited, 'and bait a couple of shark hooks and keep 'em ready, together with some wire rope. Git 'im to foller us as far as he will, and then hook him. We might git him in alive and show him at a sovereign a head. Anyway, we can take in his carcase if we manage it properly.'

'By jove! If we only could,' ses the skipper, getting excited too.

Arter a couple o' days nobody minded the animal a bit, for it was about the most nervous thing of its size you ever saw. It hadn't got the soul of a mouse; and one day when the second mate, just for a lark, took the line of the foghorn in his hand and tooted it a bit, it flung up its 'ead in a scared sort of way, and after backing a bit, turned clean round and bolted.

I thought the skipper 'ud have gone mad. He chucked over loaves o' bread, bits o' beef and pork, an' scores o' biscuits, and by and by, when the brute plucked up heart an' came arter us again, he fairly beamed with joy.

Then he gave orders that nobody was to touch the horn for any reason whatever, not even if there was a fog, or chance of collision, or anything of the kind; an' he also gave orders that the bells wasn't to be struck, but that the bosen was just to shove 'is 'ead in the fo'c's'le and call 'em out instead.

Arter three days had passed, and the thing was still follering us, everybody made certain of taking it to New York, an' I b'leeve if it hadn't been for Joe Cooper the question about the sea sarpint would ha' been settled long ago. He was a most eggstraordinary ugly chap was Joe. He had a perfic cartoon of a face, an' he was

98

so delikitminded and sensitive about it that if a chap only stopped in the street and whistled as he passed him, or pointed him out to a friend, he didn't like it. He told me once when I was symperthizing with him, that the only time a woman ever spoke civilly to him was one night down Poplar way in a fog, an' he was so 'appy about it that they both walked into the canal afore he knew where they was.

On the fourth morning, when we was only about three days from Sandy Hook, the skipper got out o' bed wrong side, an' when he went on deck he was ready to snap at anybody, an' as luck would have it, as he walked a bit forrward, he sees Joe a-sticking his phiz over the side looking at the sarpint.

'What the d— are you doing?' shouts the skipper. 'What do you mean by it?'

'Mean by what, sir?' asks Joe.

'Putting your black ugly face over the side o' the ship an' frightening my sea sarpint!' bellows the skipper. 'You know how easy it's skeered.'

'Frightening the sea sarpint?' ses Joe, trembling all over, an' turning very white.

'If I see that face o' yours over the side agin, my lad,' ses the skipper very fierce, 'I'll give it a black eye. Now cut!'

Joe cut, an' the skipper, having worked off some of his ill temper, went aft again and began to chat with the mate quite pleasant like. I was down below at the time, an' didn't know anything about it for hours arter, and then I heard it from one o' the firemen. He comes up to me very mysterious like, an' ses, 'Bill,' he ses, 'you're a pal o' Joe's; come down here an' see what you can make of 'im.'

Not knowing what he meant, I follered 'im below to the engine-room, an' there was Joe sitting on a bucket staring wildly in front of 'im, and two or three of 'em standing round looking at 'im with their 'eads on one side.

'He's been like that for three hours,' ses the second engineer in a whisper, 'dazed like.'

As he spoke Joe gave a little shudder; 'Frightened the sea sarpint!' ses he. 'O Lord!'

'It's turned his brain,' ses one o' the firemen. 'He keeps saying nothing but that.'

'If we could only make 'im cry,' ses the second engineer, who had a brother what was a medical student, 'it might save his reason. But how to do it, that's the question.'

'Speak kind to 'im, sir,' ses the fireman. 'I'll have a try if you don't mind.' He cleared his throat first, an' then he walks over to Joe and puts his hand on his shoulder an' ses very soft an' pitiful like, 'Don't take on, Joe, don't take on, there's many an ugly mug 'ides a good 'art.'

Afore he could think o' anything else to say, Joe ups with his fist an' gives 'im one in the ribs as nearly broke 'em. Then he turns away 'is 'ead an' shivers again, an' the old dazed look comes back.

'Joe,' I ses, shaking him, 'Joe!'

'Frightened the sea sarpint!' whispers Joe, staring.

'Joe,' I ses, 'Joe. You know me, I'm your pal, Bill.'

'Ay, ay,' ses Joe, coming round a bit.

'Come away,' I ses, 'come an' git to bed, that's the best place for you.'

I took 'im by the sleeve, and he gets up quiet an' obedient and follers me like a little child, I got 'im straight into 'is bunk, an' arter a time he fell into a soft slumber, an' I thought the worst had passed, but I was mistaken. He got up in three hours' time an' seemed all right, 'cept that he walked about as though he was thinking very hard about something, an' before I could make out what it was he had a fit.

He was in that fit ten minutes, an' he was no sooner out o' that one than he was in another. In twenty-four hours he had six full-sized fits, and I'll allow I was fairly puzzled. What pleasure he could find in tumbling down hard an' stiff an' kicking at everybody an' everything, I couldn't see. He'd be standing quiet and peace-able like one minute, and the next he'd catch hold o' the nearest thing to him and have a bad fit and lie on his back and kick us while we was trying to force open his hands to pat 'em.

The other chaps said the skipper's insult had turned his brain, but I wasn't quite so soft, an' one time when he was alone I put it to him.

'Joe, old man.' I ses, 'you an' me's been very good pals.'

'Ay, ay,' ses he, suspicious like.

'Joe,' I whispers, 'what's yer little game?'

'Wodyermean?' 'ses he, very short.

'I mean the fits,' ses I looking at 'im very steady. 'It's no good looking hinnercent like that, 'cos I see yer chewing soap with my own eyes.'

'Soap,' ses Joe, in a nasty sneering way, 'you wouldn't rekernise a piece if you saw it.'

After that I could see there was nothing to be got out of 'im an' I just kept my eyes open and watched. The skipper didn't worry about his fits, 'cept that he said he wasn't to let the sarpint see his face when he was in 'em for fear of scaring it; an' when the mate wanted to leave him out o' the watch, he ses, 'No, he may as well have his fits at work as well as anywhere else.'

We were about twenty-four hours from port, an' the sarpint was still following us; and at six o'clock in the evening the officers puffected all their arrangements for ketching the creetur at eight o'clock next morning. To make quite sure of it an extra watch was kept on deck all night to chuck it food every half-hour; an' when I turned in at ten o'clock that night it was so close I could have reached it with a clothes prop.

I think I'd been abed about 'arf an hour when I was awoke by the most infernal row I ever heard. The foghorn was going incessantly, an' there was a lot o' shouting and running about on deck. It struck us all as 'ow the sarpint was gitting tired o' bread and was misbehaving himself, consequently we just shoved our 'eads out o' the fore-scuttle and listened. All the hullaballoo seemed to be on the bridge, an' as we didn't see the sarpint there we plucked up courage and went on deck.

Then we saw what had happened. Joe had 'ad another fit while at the wheel, and, *not knowing what he was doing*, had clutched the line of the foghorn, and was holding on to it like grim death, and kicking right and left. The skipper was in his bedclothes, raving worse than Joe; and just as we got there Joe came round a bit, and letting go o' the line, asked in a faint voice what the foghorn was blowing for, I thought the skipper 'ud have killed him; but the second mate held him back, an', of course, when things quieted down a bit, an' we went to the side, we found the sea sarpint had vanished.

We stayed there all night, but it warn't no use. When day broke there wasn't the slightest trace of it, an' I think the men was as sorry to lose it as the officers. All 'cept Joe, that is, which shows how people should never be rude even to the humblest; for I'm sartin that if the skipper hadn't hurt his feelings the way he did we should now know as much about the sea sarpint as we do about our own brothers.

A Sting in the Tail of Harry's Summer

DOUGLAS RAILTON

Spring every year, Harry Marquis loaded fifty hives of bees on his truck and headed north for orchard country where he rented out the colonies to pollinate apple-blossom.

When the blossom was past, Harry would turn his truck south and east and work the bees on the black-locust trees in early June, the clover late June, wild thyme July, second and third-cut alfalfa in August and goldenrod through to mid-September.

Then it was home again, the surplus honey extracted, blended and marketed, the bees packed up in late fall for wintering-over and nothing much else to do but mend equipment and worry about next year's tax schedule . . .

The routine had not changed in half a lifetime, but Harry had a feeling this trip was going to turn out differently.

For one thing, he'd just that week come up to his fiftieth birth-day. Nothing special about the occasion, he assured himself; all the same he wasn't going to argue he was getting any younger.

Then, the weather. Nobody could remember so much rain and the wind never letting up all the month of May.

Finally, the recession. Trade down twenty per cent, costs up by the same factor.

There'd never been a year like this one, that was for damn-sure . . .

Travelling up the state highway, Harry listened anxiously to the radio weather-casts, ready to change his run if there was a promise of settled conditions. But the pattern of washouts and gales seemed fixed.

Then he had an idea. He was quite near the Canadian border. Crossing the line was no more than a formality. In a few hours, his decision was rewarded with clearing skies and a flow of warm air through the cab windows. An hour before sundown he saw the first scattered groves of apple trees on fertile land above the muddy river.

He pulled his truck off the highway on to an unmade red shale road that ended at an isolated farmhouse. An oldish woman and a girl of about twenty came out on to the porch, as he drove up and killed the motor.

'Whatever you're selling, mister, I'm not buying,' the elder woman called down from the porch. 'But you're welcome to a bite of supper . . . C'mon up . . . Ma Harker's the name . . .'

Gratefully, Harry followed the two indoors.

'Merle, get the gennelman a drink . . . Rye, is it, mister?'

Ma Harker was thick-set, with an untidy pug of greying hair, eyes like nickel and a hard, mean mouth.

'Merle here's my hired girl,' she explained. 'Been with me since she was in pigtails. Folks abandoned her. She's none too bright. Gets her bed and keep and a dollar or two. Helps around the place some, but she's the laziest critter alive . . .'

Harry glanced at the girl. She might have been quite pretty except for that pinched look. Kind of funny eyes, hadn't she? Empty, as if something behind them died a long time ago . . .

Ma Harker quizzed him as he ate bream with buckwheat cakes washed down with root beer.

Where was he from? What was the weather like down south? How much did he rent out the bees at?

Harry told her the charge was sixty cents a day for one hive.

'A hive'll work three to four acres,' he said, talking with his mouth full. 'How many days? Depends on the weather. Bees won't fly if it's windy, for instance.'

'I've thirty acres,' Ma Harker said. 'Apples, mostly. And some blueberries and cucumber. Okay?

'Okay,' Harry said. 'I'll set it up first thing in the morning.'

He wiped his mouth on a grubby napkin and stood up to go.

'Thanks for supper . . .' He'd noticed Merle got cornbeef hash. Ma Harker smiled without humour.

'It's deductible,' she said.

Early-bright next morning, Harry took seven hives off the truck and set them in the orchard. He unstopped the entrances to the hives and watched the scout bees fly out to reconnoitre, then return to report. Within minutes brown clouds of worker bees were flying out to start the day's work.

Busy, Harry hadn't noticed Merle come up until he heard her quiet voice from behind him. 'Don't you never get stung, mister?'

He half turned, preoccupied with what he had just seen in the last hive he'd opened.

'Sure,' he said. 'Fifty times in a day. You get so you don't notice it.'

He drew out a frame from the seventh hive and examined it, frowning, his eyes hunting for the queen bee.

'The old bitch,' he said when he found what he was looking for.

'Something the matter, mister?'

'Queen's lost weight,' Harry said, putting the frame back and taking out others, squinting at them irritably.

'Is that bad?'

'You bet it is . . .'

One of the frames of wax comb showed cells bigger than the rest. Queen-cups . . . He took out a tool from his khaki coveralls and cut these cells out. The bees on the comb buzzed angrily, stinging his hands. He put the frame back and closed up his hive.

'They're getting ready to swarm,' he said.

'To what?'

'Quit the hive . . . Set up business some place else. The queen's old, see? Wore plumb down . . . They'd raise a new one and take off to god-awmighty knows where, if I don't stop them . . .'

Merle giggled. Her dull eyes showed a flicker of interest. 'You mean, a new queen would get the old gal's boyfriends?'

'That's right . . . Only, I'm the one fixes them up with the new queen, when I'm good and ready.'

'Meantime –' Harry was picking a small wire-cloth cage from inside the truck cab – 'the old one gets put in here. Cools things a piece . . .'

Merle seemed to have forgotten about the bees.

'I never had a boyfriend,' she said: 'Guess I *could* have, but Ma Harker don't allow it. There was one or two fellers hung around but Ma Harker she shoo'd them off. Then she whupped me so hard I couldn't lay down for nearly a week . . .'

Harry wasn't sure what to say so he didn't say anything. The girl walked back with him to the house, lost in half-formed speculation.

Ma Harker was on the porch.

'Bees are flying all right,' he said. 'If'n this weather keeps up, they'll be all through in a week. Pay me then. No hurry . . .'

He rolled the truck out of the yard and down to the highway.

There was plenty of business along the valley and it was nearly three weeks before he started back to Ma Harker's place.

Merle was gone . . .

And Ma Harker was gazing at him with lifeless eyes through the steel bars of a locked bear-trap . . .

Mango Millionaire

ANTHONY STEEL

O n my first Sunday in Amba I walked in the hot sunshine to the Clubhouse. I sat in an alcove amongst a group of British expatriates and, although I knew no one, the atmosphere was cheerful and friendly.

We got on to the subject of how many whites there were in the town, five years after independence. From that we progressed to talking about the more eccentric individuals amongst the expatriate colony. Then someone mentioned 'the mango millionaire'.

'That must be the man I saw in the market today,' I said.

'Oh, you will find him there with his mangoes most market days,' somebody said.

'I was surprised when he told me that all those mangoes he brought in the truck were from his village.'

I said, 'What did he mean by that? Where does he live?'

'Well,' said another, launching into what was obviously a popular subject, 'for years he has lived in Bam, a village thirty miles along the coast.'

'Nobody except Fraser and his villagers know how he first came to live there,' added a local plantation manager. 'Bam is one of those places where the native people are outnumbered by strangers.'

'One story is that in the days when Kenneth Fraser was in the Colonial Service he was on tour to the place and was bewitched by the ju-ju there into serving the native villagers. They feared that the newcomers would drive them from their own homes. It is true that the Bam people have very strong magic.'

I looked round at my friends, but they did not show any surprise at the statement.

'This reputation for magic has been their great protection,' said Ben Edwards, the World Health Organisation doctor, a veteran of more than two decades in tropical medicine. 'No one likes to rub them up the wrong way just in case there is something in it after all.'

A burly beer drinker put down his glass. 'I heard that Fraser embezzled a big sum from the Treasury and hid it in the Kwala Society ju-ju house at Bam because he knew that none of the native police would dare search for it there. Then he had to work himself in with the village people and be accepted by them so that he could watch over his hoard. Let him stay there if he's happy like that.'

I noticed how he disliked the man.

'And how do all the mangoes come into it?' I pursued.

'The mangoes grown round the village are just about the sweetest and best in the country,' replied Dr Edwards. 'Fraser organised their production and marketing along sensible commercial lines. In return, the village as a whole seems to maintain him. He lives alone in a big wood-and-zinc bungalow. He is always with the Chief, a young chap probably very dependent on Fraser's advice. The village makes a packet out of the mango sales, although you wouldn't think so if you saw their poor, broken-down houses.'

'None of you seem to know him very well,' I remarked. 'Surely he must sometimes need English company.'

'Maybe,' said the beer drinker, 'but not ours.'

'I see him from time to time at my clinic at Elenasa,' said Ben Edwards. 'In fact, he should be coming the day after tomorrow to pick up some pills.'

It was getting hotter and hotter as the afternoon approached and I got up to get another iced drink. When I returned, the conversation had moved on to other matters, but when the doctor rose to leave a little later, on the spur of the moment I asked if I could take the pills to Mr Fraser.

The next afternoon, after work, I borrowed a Land Rover and by evening was sitting outside the Chief's house at Bam, watching dancing and drumming in the grass compound put on in my honour. Wood fires and paraffin lamps lit up the dancers, and the lines of men dancing in one great circle, married women in another, and the unmarried in a third enthralled me.

The Chief, a personable and educated young man, made me very welcome. He spoke English well. Like many of the people from the coastal area, he was rather paler in complexion than those who came from the deep inland forests.

He sat on my left and Mr Fraser, straight-backed and grey-haired, on my right. The Bam notables and elders were with us. We ate goat meat and chicken off the bone, and were served with dishes of hot rice, plantains and fried cocoyams. The night was heavy with scent from the trees and strange calls sounded from the shadows. It was the African night.

'How is it you are held in such honour here?' I asked Fraser after a time.

'The Chief should answer for his village,' he parried.

'There are many, many reasons,' began the Chief. 'Once, long ago, before I was born, the government took a decision to stamp out our customs and to destroy our possessions, such as these Kwala ju-ju masks, those drums.' He indicated in turn the masked dancers and the great hollowed-log drums. 'Our friend, who knew us well, risked his whole career in the Colonial Service by coming to warn us so that we could hide all our treasures.'

'It's lucky he reached you in time,' I said.

'He didn't. The government soldiers got here as he did and started to ransack the religious house and seize our most sacred and secret objects. They would have desecrated our life by throwing them all into this very compound before the eyes of the women and children, but this man –' he pointed to Fraser, who sat very still '– sacrificed his future by using his authority as an officer to order the soldiers away. By the time they returned we had hidden everything in a secret shrine known only to the elders.'

As he finished, the drumming grew louder and wilder.

'And that is why the Bam treat Mr Fraser with such reverence?' I concluded.

'Well, that is one of the reasons,' explained the young Chief, 'but the main reason, I think, is that he is my father.'

Semaphore

WILLIS CARSTAIRS

I was curious to know what had gone wrong with the Second Train Robbery. I went and called on Jim Outhwaite in Slattersby North Box.

In spite of all the blurb you read about multi-aspect colour light signalling, and electrified boxes controlling umpteen hundred miles of track, there are in fact still long stretches of main line controlled by the old 'semaphore' signals. Those are the red or yellow arms on tall posts, forbiddingly horizontal or permissively dropped to forty-five degrees. These lines are split into sections, and each section is controlled by a signal box; the old type of box with big shining levers, and a series of bells by which the signalman 'talks' to the next boxes up and down the line.

The robbery had occurred in a section north of Slattersby, but Jim always knew everything that went on all the way to Carlisle. I knew a bit myself. I knew that the job had been planned by Monty Blowick, who worked in the head City office of one of the big banks. I knew it involved a quarter of a million in ten-pound notes, being sent to Glasgow. I didn't know the details.

Jim did. He brewed a cup of tea, gave the two-one (Train out of Section) on the bell to the next box south, and told me. You must imagine his story as being punctuated by the bell signals, and by the pulling and releasing of levers.

Jim accepted an express freight, and offered it northward.

'Aye,' he said. 'There were four of his mates, on the train. All with guns, and by what I've heard all of 'em the sort that'll *use* guns. They worked it all from the train.

'Now if you want to get the hang of this you'll have to understand the bell code. Have a look there, on the desk.'

I did so. A bell rang four times.

'What's that?' asked Jim, tapping keys.

'Is line clear for express passenger train,' I said proudly. It was at the top of the list.

'Aye, you're getting it. Now listen. The box north of here is Moxton Cross, and the one north of that is Wingatestone, north of that again is Wingatestone Tunnel. Think on, now, and remember that.'

Jim went on, 'Now look, when a train comes past, you see me go to the window there.'

I nodded.

'Well, I'm not just doing it to amuse myself,' said Jim. 'Look down that list again. You'll see "Train Passed Without Tail Lamp". The tail lamp should be on the last vehicle. If it isn't, part of the train's adrift, and I've got to tell them.'

I nodded again.

'Now look just above that,' said Jim, 'and you'll see "Stop and Examine Train". Seven beats.'

'Why?' I asked.

'Because there's something wrong, yer daft idiot! Now listen. Just after this train with the money had passed here, going north, one of these four jokers opened a door. On this side, there it was, flapping about, and old Joe Binshaw at Moxton Cross Box couldn't miss it.

'So he sends "Stop and Examine Train",' I said, 'to . . . to . . .'

'To Wingatestone. Tom Billington at Wingatestone, puts his distant and home signals at danger and the train stops by his box. Out jumps one of these jokers, with a gun, and up the steps and into the box. Another one jumps on to the engine. The other two are pointing their guns at the chaps in the van with the money bags. The chap in the box produces a pair of scissors, and cuts the wires on the speaking telephone – like that one there.'

' "You're incommunicado," he says. "We're going to run the

train up to the mouth of the tunnel, where we've got a car. Just keep quiet and you won't be hurt."

'Just then the bell rings four beats. It was offering a southbound express, but the joker doesn't know this.'

' "What's that?" he says. And Tom Billington, without batting an eyelid, says "They're asking what's happened to this train. And if I don't tell them," he says, "they'll have someone here quick, because they'll think I've fallen ill."

' "Then tell them," says the joker, and Tom sends five beats, which means Obstruction Danger. Then he starts sending two-one-two and keeps repeating it at intervals, sending a seven now and again just to reinforce the message.

' "I'm just clearing the line for you," says Tom.

'Well, this joker is beginning to learn that there's a bit more to running signal boxes than what he'd thought. But there's nowt he can do about it.

'Jim keeps on playing tunes on the bells, and at last he says: "All right, tell him to go now – but to go slow."

'So this joker leans out and shouts down to the engine, and off goes the train. Well, it has to, with another joker *and* a gun in the engine cab.'

'But what went wrong?' I asked. 'Wasn't the car there, by the tunnel?'

'Oh, aye, it was there. But so was almost everybody else. Police, ambulances, fire brigade, the lot. Those jokers hadn't a chance, even with guns.'

'But *why*?' I asked.

'Well, you see first of all that six beats. Obstruction Danger, that alerts everybody on a railway. They tried to get Tom on the speaking phone, but of course it was dead along of the joker having cut the wire. And then Tom kept sending two-one-two.'

I turned to the desk.

'Don't worry,' said Jim. 'It's an old one that isn't often used. It asks "Is line Clear for Trolley Requiring to Go Into or Pass Through Tunnel". Well of course that sounded pretty daft, but they got the message. Something, they didn't know what, was happening at the tunnel. So they switch on the emergency procedure, police and everybody like I said.'

'I see,' I said. 'So the only one who got anything out of it was Monty Blowick, on his way to Buenos Aires.'

'Well, he didn't, neither,' said Jim. 'He didn't trust London Airport, so he took the Newhaven train to get a plane at Paris. And there was an electrical signal failure. Two hours the train was held up, and by that time they were waiting for him.'

He shook his head. 'No doubt about it, semaphore is best.'

Love was Quite a Blow to Adam

WILLIAM GLYNNE-JONES

'You ask me if you should go to Fanny Withersnee's farm-house an' pull down that sign?'

Old Josiah Brewster shook his head. 'My advice is – no! You heard me, Adam – NO! You'd be a fool to try it. That sign's been on her gate for as many years as I care to remember.'

Adam Grove's grey eyes clouded.

'But she got no right to have it there on the gate. *Private – Trespassers will be prosecuted*, my eye! I tell you there's public right o'way through the farm and I got papers to prove it . . . and a map.'

Josiah sighed.

'Now you listen to me, Adam. I've been sixty an' six years here in Potters Folly. You've seen three less'n I have but never in all that time have I fancied an argument with Miss Fanny. She's a spirited woman, that, and a match for any man.'

' "Woman", did you say?' Adam snorted. 'She's a crusty old spinster. Hard as nails, with a heart o'flint.'

Josiah remained patient. 'I'll mind you remember, Adam, that you've been a bachelor just as long as Fanny's been an old maid – and there's been rumours you were a bit keen on her yourself one time.'

'W-what!' Adam dug a hand into his pocket and drew out a bundle of papers and a torn, grubby map. 'I tell you, Josiah, I'm going to settle that Miss Fanny once and for all. See these papers? Been over to Ditchley library an' I've had a word with the registrar at Newton. I can prove she got no right to put up that sign.'

The next day Adam took the law plus a heavy hammer into his own hands and tramped across the fields to Miss Fanny's farmhouse.

Had he been watchful he would have noticed Miss Fanny standing, arms akimbo, behind a lace-curtained window, a ruddy glow on her cheeks, and he would have been forced to admit that she was, indeed, a very handsome woman.

But Adam's eyes were set on the object of his destruction. He knelt on the footpath and began to attack the wooden sign. He was a strong man, and as the sign had been exposed to all weathers for many years it was soon lying in splinters at his feet.

As he gathered up the bits and pieces, he suddenly felt a heavy blow on his head, and remembered no more . . .

Miss Fanny dropped the heavy rolling-pin. Her hands trembled, and she swayed slightly as she looked at the prone figure on the ground. Oh dear, oh dear! . . . What had she done? Adam Grove . . . He lay there unconscious a trickle of blood on his broad forehead. Agitatedly, she knelt beside him. She loosened his collar. Heaven forbid that she had seriously hurt him. She had meant only to dissuade him from his purpose, for she knew that words would be useless. Adam Grove was a stubborn man.

Oh, what a fool she had been to act so impulsively. But what else could she have done? She had to show him she was his equal, that she was not to be subdued or frightened.

Fanny placed her hands under his armpits and dragged him slowly up the pathway and into the kitchen.

A bowl of hot water, some iodine, and presently Adam revived. He looked about him, dazed.

'Something – something hit me.' He saw the vague form of Miss Fanny bending over him.

'Yes, Adam . . . I did.' Miss Fanny was almost in tears. 'But I – I didn't mean to hurt you so. Oh, why did you do it?'

'Do it?' Adam's brain was still numbed by the blow from the rolling-pin.

'The sign,' said Miss Fanny. 'If only you had reasoned things out with me, then perhaps we would have been spared this – this unfortunate episode. Oh, what it is to be such a stubborn man.'

'You – you are a stubborn woman,' said Adam, and he was amazed to find how soothing was her touch as she bathed his wounded forehead. 'A woman of much spirit.'

'Yes, Adam. We are both spirited, maybe too spirited. I only wish – ' she paused – 'that we could be friends – not quarrel and wrangle over a stupid gate and a sign with a few painted words on it. But I'm sorry I hurt you, indeed I am.'

Adam began to melt. His bitterness towards her slowly evaporated. Then he felt a twinge of pain as he moved his head, and the thought of the rolling-pin resurrected the resentment he had felt against her.

'That sign was a challenge,' he said. He remembered Josiah's words. 'Fair play's bonny play, and you had no right to stop people walking through the farmyard.'

'Please, Adam – not another word,' Miss Fanny pleaded. 'The sign shall stay where it is – in pieces. It will never be put up again. To think that I might have killed you! It's too awful to think of.'

To Adam the world was still dizzy. But Miss Fanny's voice was sweet and kind, and her manner so thoughtful and considerate. She had surrendered so gracefully.

Golly! A mighty fine woman she was, yes sir! – in spite of the rolling-pin.

'I admire any woman who will defend her rights as you have, Miss Fanny,' he said. 'We have much in common, aye indeed. A woman of spirit, that's what you are, and it's a great pity that we should have been enemies.'

'Nonsense! We were never enemies,' Miss Fanny hastened to say. 'Stubborn-minded, perhaps? But this life is too short for quarrelling.

'I am a very lonely woman, and we folks should love one another as the Good Book says.

'We'll say no more, eh? I'll make you a nice cup of tea.'

117

As Adam sipped his cup of tea he thought how delicious it tasted. A far better cup than he had brewed in his lonely house. A cup of tea made with a woman's touch, he mused.

Ah, but the blow that felled him – that was not so gentle! Still, it was good for a woman to show some spirit. She was certainly one to admire. In fact, old Josiah was right. He, Adam Grove, had always had an eye for Fanny Withersnee – but she had always been so aloof, so unattainable.

The time came when Adam had to leave. Miss Fanny escorted him to the door and along the farmyard. As he passed the barn he saw three fallen tree trunks lying across the grass. A feeling of chivalry, or atonement swelled within him.

'Miss Fanny,' he said, pointing to the trunks. 'You can't cut them into logs all by yourself. There's a good lot o' firewood for the winter to be got from them there. Now – I have a strong pair of arms . . .'

'You are welcome here at any time, Adam,' said Miss Fanny. 'It was a very kind thought, and I am indeed truly grateful.'

Adam nodded thoughtfully. 'We have much in common, Miss Fanny. And I'm really sorry for the damage I did.'

Three months later old Josiah Brewster became best man at their wedding, and the couple made their new home in the farmhouse. Six months later he paid a call to see how the newly married couple were getting on.

As he approached the farm he found Adam kneeling before the gate, paintbrush in hand, a hammer and a box of nails beside him. A brand new wooden sign had been fixed on the gate.

Josiah stood for a moment to watch as Adam finished with a flourish the last word on the sign, which read, *Private – Trespassers will be prosecuted.*

Short Measure

LESLIE THOMAS

That day Miss Worpleton really *knew* the years were adding up. It was her birthday but she was not happy about it. She got up that morning and looked resentfully in the mirror. It was unmistakable.

All the warm days of youth had gone, it seemed to her, and she had hardly noticed them. She felt that life had given her short measure.

With a quick jerk of her head as though she could hardly bear to look any longer, she turned from the mirror. She put on her shabby green dressing-gown over her nightdress, went to the window, pulled back the faded curtains and let in the sudden sunlight of the new day.

Then she fumbled with the matches, lit the gas ring and put the kettle on to boil. In Miss Worpleton's frame of mind it came home to her like a blow that the action was automatic. She had done it for so long and she would go on doing it, she supposed. Always and always, and it was all her own fault.

Slowly she returned to the window, gazed through the narrow panes, and then, fumbling with the catch for a moment, pushed the sash up. The sweet morning air invaded the stuffy little room and the sounds of the street floated up to her. The janglings, whistlings, hoots and cries of a bright, busy morning.

Miss Worpleton leaned out. There were cars and vans and

people passing up and down the street and some small boys were jostling each other at the corner. A girl in a yellow sweater and bright tartan trousers was walking her dog jauntily along the opposite pavement, a delivery boy was teasing a girl in a white apron outside the grocer's shop and she was laughing, a young couple were going shopping, both holding the basket, with their hands touching on the handle. They could not have been more than nineteen . . .

Everything seemed so young. Miss Worpleton pulled down the window with a crash. Then, her anger dissipated by the action, she walked sadly away to make the tea.

She had thought that there was so much time. When she was nineteen the years seemed to stretch before her to an horizon that could not even be seen. That was the winter when she had gone skating with Henry on the lake on the common. A nice boy, Henry, but strictly for amusement, she had thought.

That afternoon, she recalled, was as sharp as a knife edge; the ice was thick and the air almost crackling. The sun, like a shrivelled apricot, was low over the winter landscape. As she and Henry had spun across the lake she had felt the wind stinging her face to a rosy glow. She laughed and shouted aloud, and Henry came skating breathlessly after her. She knew how he felt for her and it made her feel exultant and grown-up – but not too grown-up.

They had skated very fast and suddenly found they could not stop. They piled up on a bank crisp with snow and lay there laughing and breathless. Then Henry stopped laughing. He sat up and looked down at her with a funny half-choked look.

'Nancy,' he had said, 'please marry me.'

A little, sly, triumphant thought jerked itself into her mind. Then she felt sorry for him.

'Don't be silly, Henry,' she had said, pushing him gently away. Then she had laughed and got to her feet. 'Come on, let's skate some more,' she had said.

That was the first one. There had been plenty of others. But the horizon seemed always so far away and she had been having such a good time. The answer had always been 'No'.

Then, suddenly and cruelly, it seemed to her, it had all changed.

The years had gone unnoticed. All those who had been young with her were not there any longer. All the gay people these days seemed to be very youthful. And there she was with a bed-sitter, a gas-ring and faded curtains. A cat and a parrot would be next, she thought wryly.

It was Saturday, so she took her time dressing. Then she went down to the street. She wondered, as she walked, how old the people passing would think she was. Once she thought a young man hurrying by had turned and given her a second look. But he turned and walked right past her to raise his hat to a young girl looking in a milliner's window.

Miss Worpleton walked sadly on. She turned off the main street and took the road that led up to the common. The houses dwindled and soon she had walked across the firm grass towards the stream that flowed sluggishly from above the town.

Under the wooden bridge across the stream the vicar was fishing. He was a kindly little man, fat as a pie.

He took one hand from the rod as she approached and raised his hat. 'Morning, Miss Worpleton,' he said. 'Please forgive me for not getting up, I think I might have something here. Sometimes I think fishing this way needs even more patience than fishing for men.'

She smiled. He was such a nice little man. The sort of man you could talk to.

Suddenly, so suddenly that she surprised herself, she was telling him all her thoughts of that morning. She stood on the bridge above him and talked while he sat gazing at the bobbing float and now and then nodding his round head.

If she could have seen his face when she had finished, she would have seen he was laughing. The laughter was still in his eyes when he turned about.

'We all grow older every minute, Miss Worpleton,' he said kindly, 'but I don't think you should worry very much. If you don't mind my asking, just how old are you?'

Miss Worpleton looked down and not noticing his eyes, said, very seriously: 'I'm twenty-five today vicar.'

The Russian Princess

WILLY TREBICH

'It is the head of the firm I wish to see.'

I had been standing in the outer office when the stranger came in, eyeing me coldly. The firm of Jean Tailleur et Fils, estate agents in the South of France, had offered me the job of assistant manager, and I was learning fast. Tact is essential.

'But certainly, sir. What name is it?'

He threw a card at me.

'Prince Feodor Youssoutzine,' I read.

I went into the inner office and gave the card to Monsieur Tailleur.

'This way, Your Highness.'

The French Riviera in the mid-thirties was a haven for many white Russians, most of them penniless, but I had not met this one before. Some ten minutes later I was summoned into the inner sanctum.

'Willy, Prince Youssoutzine is here on a delicate mission, but I know I can rely on your discretion.'

I bowed appropriately.

'I am looking for a villa on Cap Ferrat which must be worthy of its future occupant,' the Prince said pompously.

'I have the Prince's permission to tell you that a very illustrious lady may be honouring us with her presence before long,' Monsieur Tailleur added. 'Therefore I want you to escort His Highness through the properties which are available.'

The Villa des Fourmies is delightful, situated as it is facing the small harbour of Saint-Jean-Cap-Ferrat. Prince Youssoutzine looked over the house arrogantly. He treated the old caretaker like a serf.

'Tell your employer, young man, that I will be considering this property. See that it is shown to no one else.'

A few days later we received a telegram from the Prince saying he was bringing a lady to inspect the villa and advise on decor.

La Naroskaya, one of the most vivacious women you could imagine, had been Prima Ballerina in the days of the Tsar. She had known me all my life.

'Willy, darling! Fancy seeing you here!'

The Prince gaped. 'Do you know this young man?' he managed.

'Know Willy? I used to bath him. He did *pipi* one day all over my dress.'

My face was scarlet as I returned her embrace. I took them to the villa. La Naroskaya went into rhapsodies and the Prince, thawing, offered me a cigar.

'Madame Naroskaya! Do tell me who is coming.'

'No, Willy, and you must not ask me.'

'Is it the Dowager Empress? She must be feeling the cold up there in Denmark,' I persisted.

La Naroskaya shook her head.

'Then are we to expect someone romantic?'

I think she was about to tell me when we were interrupted by the Prince. She just squeezed my arm and winked.

'Every impression is favourable so I will be reporting direct to my colleagues,' he informed me.

Before they left La Naroskaya had a final word.

'We are holding a reception in honour of the Prince while he is down here, Willy, so you must buy two tickets for me.'

The great day came and a ballroom was hired. I arrived early with a girlfriend. The other guests were dressed mostly in faded finery resembling Court dress, but the men's uniforms and decorations were impressive. The most important guest was Romyshkin, a distant cousin of the late Autocrat of all the Russias.

'Champagne, Monsieur?'

I took a glassful. It was Vin Blanc fizzed up with lemonade.

I wandered about with my companion and then spotted two fellows of my own age. Artemy was the son of a former Tsarist Ambassador. He had a reputation as a lady-killer and stealer of other men's girlfriends. The other one was Serge Braiski. He was incredibly handsome and made a living as a film extra. I was talking to Serge when I noticed my girlfriend was at the other end of the room being given a drink by a smiling Artemy. And that was the last I ever did see of her.

'Pray silence for Her Imperial Highness and the Prince Feodor Youssoutzine!'

The Master of Ceremonies, an ex-colonel of the Tsar's Body-guard but currently a part-time waiter, announced their arrival with a flourish. To the accompaniment of the Imperial Russian anthem from a cracked gramophone record, the couple made their dignified way towards two chairs placed like thrones beneath a large portrait of Nicholas II. The aide-de-camp for the occasion would have been recognised as the man who ran the Café de Moscou in the rue Gioffredo. His uniform was too tight for him and I did not once see him sit down.

I introduced Serge to Madame Naroskaya.

'How he is beautiful!' she exclaimed.

We then queued to be presented, a ritual which no Russian function is without. I mumbled my name to the Master of Ceremonies but he got it wrong when he announced me.

'Don't smash the wineglasses – they have to be paid for!'

The whisper was passed from mouth to mouth. Waiters circulated bearing trays of glasses for the toast. The Master of Ceremonies again called for silence. Prince Youssoutzine stood up.

'To Holy Russia, and to our beloved Imperial Family!'

Heads were flung back as the vodka was drunk in one gulp. It was well watered.

'To Holy Russia!'

Eyes became moist. There were a few moments of complete silence before the glasses were put down carefully.

'Willy! I have news for you!'

I was standing before Monsieur Tailleur in his office a few days later.

'I have received a letter from Prince Youssoutzine. There will be no Illustrious Lady taking up residence in the Villa des Fourmies.'

And that was that. If M Tailleur knew the explanation of the whole business he was sworn to secrecy. Probably he didn't know. Years went by and I thought I would never know the answer. Then one day, by pure chance, I ran into Prince Youssoutzine.

'Oh *that*,' he said 'the Very Illustrious Lady? Well you see, we really did think she was the Grand Duchess Anastasia.'

My Husband Says it All with Flowers

MARTHA DUNCAN

They say it is a mistake for husbands and wives to take separate holidays but Robert and I had always done so.

This was partly because Robert could not take his during the hot summer months and I simply could not stand the heat and was glad to escape back to Scotland for them.

Then when the island cooled slightly we took the boat and visited together the other islands that made up Robert's beat.

Far from weakening our marriage it had strengthened it. Even the short sharp affair I had had with Justin one summer had strengthened it. I had confessed and been forgiven and the marriage had been all the sweeter.

I was, however, taken aback when several months later Justin arrived on the island as a replacement for one of the other officials.

He arrived just before the New Year and as always the Scots gathered for Hogmanay and celebrated well – if not wisely – everything to do with their homeland from whisky to Burns and back again. Mostly back again.

Naturally, Justin was included in the party. To be fair to him he never so much as blinked when we were introduced and as far as the rest were concerned we were meeting for the first time.

The casual friendship that grew between us was no more than

the normal one of a young man taking advantage of the open house that Robert and I had always held for lone bachelors. What was of more interest was the deeper one that sprang up between him and Robert, for I had not realised how much they had in common.

There was, for instance, the garden. They would spend hours working in it and while they loved the garish tropical plants that throve there, they both craved for the more delicate flowers of a northern climate. So, while pruning the geraniums, they would murmur about primulas. While cutting back the oleander, they were apt to grow misty-eyed over laburnum and lupin.

Every year I brought back seeds with me; often I dropped a handful from a friends's garden into a letter, and every year they failed. Sometimes they pushed shoots through the ground only to bolt in the midday sun and die by nightfall.

When June came round again I left them to it and returned to Scotland.

In July, Robert disappeared.

They found his car on the edge of a cliff where I knew he used to walk. They found a newly dislodged wedge of earth above a three-hundred-foot drop on to the rock at low tide and crashing breakers at high.

Justin was kindness itself. I think he felt the sheer awfulness of not only being one of the last people to see Robert alive, but of also being the one to step into his shoes.

He went to great pains to tell me everything that had been done, even to how he had met Robert coming out of the Post Office and how he had asked him to come back to the cottage for a drink and how Robert had said he had another engagement.

Nobody knew what that engagement was and it remained a mystery.

He told me how they had searched the water's edge and dragged the various pools in the vicinity. A helicopter had hovered inches above the clear water and found nothing. Perhaps his body had been sucked beneath the cliffs and held under some overhanging rock. Perhaps, and this he did not like to have to suggest, but there were sharks along the coast and while they didn't normally come in that close . . .

He left the dreadful thought unfinished.

He put his arm gently around my shoulder and said I would feel better later. Time was a great healer. No matter how dark the night, the sun must rise.

Perhaps, he suggested, it would be better if I returned to Scotland. After all, there was nothing now to keep me on the island. Maybe later I would return.

But I stayed. I stayed through the autumn and winter and into spring. I stayed because for some reason I felt I could not run away from the grief of losing Robert. I wanted to stay close to him for as long as possible. I think if I could have seen him dead . . . wept at his funeral . . . taken flowers to his grave . . . I would have recovered more easily. As it was, I spent long hours stretched out on a deck chair on our verandah just staring down the garden that he had loved so much.

The oleander had grown so that the two hedges now met over the path making a cool cavern lined with their fallen pink and red petals. The bougainvillea threatened to pull down the garden shelter and the Pride of India was about to burst into flower.

One afternoon, as spring was turning into summer, I walked across to Justin's cottage to tell him that I had decided to go home for the summer as usual, but that I would return in the autumn, to take up life again, so to speak.

He got up from where he had been kneeling beside a bed of zinnias and turning me round so I could not see his face, he asked me to marry him.

No rush or hurry, just a gentle proposal that he would wait until I was ready . . . after all we had that brief affair . . . he would be a good and kind husband . . .

I was touched by his caring and gentleness. I was tempted.

He dropped back to his knees and went on with the work of loosening the soil around the zinnias. His hand brushed against a clump of long-fingered leaves and then curled around them as if to pull them out.

'Don't!' I dropped on my knees beside him.

He looked up, startled.

'Don't what?'

I leaned closer to the plant. Broke off a leaf.

'That's a lupin. We've tried over and over . . . Robert would have loved to have grown them . . . how on earth did you manage it?'

He looked blankly at me. 'What are you talking about? Come inside, the heat is too much for you . . .'

But I was no longer standing in a tropical garden but back in a cool, shaded, Scottish one, idly pulling off the pods of the lupins that had gone to seed . . . laughing as I put them in the letter I had just written to Robert. The letter that Robert would have collected at the Post Office and stuffed into his pocket when Justin asked him home for a drink.

It was extraordinary that these seeds, out of all I had ever put into letters, had germinated and sprouted and had survived long enough to point Robert's grave.

And to his murderer.

Ratcatcher

HERBERT HARRIS

As Luigi left the lift on the hotel's third floor he saw the girl outside the door of room 101. He watched her hesitate before tapping quietly on the panel.

Luigi shook his head sadly. He had seen her before and noticed how young and pretty she was. But the dissolute man in room 101 liked them young – just out of school preferably. Blayne, his name was, some sort of entertainment tycoon.

The kid with the nice fresh young face must be the latest innocent Blayne had marked for seduction. Luigi, hardened though he was by hotel life, felt sick and angry when he thought about it. Luigi liked the look of the girl. Maybe he would have tried to get friendly with her if it hadn't been for Rosa, his own lush, flashing-eyed Rosa, to whom he was now engaged.

Luigi went on his way with a tray of supper for one of the old ladies. The old ladies adored Luigi. Pretty well everyone liked Luigi. He did everything he was asked to do, willingly and cheerfully, and turned his hand to anything. Once they had got him to catch a rat in the cellar after he had boasted of his ratcatching in Italy. Pity, he thought, that he couldn't exterminate that rat in room 101, the rat called Blayne.

When Luigi came back with his empty tray, the girl was still standing outside Blayne's door. She turned to look at the young

Italian as he approached, her eyes bewildered, flustered, guilty . . .
Poor kid. Hardly yet a woman. It made him very sad.

He paused beside her, hoping his beloved Rosa wouldn't pop
up from somewhere and catch him shooting a line. But Rosa –
even if she had followed him from Milano to work beside him in
the same hotel – wasn't really a jealous type.

'No answer from 101, *signorina?*'

'Er . . . no,' she answered in a nervous small voice.

He flashed her a smile. 'I'm on the staff. A sort of – how you
say – dogsbody.'

'Oh . . . I see.' She had a half-scared look as if she feared she'd
be thrown out of the hotel.

'Mr Blayne was expecting you?'

'Er . . . no . . . I . . . I came on the off chance.'

Her dimpled schoolgirl face wore a timid smile. He had an
overwhelming urge to help her, to rescue her from this evil man
Blayne, who used promises of star opportunities to deceive the
innocent.

'I . . . I expect he's gone out,' she added.

'Ah, *si, signorina – si!*'

But that wasn't true, was it? Blayne was right there in his room.
He had heard him clearly only a little while ago. And Luigi had
heard not only Blayne's voice but the voice of yet another of the
rat's girlfriends, the ones Little Miss Innocence standing here had
never heard of. Luigi had heard laughing voices inside the room.
If Blayne had heard the girl's quiet knock, he had chosen to ignore
it. He disliked being interrupted while 'in conference'.

A sudden malicious idea came creeping into Luigi's mind. It
would be hard on this decent little girl, but one had to be cruel
to be kind, no?

'He will be disappointed if he finds out you called during his
absence, *signorina!*' He tapped his chest, smiling. 'Me, I would cry
on my pillow all night to think I had missed this so attractive
visitor!'

She blushed pink, the dimples showing again.

'I think Mr Blayne has popped out for a little while,' he said.
'He is always at home on a Sunday evening . . .'

'Then . . .' she faltered. 'You think I should wait?'

'You can wait in his room if you like,' Luigi told her. He spoke in a low conspirator's voice, looking over his shoulder.

'In his room?' she reddened again. 'I . . . I haven't a key, I'm afraid.'

'No problem, *signorina*.' He grinned. 'I can get a passkey whenever I like.'

The girl stared at him, lips parted uncertainly.

'Don't be alarmed, *signorina*. Mr Blayne will be so grateful. He will reward me perhaps. He will be so glad in his heart to find his pretty one waiting for him, no?' He frowned. 'You are in love with this Mr Blayne?'

'Oh, yes . . . he means a lot to me!'

Luigi gritted his teeth, but kept smiling. 'Very well. You wait here. I'll get a key and let you in.'

His heart thumped with excitement as he hurried away. At last, he thought, he would make this Blayne rat suffer. A pity, certainly, to disillusion the nice little girl waiting in the corridor, but better some disillusionment now than disaster later . . .

In his mind's eye, Luigi could picture Blayne's surprise when this girl was admitted to his room with the passkey – just when he was busy 'entertaining' another of his innocent little worshippers . . .

Luigi hurried back with the key. 'So! We go in now, yes?'

He threw open the door with a dramatic flourish. He stood back a little, urging the girl forward with little prods. But almost at once she was recoiling, staring with horrible fascination.

The girl already inside the room had shrieked, and was now trying to hide herself in a pathetic and ludicrous way. Blayne, similarly undignified, was white-faced with rage. He glared for a while at his intruders, then came pounding across the room to slam the door shut in their faces.

The young girl beside Luigi stood in shocked silence, her face pale.

'Sorry about that, *signorina*,' Luigi said. His voice was strangely quiet. 'But it was better for you to see the kind of man you had got mixed up with . . .'

'Yes,' she sobbed. 'Thank you.' She turned and ran away suddenly towards the lift. Her dream-world had turned in an instant into a nauseating nightmare but tomorrow reality would be even more cruel.

She would learn that Blayne was dead, stabbed to death; that the nice Italian who had helped her at the hotel was now in a cell, accused of murder; and that the girl in room 101 was somebody called Rosa who apparently had meant a great deal to Luigi.

Elementary, My Dearest Watson

ERIC BEAN

She put a bunch of flowers on the bookstall while she opened her purse and the flowers started sliding towards the edge. I put out a hand to stop them and she gave me a quick, warm smile. But only for a second. Then she picked up her magazine and flowers, and walked away.

I watched her at the barrier of Number 4 platform. A small, pretty face, brown hair and calm eyes. And then she walked down to the train.

Number 4 platform. That was my train! I followed her at a distance, counting the coaches. One – two – three – four. The fourth carriage.

I don't know how I found the courage, but I got in the fourth carriage and found her compartment.

'Anybody sitting here?' I said, indicating the seat next to her.

She looked up from her magazine. 'No, it's all right,' she said.

So I sat there, very much aware of her beside me. But I didn't know how to start up a conversation. It was ridiculous. Then I looked at the luggage rack. Her flowers were there. And her small blue suitcase.

I tried to read the initials on the suitcase through the netting. The letters seemed to be, Z.Y. Unusual, I thought.

The train started, and the girl looked out of the window. Her brown hair was curled in neatly at the back. Then she stood up and pushed at the window.

'Here, let me help you,' I said. I jumped up and pushed the window open wide.

'I was trying to close it,' she smiled. So of course I apologised and closed the window. And from then on it was easy. We were speaking to each other.

'Going on holiday?' I asked.

'No,' she said. 'I'm just going to spend a few days with my parents.'

'Me too,' I said. 'For a week.'

When the attendant came, I offered her a coffee. 'Thank you,' she said. 'I haven't had a drink since four.'

We talked for a while, and then she stood up and took her things from the rack. I asked her if she was getting out, and she said yes, she had to change trains.

'I hope I'll see you again,' I said.

And she said, yes, she hoped so too. And then she was gone. I watched her walk up the platform. Prim, and neat, and very beautiful.

And then my folly struck me. I hadn't asked her name. I didn't know where she lived. I didn't know where she worked. I could walk about the city for years and never see her again.

And I just *had* to meet her again. But how? What did I know about her? Well her initials were Z.Y. What name could I make out of that? Zoe? Yeadon? Zenobia Yarrow? Everything sounded false, no matter how I permutated the possibilities.

When I got back to the city I looked through the phone book. I found a few pages of Ys, but not one had a Z in front of it.

The electoral rolls didn't help me, either. Probably because her parents' home was elsewhere, away from the city.

I wonder where her real home could be. So I checked at the railway station where she changed trains.

'What trains were booked to connect?' I inquired.

Well, I found that four trains were listed as connections to the one she'd been on. And the four trains stopped at a total of thirty-two stations. Some of them quite large towns. Impossible.

It seemed hopeless. I back-tracked my brain. What else did I know about her? She had a case with initials on it. She also had a bunch of flowers. Flowers!

She couldn't have bought them that morning, because the shops didn't open until nine, and we had caught the 8.50. But perhaps she could have done – there was a flower stall on the west side of the station, and that was open. And to see the stall, she must have approached the station from the west side.

What buses stopped on the west side of the station? I checked. There were three routes, all of which went to the outskirts of the city. It narrowed my search to a quarter of a million people. Not exactly encouraging.

I decided to go back to the station and go through all the moves she'd made: re-enactment, as it were.

What did I remember? A quick smile when I stopped her flowers from rolling off the counter. What else? She bought a magazine. What magazine? I didn't know. I didn't notice. But I did see where the assistant got it from – the pegboard wall behind her.

The magazines on the pegboard were the more serious types: the *Builder's Gazette*, the *Electronics Review*, the *Teachers Monthly*. Could she have been a teacher? No. It was term time and a school day when she travelled.

There were a few more: the *Chemist and Druggist*, *Hi-Fi Illustrated*, the *Nursing Journal* . . . could she have been a nurse?

And then it hit me. On the train I asked if she'd like a coffee. And she said yes, she hadn't had one since four. Four a.m. She'd just come off night duty.

I looked at the bus routes again. One of them passed a hospital. The Royal Infirmary.

I stood in the hospital drive-way, trying to decide where to go first? Outpatients? Ear, Nose and Throat?

And then I saw the ambulance coming fast. I felt stupidly disorientated, I started to go forward, jumped back – and messed it up thoroughly. I felt the wing hit me and then I felt nothing more till I woke up in bed, saying, 'Where am I?'

'You're in hospital,' said a face.

'Is there a nurse here with the initials Z.Y.?'

The face bent down to hear me better. 'I don't know, let's see. Yes, it could be Zena Yates, the night sister.'

'Could you ask her to come and see me, please?'

'You'll see her tonight. But you're to rest now.'

It seemed an eternity. And then the sister bent over me. There was grey hair peeping from her cap. She was a kindly old soul.

'You wanted to see me,' she said. 'I'm Zena Yates.'

'You can't be,' I said. 'There can't be two people in any one hospital with the initials Z.Y.'

I lay there for hours. Thinking. And then the simple solution struck me. I asked again to see the night sister, Zena Yates.

'Yes,' she said. 'I lent a little weekend case to Valeria Watson, one of the nurses.'

And at last Dream Girl was there, sitting beside my bed with just a trace of amusement wrinkling a corner of her mouth. This was it, all right. Not the tiniest trace of doubt. The only girl in the world for me.

'How did you find me?' she asked.

'Deduction. A simple matter of deduction. I'm in the police. I'm still only a detective constable, I'm afraid. But I'm very ambitious.'

She smiled broadly now and bent down. She whispered in my ear: 'I like an ambitious man.'

Donald the Diplomat

JOHN HYNAM

Yes sir, Desmond Donald's the name. Fifty years' service in the Harborough family from pantry boy to butler which I have been for the last twenty years.

We read a lot in the papers, even today, about class distinction and the old school tie; me being what I am, you might think that I know all about it. To tell you the truth, I've never noticed it.

Mind you, if there's one thing the so-called upper-class families still manage very well, it's in the matter of discretion. That's one solid lesson I have learned in all my years of service. But take my word for it, diplomacy and discretion pay.

Every family has its black sheep, and the noble Harboroughs are no exception. In the eighteenth century there was Lord Roger, who scarpered to France when the law got after him for a duel killing. In the nineteenth we had Lord Eustace, who would gamble on which fly would get to the top of the window first. It was rumoured that this chap sold half the family portraits to pay his gambling debts. He died, suddenly.

But the family strains keep on coming up, time and time again; the Harborough face comes along every so often, and similar ways of behaviour too.

Discretion is not merely the better part of valour; it's a factor which makes for a pleasanter existence. Take, for example, Master Richard. That's not his real name, of course; you wouldn't expect me to give that, would you? Captain Master Richard got four years – dishonourable discharge followed by court proceedings.

Now, although I have served nearly all my working life up at Harborough House, I do have a friend named Masters who has worked long years in a fine establishment in Eaton Square.

One day he rang me and said that Master Richard was being pursued by some gambling club strong-arm types. I bore this in mind, but said nothing to the family, particularly as Master Richard had been forbidden by his lordship ever to come there again, and his present lordship knows the value of discretion.

It was at this time that I directed the housekeeper to change rooms with me, so that I was near to his lordship's office, which was halfway down the Great Gallery. I also borrowed a serviceable shotgun from Bostock, the head keeper, and awaited events with a certain amount of placid anticipation. You see, I know the Harboroughs.

I awoke, one morning, at three o'clock. I thought that I had heard, through the gusty night, the sound of breaking glass. I got out of bed, put on dressing-gown and slippers, collected the loaded shotgun plus two cartridges. I pushed my door slightly ajar, placed my ear to it, and listened. Two creaking boards – coincidence. Three creaking boards, in measured time, means that you have burglars.

But, even with burglars, you have to be discreet.

When a torch was switched on, and I saw by the reflection that the intruder was Master Richard, I knew that I needed no valour, only discretion. He was shaking like a jelly.

I watched; he was going along the line of family portraits. He walked slowly past the Gainsboroughs, the Romneys, the Constables. I noticed that he passed by the large and heavy ones with merely a glance, while the smaller ones were considered at some length.

Finally he stopped about twenty yards away from my bedroom door, at the end of the gallery, interested in the Romney of Lady Eustacia. I understand the Lady Eustacia, in her youth, was a girl who found the word 'No' difficult to pronounce, but this could not be divined from an examination of the portrait; she was a true beauty, and innocent-looking with it.

And Master Richard picked this one. He found a chair upon which to stand. Cautiously, he took hold of the frame, and eased it upwards. I approached quietly and, raising my gun, I said, 'Master Richard, sir, if you move I may blow your head off.'

He swayed, staggered with the weight of the frame, regained his balance and stared down at me, his torch stuck in his mouth. He looked stupid.

'Descend, sir, with caution,' I requested.

He got down. 'Look here, Donald, I can explain . . .'

'In this situation, sir,' I suggested, 'no explanation is necessary. You have come to obtain the wherewithal to pay your debts, otherwise a couple of heavies from a certain club will do you up more than rotten. Is that so, sir?'

He goggled a bit. 'Yes.'

'Then, sir, I must point out that your selected picture is worse than useless. The notorious Lord Eustace – whom you so resemble – had a copy made a hundred years ago, took the genuine one, and so paid his debts.' I was severe, and it registered.

He sagged. I knew he would. I took the Romney and leaned it against the wall. 'Now, Master Richard, if you want a picture for cash with which to leave for the colonies – it can be done for ten pounds, I believe, in the case of Australia – I suggest that you take that little one *there*, of the eighth earl in dress uniform of the first of foot.'

He didn't seem to understand, at first.

'That one,' I said.

'My God, Donald, you're a brick!' he said. He grabbed the eighth earl, and was gone.

I replaced the Romney; that picture of the eighth earl the whole present household knows to be a copy, and its disappearance will cause little fuss.

Nevertheless, I shall have to have a quiet word with his lordship. You see, though the picture of the soldierly eighth earl is a fake, it will yield fifty pounds at least.

The Romney I rescued is also a fake, the difference being that his lordship, with my assistance, twenty years ago did a switch with the Romney. Thus he was able to pay off a young lady who had given herself freely and, indeed, bore him twin sons to prove it.

As it would be most awkward – nay, unthinkable – to lumber the present succession with a pair of heirs born on the wrong side of the blanket, one has to be discreet, especially as it might make difficult my extra quarterly cheque from his lordship, which is for discreet services discreetly rendered.

Another Scotch for you?

Against the Bidding

DENYS VAL BAKER

Mr Watson was a tough, balding and somewhat disillusioned auctioneer. He was very well used to the odd ways of mankind, and even womankind. Consequently, when the little old lady called Miss Palmer was ushered into his office clutching her precious parcel, he knew from past experience that he would have to be patient for a while.

'. . . quite a family heirloom in its way,' she confessed at last, undoing her parcel and revealing a middling good Toby jug. 'Once upon a time it used to belong to my mother.'

Miss Palmer winced at the 'used' of the past tense, and her eyes went a little moist. Mr Watson looked away uncomfortably.

'Of course, I, er, suppose I'm just a sentimental old thing,' said Miss Palmer, half to herself. 'But you see – well, I can remember my mother telling me how her dear grandmother always kept the jug on her mantelpiece – and then my mother, she, er, was rather the same.'

'And I suppose you've got rather attached to it, too?'

Miss Palmer smiled, a faded, rather sad smile. 'Yes . . . but . . .' Her voice was very quiet. 'In my present circumstances, well . . .'

Mr Watson coughed, and stood up. 'Quite. Don't worry, ma'am. I'll do my best.'

Miss Palmer went out then, with one last lingering look at the

Toby jug. Mr Watson watched her go with some misgivings: it was, after all, several days to the auction.

As he expected, the next day Miss Palmer was back in the office again, all tight and taut and full of new determination, saying that she had decided not to part with her precious jug after all.

The following day, of course, sheepishly, she brought it back again. And after that, she kept away, though Mr Watson had some faint idea of the turmoil raging in her quiet and normally placid little heart.

On the day of the auction the hall was crowded to capacity with the usual conglomeration of dealers, buyers, and the merely curious. There were several lots to get through that day and Mr Watson found himself busy with his gavel, shouting the numbers and taking the bids up sometimes into the eighties and nineties, for some inlaid walnut furniture.

He was so busy, in fact, that he hardly remembered Miss Palmer, until at last he came too: 'Lot 145, a period Toby jug . . .' and he paused and looked around. There she was, tucked in a distant corner seeming almost to belong to the furniture and the period pieces.

Mr Watson smiled and nodded, as if to convey again 'Don't worry, ma'am, I'll do my best,' and then in a brisk, businesslike voice, he drew attention to the superlative qualities of this genuine and most original piece of real Staffordshire pottery.

The bidding, as Mr Watson had secretly feared, was not half as brisk as his introduction: Toby jugs were, these days, an uncertain element. However, there was one dealer he had his eye on who specialised in the jugs, and he was hoping to land the sale with him. 'Forty pounds,' said Mr Watson at last, repeating the dealer's latest bid with some satisfaction; it was in his opinion a fair price. 'Forty pounds I am bid for this – '

Mr Watson's stentorian voice was cut short by a bid of forty pounds two shillings and sixpence; he frowned, looked puzzledly around, and then inquiringly at the dealer–specialist who, much to Mr Watson's relief, nodded.

'Forty pounds five shillings,' said Mr Watson quickly, and then, hurriedly, 'Going – going – '

'Forty pounds seven shillings and sixpence.'

Mr Watson glared, and then looked beseechingly at the dealer. By some supreme effort he willed the dealer to bid another half-crown. Back came the answering bid by which time the dealer himself was perhaps a little piqued. But he went on twelve and six and then even up to forty pounds seventeen shillings and sixpence. Mr Watson took the bid himself up two shillings.

But there, Mr Watson could see quite clearly, the dealer was sticking; and it was with real anguish that he heard the firm, clear, rather reed-like voice pipe up from the back of the hall, 'Forty-one pounds . . .'

At the end of the auction Mr Watson was still muttering to himself about women and sentiment, and old fools who bothered him and all that sort of thing; and moving sheets of paper about, trying to get his things cleared up. He was not too busy, however, to observe the frail old lady who sidled, shamefacedly, up to his table.

'Well,' said Mr Watson, with heavy sarcasm. 'Well, well – '

He was about to say something more when he took a good look at the face of Miss Palmer, who had just quite crazily bid forty-one pounds for her own Toby jug. It was a finely formed, once pretty face of a sweet old lady, and Mr Watson didn't like to see the rings under her eyes, and the generally pinched look.

'Oh, dear,' said Miss Palmer apologetically. 'I'm afraid that when I thought of my jug going to that dealer and being put in a shop window like an orphan, I just couldn't help bidding.'

'Ummh,' said Mr Watson, sternly. He cleared his throat officiously. 'Well, as it happens I'm afraid your bid was too late.'

For a few seconds Mr Watson paused in order to punish Miss Palmer a little with her own dismay, then he went on.

'Your jug was sold for forty pounds nineteen shillings and six-pence. However,' Mr Watson coughed and busied himself with a cheque-book. 'As it happens the bidder decided he didn't want the jug after all and he, er, asked me to return it to you with compliments.'

'But – ' began Miss Palmer tremulously.

In one magnificent movement Mr Watson, who could be most efficient when he wanted, placed in Miss Palmer's arms a Toby jug and a cheque for forty pounds nineteen shillings and sixpence and escorted her towards the office door. Allowing Miss Palmer to but no more buts, he propelled her gently out into the wide world.

For a time he stood watching her frail, bewildered figure as it disappeared down the street. She wasn't the only fool in town.

Simple Sailor

BARTIMEUS

It had been raining, and all the wagons that could be mustered were out in tow of tractors to collect the sacks of barley which the combine had cut, threshed, winnowed and bagged.

The buyers were particular about the correct degree of moisture in the grain.

Jorgen Anderson, who had mastered the technique of testing the grains for moisture and the rather complicated process of drying and bagging, was in charge of the drying plant. He was a big, bald, muscular man with gentle movements and quiet eyes, steady in their regard like a seaman's. Jorgen's forebears had been Danish seamen for centuries, fishermen mostly. But his grandfather had turned inland when he married a girl who had been widowed very young by the sea.

Jorgen had a little white dog, with no tail to speak of, called Sofie. In the evenings, while the grain was drying and there was nothing to do but listen to the hum of the machinery, Jorgen sat in a deck chair in the drying loft with Sofie on his lap.

There was an Englishman staying on the farm who had been a sailor. Between him and Jorgen there was some mysterious mutual sympathy and liking which included Sofie. The Englishman spoke practically no Danish and Jorgen no English whatsoever.

The Englishman sometimes visited Jorgen in the drying loft during what he, the Englishman, would have called the second dogwatch, and he came the night the rain stopped when they were drying the last of the grain.

Later, one Magnus came to relieve Jorgen, bringing a bottle of beer and some *smørrebrød* in a piece of newspaper.

Jorgen, who was proffered the bottle, removed the metal cap with his teeth, said '*Skål!*' drank, passed his hand over the neck of the bottle and gave it back. '*Tak!*' he said. 'The Englishman has been here for a chat with me. He was in the English navy. Now, my grandfather was a sailor and his grandfather, and back and back to the Vikings, one of whom as you know lies buried in the field where they cut the barley today. This Englishman and I, we understand one another.'

Magnus nodded uninterestedly. His immediate forebears worked on the farm. Before that they were woodsmen. Back and back. They had no dealings with the sea, but Magnus had once known a sailor who was a simple man. From this Magnus deduced (having himself a rather one-track mind) that all sailors were simple folk. You could easily get the better of them – not that he, Magnus, would ever want to. But if he did, they were . . .

Jorgen softly whistled Sofie to his heel, wished Magnus good-night and disappeared down the ladder, leaving Magnus in charge.

Next morning saw the task of gathering the harvest completed. The contents of the last forty sacks were to be stored in a convenient loft for consumption on the farm. Each sack weighed a hundred and sixty pounds and it had to be carried up a steep staircase – ten steps high – and the contents tipped on the floor. The pile of grain spread gradually over the floor, threatening at last to overflow down the stairs. To prevent this, one of the men stemmed the encroaching flood with a broad long-handled shovel, flinging the grain towards the rear of the loft. The men tipped their loads as far back as they could, labouring in up to their knees. Shovelling without a pause and by flinging the shovelfuls well back, it was just possible to keep pace with the inflow.

There were four men carrying the sacks and they were getting tired, as indeed was Magnus, who was shovelling. There were only twenty sacks left to finish the job and it was nearing the dinner hour.

Work of a character unfamiliar to him attracted the Englishman.

He watched Magnus shovelling the encroaching grain back from the stairs up which the weary men staggered in turn with their burdens. Something came back to him from the past when he occasionally shovelled coal into bags in a collier's hold. Some impulse to lend a hand and get the job finished came to him. He took the shovel from the surprised and sweating Magnus, who stood back watching him awhile.

Then unobtrusively Magnus descended the ladder. There were fifteen sacks left on the wagon. It was nearly time for dinner. The Englishman seemed to like shovelling grain against time in a dusty loft on a hot day. Magnus decided to indulge his whim. The Englishman was a sailor, after all. He disappeared round the corner.

After a while the Englishman decided he had had enough. His muscles ached, his mouth was dry with dust, and he was drenched with sweat. He looked round for Magnus who wasn't there, so he went on shovelling. If he stopped for breath the golden cascade slid forward towards the staircase with the inexorable advance of a glacier, but a lot faster. Still the sacks arrived and their contents multiplied what assumed in his mind the proportions of a catastrophe.

The thing had almost become a matter of international prestige . . . Sweat blinded him. He reminded himself that he wasn't as young as he had been . . . He wondered whether this wasn't how people strained their hearts.

He was aware of the engine of the tractor down below, and looked round. He was alone. After throwing down the shovel, he descended the staircase and gazed round the yard. The wagon had gone. Leif, the youngest of the farm workers, had stayed behind to fold the last of the sacks into bundles. He grinned at the Englishman who it was understood spoke no Danish.

The Englishman merely sat on a bundle of sacks and panted. Leif clumped off to get his dinner and a bottle of beer. At the corner of the outhouse he looked back with another grin, and for the Englishman's benefit went through the pantomime of raising a bottle to his mouth.

The Englishman had recovered his breath and, presumably, his sense of humour. He laughed back.

Family Funeral

GIOVANNI CECCARELLI

Carlo the young Sicilian policeman sat down on a rock along-side the dusty road. He wiped the sweat from his forehead with a handkerchief and loosened his tie. He felt the skin of his face burning under the hot sun; the walk up those stony hills had exhausted him.

He thought about the promotion day and the chance to leave the uniformed *Carabinieri* to become a plain-clothes detective. He had joined the police with rosy ideas of high adventures in big cities and the chance to solve sensational cases. He was highly intelligent and had the fine sense of perception necessary for a good detective. He felt he was wasting his time as a *carabiniere*. When he finished his training he least expected to be posted to a rustic village lost in a forgotten part of Sicily where the police had little or no power against the Mafia who had ruled unchallenged since time immemorial.

Carlo adjusted the rifle across his shoulders and scanned the hilly horizon. He knew he had to be patient; he was at the begin-ning of his career and the routine jobs had to be done, but it seemed as though the Inspector always picked on him for the worst duties.

He wished he had not been sent to investigate the theft of a couple of sheep some ten miles from the village – that day of all days. The day of the funeral of Don Fredo. He wanted to be in on that. 'Now that that Mafioso is dead there will be some real peace around here,' Carlo said to himself as he passed the handkerchief round the back of his neck to dry the sweat.

Don Fredo had been a fat and cruel overlord with strong American connections. He had been sent back from New York to replace another overlord who had displeased the Family and had passed away under a shower of bullets. Don Fredo's job had been to organise the despatch of drugs to America. After one look at him the villagers thought it would not be long before some other branch of the Family disposed of him but he had reigned for many years and then apparently died of a heart attack.

The wind came up mysteriously, bringing giant black clouds. The sun quickly disappeared leaving the arid hills in a strange eerie light. The smell of rain filled the air and minutes later a summer storm broke in fury.

Carlo ran towards a half-hidden farmhouse he had seen not far away and found it empty. All the doors had fallen apart and the place was almost covered by overgrown trees and weeds.

He entered a large stone-floored room, leaned against a wall to catch his breath and wiped the rain from his face with the back of his hand. He looked around and saw a few farm implements rusting away. The house appeared to have been abandoned for many years and yet . . . There was something, a strange smell.

He moved towards the fireplace and saw a pile of ashes, a broken pot and a few brown stains on the floor leading to a heap of masonry and rubble. He suddenly realised what it was. He shifted some of the rubble and found the decaying body of a man. Carlo could not believe his eyes. He stared at it. There was no mistake. Don Fredo had not died of a heart attack after all. The bullet hole in his head made that clear.

Carlo ran most of the way back to the village. He reached the police station wet through and out of breath. The Inspector looked at him surprised as Carlo explained what he had seen.

The Inspector paled and shook his head. 'You must be mistaken,' he said coldly. 'Don Fredo is lying in the church at this very moment. We are waiting for some of his friends to arrive from Palermo to collect the body and take it to the airport. His

American relatives want to give him a family funeral in America and bury him there.'

Carlo was baffled. 'I can assure you, sir . . .'

'I would advise you to forget it,' the Inspector said sharply. 'The man you have found in the farmhouse cannot be Don Fredo.'

Carlo turned towards the door ready to leave.

'Where are you going?'

'To the church to make sure I am not going out of my mind.'

The rain stopped and the wind was chasing the clouds away. The sun shone, turning the water pools into sparkling mirrors. Carlo walked along the maze of cobbled streets flanked by whitewashed houses, reached the main square and the old, poor church.

He went inside where a handful of old women were whispering a mournful prayer. As soon as they saw the policeman they stopped praying and stared at him with their beady eyes. Carlo had the impression that they were watching the body more than praying for its soul.

He looked down at the open coffin and thought that the face of Don Fredo was thinner and smoother. It looked as if death had given it the translucency of wax. The policeman was utterly confused. He noticed that the collar of the shirt was too big for the neck and he could see the naked body underneath.

Carlo realised what had happened. He moved away from the coffin and sat down on a bench away from the old ladies and waited patiently.

The men from Palermo arrived together with the Inspector and several other policemen. The Inspector looked at Carlo as if to warn him to keep quiet. The young policeman felt nervous and did not know what to do.

The priest arrived shortly after, said a few ritual prayers and the men from Palermo put the lid on the coffin and lifted it on to their shoulders. Carlo went out into the square, unstrapped the rifle from his shoulders, loaded it, and waited.

'Drop it!' Carlo ordered the men as soon as they were out of the church. 'Drop the coffin!'

The old women ran away in panic. The men gently lowered the coffin to the ground. The Inspector tried to say something but remained silent behind the group.

Carlo lifted the coffin lid. He gently slid his fingers under the shirt collar on the corpse and pulled off the wax face-mask, revealing the mass of raw opium shaped to look like the body of Don Fredo.

The Inspector and Carlo stared at each other for a while.

'I told you to leave it,' the Inspector finally said. 'The Regional Commander and I knew of the whole thing. We wanted it to go as planned. These men are only the small fry. We were after the big bosses in America. But you had to mess it up.'

The Brand of Eve

C. S. FORESTER

My Grandmother Betty is one of the very nicest women I know, and nearly the oldest. She was eighty this year, and I am not committing any breach of confidence in saying so, because as soon as she left seventy-nine behind she announced that she did not care any longer who knew how old she was. Up to that time she was always a little reserved about her age, only telling it in the strictest confidence to everyone of her acquaintance.

But it is only quite recently that she told me about how she came to be married.

It appeared that Grandmother Betty was the daughter of a family of advanced views – in the seventies and eighties my great-grandparents had very peculiar and suspicious opinions about the Higher Criticism, and the Emancipation of Women, and the Origins of Species by Natural Selection, and all the other matters about which there was such hot debate.

Yet it had the unfortunate result, in Betty's case at least, of making it very hard for her to find a husband, because the eligible men of the district naturally shied away from a young woman of such doubtful upbringing, so that she had reached the age of twenty-three and was practically an old maid without ever having received a proposal of marriage.

Her elder sister, Charlotte, was more fortunate – she married

Soames, the portrait painter, who, being an artist, and therefore more tolerant of outlandish ideas, took the risk, and installed himself and his wife in a comfortable house in Kensington and flourished exceedingly on painting portraits at his customary fee of three hundred guineas for a full length.

It was while making her way to London to pay a visit to Charlotte that Grandmother Betty received the Brand of Eve and caused this story to be written.

It was May Day, and, appropriately, a fine sunny morning when Betty started off to walk through the lanes to the station.

At a corner of the lane she met the Captain, who was taking his retriever for a walk.

The Captain had a local reputation as a bit of a rip, I fear; anxious mothers discussed his latest peccadilloes in hushed voices in retired corners of their drawing-rooms. Betty, for instance, knew that the Captain was a man in some way of a sinister and therefore romantic reputation. For all her emancipation it gave her a little thrill to be walking alone with him in that quiet lane.

For some hundreds of yards they walked along together, talking of larks and cuckoos and primroses, with the retriever scampering round them.

And all that time, I fancy – Grandmother Betty's own reticence on the point nearly convinces me of it – the Captain was eyeing her sidelong and meditating a new conquest.

After all, he was quite justified in his own eyes, for any young woman allowed to stray alone in country lanes and to travel by herself all the way to London – let alone being an artist's sister-in-law – must necessarily be of easy virtue and fair game for any rusticating Captain. However it was, when they had nearly reached the point where the lane emerged into the highroad close to the station, the Captain made his plunge.

They had halted to admire a bit of the countryside of which Betty was particularly fond, and when she was expecting to start off again the Captain put his hands on her shoulders.

He smiled at her for a moment, and then he said, 'May I?' Nor did he stay for an answer, for the next second he had Betty in his arms and was kissing her on the lips which – for all her emancipation – had never been kissed by any man save near relations.

He kissed her several times, and Betty, who had not time to feel ashamed, actually enjoyed it.

He said nothing after that first 'May I?' and she said nothing at all, while the retriever sat and wondered and the lark sang in the blue sky.

And then Betty suddenly heard the distant whistle of the train, and she came to her senses with a jerk. Not merely was she courting the very gravest risk but she might miss her train – and there were only two trains daily to London.

She tore herself from the Captain's arms and with a cry of 'My train!' she ran away down the lane to the station, leaving the Captain staring after her.

She only just had time to buy her ticket – she had to hold it in her mouth as she ran, her hands full of her muff and purse bag and parasol, on to the platform, and she jumped into the carriage (containing two elderly ladies) whose door the guard held open for her.

When she sat down she was still quite unrepentant. She felt no prick of conscience whatever; merely a muddled exhilaration. She had been so far imbued with her parents' dangerous ideas as almost to have come to believe that a double standard of behaviour was unfair – that if men could go round kissing girls, then girls could go round kissing men.

She told herself this, rebelliously, when at length her conscience began to trouble her, and she tried to distract her mind from any sensation of guilt by going back in memory through her recent experience – the smile on the Captain's lips when he said 'May I?' and the thrill which the touch of his waxed moustache had given her, and the pleasant scent of tweed and hair oil which she had noticed about him.

Then she realised that she must be a little untidy; she was probably flushed and her hat was certainly a little awry. With an apologetic murmur to the disapproving old ladies she took her mirror from her purse bag, and she received the greatest shock of her life.

There, printed on her lip's unmistakably, were the words 'May I' – the very words the Captain had used before he kissed her.

First Betty paled and then she flushed as she stared at her reflection with the damning proof of her guilt.

This was the way God was going to punish her for all her wickedness of the past, for the slackness of her corsets, and the freedom of her thought, and her last culminating immorality. That kiss of the Captain's must have burnt his words into her lips. All her life she would have to meet the sneering glances of the world directed at 'May I?' on her mouth.

'Are you quite well?' asked the elder of the two elderly women suddenly.

'Y-yes,' mumbled Betty. In a panic she had caught up her handkerchief to her mouth.

'I should hardly have thought so,' said the elderly woman, pointedly. 'However . . .'

Betty scrubbed at her lip with her handkerchief, and then she took another furtive peep into the mirror. The words were still there, accusatory and damning.

She held her handkerchief tightly to her mouth all the way to Waterloo, and at the station she only took it away in order to be just intelligible to the driver of the four-wheeler which she engaged to take her to Kensington.

My Great-Aunt Charlotte was not very sympathetic when her young sister arrived at her house on the verge of hysteria.

'Nonsense,' she said, looking at Betty's mouth after her tearful explanation. 'You've got a few marks there, perhaps, but nothing anyone could read unless they had an imagination like yours.'

Betty took another look in the mirror, and there was 'May I' written as plain as could be on her lower lip.

'It is there,' she wailed. 'This is my punishment, my just punishment.'

'Fiddlesticks,' said Charlotte. 'Come along now, Betty, and leave off behaving like a schoolgirl. You'll have red eyes at dinner tonight unless you show a little more self-control.'

'I don't care if I do,' said Betty.

Later on in the day Charlotte made some concession to this schoolgirl behaviour on her sister's part. She came into Betty's bedroom with a mysterious little silver case in her hand, and in the case was a scarlet pencil with the label scratched off.

'Here,' she said. 'You had better try this. I only keep it, of course, because my lips crack so badly sometimes in the winter. It is just a salve, you see, but if you put it on your lips it will hide those marks that you seem to be so worried about. And to speak quite plainly, my girl, a little colour on your mouth won't be a bad thing. You're looking positively anaemic. For heaven's sake put some on and leave off crying.'

The lip salve certainly solved the problem of Betty's appearance at dinner that evening, for, smeared on moderately thickly, it quite covered the words painted on her lips.

She was distraught and nervous, and she slipped off to bed at the very earliest opportunity. She prayed long and deeply, vowing the sincerest repentance and the deepest reparation.

Next morning the words were gone. Her lip's – after, anxiously, she had wiped off the salve she had not had the courage to remove on going to bed – were unmarked, pure, once more.

'Heaven has been good to me,' said Betty to herself. 'It sent those words just as a warning to me of how wicked I've been. Now that I've learned my lesson it has taken them away. I shall be good, ever so good. I'll make up for my wickedness just as I promised last night. I will, really. I'll be an honest woman soon.'

Even before she reached home she had the opportunity of making an honest woman of herself, and she took it with both hands.

At that selfsame corner of the lane where the dreadful thing had happened there was the Captain waiting for her on her way home from the station.

Betty attributed his appearance there to the direct interpolation of providence, but I am inclined to doubt that. I rather fancy that she had mentioned to the Captain how long she had intended to stay with her sister, and he had come along to meet the only train by which she could arrive, in the hope of making further progress in the affair.

Betty did not beat about the bush.

'Captain,' she said, 'you've got to marry me.'

'Er-what?' said the Captain, taken a little aback.

'You've got to marry me. You must. You must,' said Betty.

Betty had the Dresden china complexion which she preserves

to this day, and the excitement of the moment flushed it to beautiful pink, and lent sparkle to her eyes, so that for all her twenty-three years and imminent old-maidishness she was really pretty; and for the first time in his life the Captain felt as if there might be something in this notion of marriage.

'What is the trouble, my dear?' he asked, temporising. He could not be expected to throw over all at once his life-long resolutions regarding bachelorhood.

'We've been sinful,' said Betty. 'It will be terribly wicked of us if we don't get married.'

There was desperate sincerity in her tone and in her expression. The Captain was surprised, pleasantly surprised, to find that Betty possessed such high moral standards. He was surprised that a girl brought up so deplorably as she had been should make such a fuss over a kiss or two. It meant that her innate virtue must be extraordinarily pure.

And there was no denying how pretty she was; the Captain told himself he would have considered her favourably as a possible wife long ago if only he had not been led to doubt her virtue on account of her upbringing. In face of this proof he had no hesitation.

'Of course, my dear. We'll get married as soon as you will name the day. May I come back with you now and speak to your father?'

But they took a long time to get home. Betty was so lighthearted at having made an honest woman of herself, and the Captain was so taken with this new idea of marriage, that they lingered, often.

Grandmother Betty says that the modern girl misses a great deal in never knowing what pleasure is to be derived from a kiss associated with a waxed moustache and a feeling of pure virtue.

Not until a long time after, when the honeymoon was over, in fact, not until a month or two before my Uncle Harry – my father's eldest brother – was due to be born did my grandmother tell my grandfather of how heaven had directly interposed in order to bring about their marriage.

'H'm,' said the Captain. 'That's queer.'

'Queer?' said Grandmother Betty. 'I don't think that's the way to describe it. It seems to me to be irreligious to call it queer.'

'H'm,' said the Captain again. Anyone who had the pleasure

of knowing my grandfather, even in his old age, would know how difficult it would be to convince him of a miracle. An idea struck him. 'Do you remember the date when it happened?'

'Yes, of course,' said my grandmother. If for no other reason, it was the first day of the year on which she had worn a starched petticoat. 'It was the first of May.'

'Quite so,' said my grandfather. 'And you had to run for your train. And I'll bet a pony you put your ticket in your mouth when you bought it. Didn't you?'

'Yes.'

'And the printer's ink was wet and came off on your lip. It wasn't "May I" but "May the first" you saw there. That's why you could read it in a mirror while Charlotte couldn't.'

'Perhaps – perhaps you're right,' said Betty miserably.

'Of course. I'm right. And the lip salve would take off printer's ink in a way nothing else would. But let me tell you this, dearest. I'm jolly glad about it all. Jolly glad.'

The Housekeeper

J. I. HOBBS

Charles Courtney stared in consternation at the trim figure in the grey dress.

'Frightfully sorry! Had no idea.' His gaze shifted somewhat guiltily to the shattered glass from the French window.

'No idea of what exactly?' The question shot crisply across the elegant room.

'Well. No idea Dr Fraser had a – a housekeeper. Thought the place was empty now he was away on holiday. Lost the key, you know.'

'Lost the key! You broke in,' she accused. If she was startled she wasn't showing it.

'Well, I had to.' With an effort he asserted himself. 'I had to get in, obviously. Of course, if I had known you were here, I'd have rung the bell.' Damn the woman!

'Who are you?' Her voice was reminiscent of a hospital matron.

'Courtney's the name. Dr Fraser's locum, you know. Surely he told you to expect me?' His tone carried now just the right amount of asperity.

Tiny pause then she murmured: 'Yes, of course. But . . .'

'But not in such an unorthodox manner,' he finished for her, smiling.

She almost returned his smile, but not quite.

'You say you've lost the key. Did the doctor send it to you?'

'Yes. Damned stupid to have mislaid it. Can't think what I've done with it.' He started to pick up the splinters of glass.

'I'll see to that presently,' she answered briskly; then observed: 'You've cut your hand.'

He shrugged. 'It's nothing.'

Stridently, so that they both started, the telephone rang. She looked uncertainly round the room then back, involuntarily, at him. Perhaps she didn't like telephones.

'Try the hall,' he suggested after a moment. He eyed her narrowly, frowningly, as she hurried into the hall.

He heard her asking who was there. Then she was back.

'Someone forgetting to put their money in,' she remarked.

'They'll ring again, no doubt.' He smiled suddenly. 'Look here! Awfully sorry if I scared you. I assure you everything is all right.' He pulled a spotless handkerchief from his breast pocket, wrapping it nonchalantly around his hand. 'And if you have anywhere you'd rather go for the weekend, I can manage perfectly well for myself.'

'Where's your luggage?'

He indicated a small case by the window. 'I've all I need for calls. I'll collect my suitcase from the station tomorrow.'

'I'll not be going anywhere,' she informed him flatly. 'I promised Dr Fraser.'

'As you wish, of course.' A calculating look sharpened his eyes as he remarked casually, 'How come you didn't know where the phone was?'

'I'm not the regular housekeeper,' she said at last. 'She's – away. The doctor asked me to come and keep an eye on things over the weekend. I live in the village.'

Charles somehow didn't know whether he believed that.

The telephone blared again through the house.

'I'll get that,' he said. 'Probably for me.'

But, smartly, she was already out of the room. He pushed the door wide, moving to look at the painting. He could hear her clearly. Not saying much, just answering.

'Call for you,' she said presently. 'Young Mrs Lawson. Her first.'

He moved slowly towards the hall, but she detained him. 'They've rung off.'

161

He could have sworn there was some sort of a glint in her eyes as she went on, 'In fact I'm told it's twins. Always come at night, don't they?'

'No peace for the wicked.' He gave an extravagant sigh. 'Well, have to be on my way. What address?'

'Her husband said it wasn't urgent. There's time for coffee. And you have your things, you say.' She eyed his case on the chair. 'Come into the kitchen. I'll fix your hand.'

'Don't bother. There may be more calls.'

'It's no bother.' She shepherded him into the kitchen, brooking no argument. Expertly she dabbed antiseptic on his hand and applied a small plaster.

'There. That ought to do.' As she poured boiling water into two cups she said shrewdly: 'Not much experience with babies?'

'Not really. Not long out of training hospital, you know.'

She handed him a cup. 'Instant, I'm afraid. But it's good and strong. It'll be all right, you know. With the twins, I mean.'

They stood silent then, drinking. But before they could finish the coffee, the doorbell rang. He couldn't help it but his cup went down with quite a bang on the table. She put hers down slowly.

'More customers. I'll try to put them off for you till the morning.'

But he beat her by a couple of strides to the door. He opened it with a flourish, then stood quite still. The police sergeant in the doorway also stood very still. Charles Courtney felt the colour drain from his face. How had the woman done it? He had heard her every word on the phone.

'Well, well! If it isn't our Charlie!' The sergeant was the first to recover.

'You know him, Sergeant?' The woman had come up behind him and sounded both breathless and relieved.

'That I do, ma'am. I see the French window is broken. Has he taken anything, d'you know?'

'Not now, he hasn't.'

The two men watched her as she took from Charlie's case the painting that had hung on the wall.

Strangely, he showed no surprise. Things just hadn't gone right for him this evening. She was clever, the woman. But he'd surprise her, though.

'You want to ask her what she's doing here, too, Sergeant,' he blurted out angrily. 'No more right than I to be here. Housekeeper, indeed! Never been in this house before tonight.'

The woman returned the picture to the wall, tapping it straight with her finger.

'That's right,' she agreed coolly. 'I arrived just before you.'

The sergeant looked at his watch anxiously. There was an air of sudden harassment about him.

'Better both get in the car,' he ordered. 'I'll drop you at the station, m'lad.' He snapped a pair of handcuffs around Charlie's wrists. Then he was turning to the woman.

'Good thing you came, Sergeant,' she said, pulling on a coat. 'Mustn't keep those twins of yours waiting.'

'After you, Doctor,' he said respectfully.

Phantom at the Head of the Table . . .

LOUIS ALLEGRI

The woman was playing some delicate Debussy on the piano. The man sitting on the sofa in the elegantly furnished drawing-room reflected that the scene was all a man could wish for.

Perfect. No! He drew his breath in sharply. He mustn't use that word – it always caused murderous feelings to erupt inside him.

As if he could murder a ghost!

But a spectre did loom over everything in that house, forming an invisible barrier between him and his fiancée, the girl at the piano, whose graceful beauty still retained much of the warm, trusting innocence of childhood. They were to be married in a few months, but the thought of that other man – the presence – sent a chill through him. How do you destroy a ghost?

She suddenly stopped playing with a massive discord and then stood up. 'I'm hopeless.'

'Hopeless? Why do you always demean yourself?' He walked over and put an arm about her shoulders. 'I thought it was per . . . quite marvellous, Esther.'

'Poor Des,' she smiled. 'It was rubbish – when you've been used to hearing real talent.'

'Well, I liked it!'

She looked up at him. 'My dear, kind Desmond. You'd say the

same thing if I played it backwards. You don't understand, I mean – '

'You mean I'm too insensitive to appreciate the difference, not like – ?'

'Let's not talk about Arnie – tonight of all nights. It's our wedding anniversary.' She turned away, shoulders bowed.

'You don't normally let me forget your perfect Adonis of a husband. He's everywhere in this place.'

He looked around and his gaze came to rest on the large painting over the marble fireplace. It showed a handsome, smiling man whose dark eyes always seemed to peer all round the room.

'Yes, he was a paragon of all that's talented and wonderful. And me? I'm not fit to lace his elegant shoes. And there are actually some of those still around. It's like some crazy fetish.'

'Don't. Please don't.' She walked across the room to stare out of the French windows on to a rain-swept, walled garden.

'Give me more time, Des,' she whispered. 'We were – so close. As if he were part of me. My whole reason for living rested on poor Arnie. I love you, Des,' she turned, a tear sparkling on her pale cheek, 'but no one can truly take his place. You know, Des,' she wiped the tear away, 'he really was like a Greek god. He could have had any woman he wanted. Yet he chose me. Six wonderful years we had together in complete harmony and trust.'

'Roses all the way,' he winced. 'Can't compete with that.' He glanced at the bunch of flowers he had brought, which lay, still wrapped on the table.

'Anything Arnie put his hands to turned to gold,' she said as though she hadn't heard him. 'Music, painting, everything. Did you know that is his own self-portrait?' She looked up at his picture. 'Arnie was the only man I'd ever loved – apart from Dad, of course. He was quite a wonderful man. Oh, and I'm not forgetting my dear, kind Des.' She hurried back to him and kissed him, her eyes filled with tears.

'I feel like a second-class intruder in this house,' he mumbled, looking at the sheen of her auburn hair, 'with a ghost at the head of the table.'

'Don't say such things.' Her voice was muffled. 'It – it's not nice.'

'Why? Do you think he's watching, surveying the crude inter-loper in his earthly paradise? The man's dead. He's no more. Why won't you accept that, Esther?'

'No!' she shook her head. 'Part of Arnie, at least, is still with me. I can still hear and feel his presence. Such a vital, conscious being like Arnie doesn't just disappear into nothing. He can't . . . *can't*.'

Almost overwhelmed by her vehemence, he pushed her gently away.

'I think I had better leave now, Esther. It's all a bit too much for me. I've done a few things in my time and am certainly far from perfect. Tonight is a night for you to commune with the gods. I'll leave you with your – your spirit of things past.' He hesitated before the melancholy in her grey eyes. 'I'll try to get here tomorrow night.'

Then anger suddenly replaced conciliation. 'I feel murder inside me for that – phantom. It's destroying you, Esther. He's been gone eight months now! He's a dead man rotting below ground. God, it's not right!'

'Stop . . . stop it!' She covered her ears. 'Please go now,' and she ran from the room.

He had to do it – for her sake. From his pocket he took the love letter that left so little to the imagination from – Elizabeth to Arnie. His whole body trembled in an ache of uncertainty, but then, in desperation, he walked swiftly to the bureau and with a shaking hand, slipped the letter at the back before hurrying out to his car in the drive.

The following night, he drove beneath a stony, grey sky towards her place hating himself. How could he have done such a thing, to have forged such a letter . . . from no one to no one. But, he couldn't let the dead control the living.

Then his mood changed. By God there would be a lot going for them both once that ghost had been destroyed completely.

He entered the house and walked into the drawing-room. The bureau was open, the letter gone. She must be upstairs.

But then he saw his fraudulent letter on a table. And there was also one from her to himself . . . and beside it an empty sleeping tablet bottle.

'Found this letter! Wouldn't believe it! But then – God, I remembered Elizabeth Thraxton – one of our friends! So much hate I felt it wasn't me . . . Poor Des. I'm not worth all that worrying. That woman's destroyed me now. Can't go on with this terrible wasteland in my head.'

'Esther!' he yelled, running out of the room and up the stairs. But he knew what he would find. That empty bottle beside the letter told the story.

The man standing at the top of the stairs said he was the police. 'You must be Desmond? Oh, she's all right. Got her to hospital in time.'

'Thank God!' He choked. 'How long will they keep her? When can we get her home?'

'Home? She is being charged with the murder of a Miss Thraxton. Miss Elizabeth Thraxton . . .'

Star Gazers

ROY BOLITHO

'A breath of romance will blow into your life this week. You will meet someone you greatly admire.'

My wife, Pam, talking. Quoting from the horoscope feature in her magazine. Blimey. She takes an excited sip of tea. 'So we must go to Priam's, Jack.' She mentions the name of a posh restaurant in the West End. '*He* may be there.'

I sigh. *He* is Grant Faulkner. You know, that fellow with the silver hair who's got this show on telly. Sings like his mother was a nightingale or something. My wife's nuts about him. Every Thursday at seven-thirty, even if she's in the middle of washing up, my wife, Pam, turns on the television to this Grant bloke. Seven-thirty, come hell or high water, it's *The Grant Faulkner Show*. She sits there on the edge of her chair, a dish-towel in her hands. She looks at him and she looks at me, and she never says anything, but this does not mean she's not thinking.

'He's a real gentleman,' she says once, during the commercial break. I reckon she must be getting at me then, for I've parked my stockinged feet on the mantelpiece while reading the sports pages.

'Yeah,' I tell her, 'and if he was on his feet for nine hours in a shop, he might have his shoes off, too.'

'There are other differences,' she mutters.

I let it go, but I can no longer concentrate on Charlton's team for Saturday's match at the Valley.

The fellow's singing I don't mind. He's quite good. It's the comparisons I object to. Comparisons with me. I can't stand the worshipping, either. Old Grant's only got to smile and my wife's ready to take off to the moon.

Sure we have our scraps now and then (I sometimes run out of insults), but it's usually over pretty soon. With Grant Faulkner, though, it's different. She doesn't argue. She gives me a look like I was something the cat dragged in.

We have this little house in Plumstead, you see, which is not too big, but comfortable. We have two kids half grown up and, apart from the mortgage, we don't owe anybody any money. I don't make a million in the shop, but there's always enough to eat on the table and the kids always look clean and smart.

My wife, actually, is very pretty. She's quite tall, my Pam, about five-ten, I guess, with big brown eyes and this nice fair hair falling softly about her neck. Really attractive, you know.

But she doesn't look attractive right now. Her lipstick's smudged, her hair's awry and her blouse is crumpled.

'Jack, we must go!' she cries again.

I fix my eyes on the wet green leaves outside our kitchen window. I try not to listen, though I'm aware that this doesn't help matters. I could, of course, simply leave the room. But I think the reason I do not is because it might snap the fine thread of communication which still exists between us.

'We'll go on Friday, yes, let's,' Pam says. She shows no sign at all of drying up.

'Look,' I point out, reasonably, 'we can't afford to go to Priam's. We've got a mortgage and two kids to feed and buy clothes for and . . .'

'Oh but we *can* afford it,' she whoops. 'You see, I've been putting away some money every week, just for such an occasion and I've saved nearly thirteen pounds!'

I blink. Thirteen quid. My God. Of course, there are lots of things I could do with thirteen quid, but not one of them includes going to Priam's. I open my newspaper and turn to the horoscope page. 'Avoid any entertainment this week,' I lie. 'Best to stay at home with a book . . .'

'Don't muck about, Jack.' she says. 'Oh, it'll be marvellous. All the celebrities go there. Grant Faulkner uses it as well, I know he does. I read it in my magazine. We might see him.'

There you are, you see. One of my wife's failings. Star struck. She sort of weaves romantic webs round these celebrities. I'm sure it doesn't do her the slightest good. Sometimes – when she's all dolled up – I tell her she's as good-looking as some of these star birds you see on the films and the telly. But the funny thing is, she never seems to take any notice of what I say. She just keeps going on about Cilla Black and Cliff Richard and Julie Christie, and, of course, Grant Faulkner.

Anyway, so what can I do now? She's saved thirteen quid for this, and what with that blessed horoscope and her determined attitude, I have to agree to go.

The last time we went up West was when we saw Val Doonican at the Palladium. Actually, this place Priam's is not far from the Palladium. It doesn't look all that much from outside. But inside it's really fancy: all red and gold and shining. Just before we go in, my wife tugs at my sleeve as a tall, good-looking blonde passes by.

'Anita Ekberg,' she whispers.

I shake my head. 'Chorus girl from the Palladium,' I say.

'How do you know?' she says, a bit suspicious.

'Tell by the way she walks,' I answer.

The grub, I have to admit, is really great, but my wife is more interested in the people round her, rather than what's on her plate. She keeps nudging me and hissing: 'Look, over there. I'm sure I know him. Look, in the corner, that's Shirley Bassey, I'm sure.'

I recognise nobody. I just concentrate on my steak.

When the waiter brings our sweet, which is served with a smashing plate of whipped cream, a well-dressed couple make an entrance. My wife goes all quavery. 'It's him, it's Grant Faulkner,' she breathes.

I stare across the room at the couple. He's about medium

height, and his hair is certainly silvery. But at this distance it is impossible to be sure. The girl with him has long fair hair.

Well, my wife goes on and on about him, and when the waiter brings us our coffee in half-pint silver pots, she really embarrasses me. Yes, she ups and asks that waiter if he knows who the silver-haired gentleman is.

The waiter is sour-looking and as thin as a broomstick. 'He isn't anybody,' he snaps.

'Oh?' My wife is put out, I can see that. 'How are you so sure?'

The skinny waiter shrugs. 'Because he's just asked who *you* are,' he says.

The Winning Secret

PETER WEY

Reg was asleep, as usual, when the postman called. It was Bess who picked up the letters from the mat in the hallway. Bending stiffly, her bulk creasing the flowered overall, she lifted the three envelopes, then hastened back to the scullery, where the kettle was boiling.

The letters lay on the Formica table-top until Bess had given the cat his milk, and carried Reg his cup of tea, receiving his bristly morning kiss by way of thanks.

She drank her own tea, then brushed her white hair into a fluffy halo, and retrieved her glasses from under the patchwork cushion on her TV chair. She sat down to read her mail. Only one letter was addressed to Mrs E. Watts personally but she opened all three. She and Reg had no secrets from each other. Well – she laughed to herself – only one . . .

First, the gas bill. Well, that's all right, she thought: the battered tea-caddy by the clock held enough fifty-pence pieces to buy the necessary postal order. Only just, but enough.

To you, on your golden wedding anniversary. With love from Paula, Mike, and the grandchildren in Melbourne. Oh, how beautiful. She stood the card up, tears misting her view. Fancy it being so early, after travelling halfway round the world. She would show Reg when he came down for his breakfast, then tuck the card behind the clock until the 12th.

She was looking forward to the day. There would be no big family reunion, of course, not with Paula in Australia, but Reg was planning a special day in Eastbourne for them both. It would be lovely. They hadn't seen the sea for so long . . .

Still musing, Bess opened the third letter; she saw the heading, the name of the pools firm. She read it incredulously, barely registering the five-figure number prefaced by the £ sign. She refolded the sheet of paper, and put it in her overall pocket . . .

Reg came running when he heard the crash. Finding Bess immobile on the red-tiled scullery floor, her tea-cup smashed, and the startled cat bristling on the draining-board, he had a moment of panic. But Bess was already reviving and, seeing his troubled face, half lathered and his pyjama cord coming undone, she started to laugh.

'Bessie,' he said, nettled, 'what's going on?' Nevertheless, he squeezed her warmly as he helped her to a chair. 'I nearly cut my throat when I heard that bang. What happened?'

'I – I had a funny turn, Reg. It's a warm day.' How easily the first lie in their fifty-year-old marriage had slipped out! It added a smaller shock to the great one.

'Not very warm, at seven-thirty in the morning!' he retorted. 'Are you sure you're all right, love?'

'Of course I am!' She gave him a little push, and after a moment he plodded off to complete his shave. He was almost more shaken than Bess, yet he still knew nothing.

Breakfast passed quietly, and Reg left for his 'constitutional'. He would inspect the roses in the municipal gardens, buy himself a paper and read it through, enjoy a beer with his cronies at the King's Arms, and return for lunch at one. Bess could complete her housework, and think.

Her little secret. Her cherished dread had come true, and the innocent deception involved in the tiny weekly wager on the pools would be discovered. It would be in the papers. She had always put an 'X' for 'No Publicity', but the papers would be sure to get hold of it. They'd photograph their little terraced house, and Reg – maybe without his teeth.

Standing in the queue at the fish shop, she waited to buy the coley for their lunch, and suddenly felt dizzy. Next week, it could be caviare! Oh, Reg, what a golden wedding celebration they would have!

Back at home, she dusted and polished the awkward little house, and she thought of a new split-level bungalow on the Isle of Wight, of electrical appliances to ease her daily round. Maybe even a daily help! The thought made her giggle. 'You're too imaginative, Elizabeth,' her schoolteacher had told her, as she sat, dreaming, beneath the high window of the schoolroom. 'You've a lively mind, but you're wasting it on daydreams.' The memory of that acid voice was still with her.

The cloth was on, and the table neatly set, when Reg arrived home. He bore a bunch of sweet peas. 'Look at those blooms!' he said. 'Better than ever.'

The sideboard drawer was perpetually jammed, so full was it with red Horticultural Society prize-cards. Sniffing the silky flowers, Bess felt a sudden pang. He'll miss his allotment, she thought, and his friends, too. She served the meal in silence. But Reg was animated, not noticing his wife's quietness. 'Bessie,' he said, his eyes sparkling, 'I've got something to tell you. I've – I've had a little secret from you all these years.'

Guiltily, he began to explain. Life had always been so hard for her – he'd longed to be able to give her a little cash to spend on herself. She'd never complained, she'd always seemed so contented and full of fun, but he knew his pension didn't stretch far. And now he had to own up. A filly had brought him a little windfall.

'It's not much,' he told her, laying down his knife and fork, and patting Bess's hand, 'but it means we can stay a week in Eastbourne, in a hotel, Bess, and still have some cash over.'

He unfolded the whole tale. The horse, a complete outsider with an undistinguished record, had seemed an unpromising bet. 'But it was her name that made me do it, Bess. Her name was Bright Elizabeth.'

She had never asked Reg to wash up before. But on this extraordinary day, she left him in suds to the elbow, a look of puzzlement on his face.

She took the tea-caddy money, the gas bill, her coat and hat, and she almost ran to the Post Office. The clerk helped her word the telegram.

PLEASE REDIRECT CHEQUE: MEADOWREST RETIREMENT HOME FOR HORSES STOP THANK YOU E.WATTS

Bright Elizabeth might be glad of it, some day.

A Reflection of Life on the Last Tram to Tooting

ROBERT QUIGLEY

Tuesday. A cold, grey day in November 1951, a day not easily forgotten, because it was the day I'd decided to put an end to it all.

I remember waking up just after one o'clock in the afternoon. I should have been at work, but having taken the Monday off, it would now require a medical chit to put me in the clear. Now it was just a matter of . . . how?

On a chair close to my head was the princely sum of five shillings and sixpence. I looked at one shining shilling. That round, shiny, little coin was going to do the job. That shilling-piece inserted in the gas oven and twenty-four years of jumbled emotions and experiences would pass to oblivion.

But before that, I had enough left over to make a day of it. Catch a tram to the High Street. Maybe see a last film? I began to dress slowly, relishing the minutes. And then I heard the old, familiar sound, that very special droning, rumbling, noise which came up four times to the hour from Tooting Bec: the one-thirty tram. I felt strangely sad. That was a sound I was going to miss, a sound that had kept me together so many nights when I'd lain cold and hungry.

I slipped on an overcoat, turned up the collar against the November fog, and made my way slowly round the corner to the tram-stop. The tram came rumbling in, and we clanked and clattered all the way up to the High Street of Streatham. The Odeon was offering a weepy with Joseph Cotten and Olivia de Havilland, the Regal an early John Garfield toughie. I settled for the first; it seemed to go with my mood.

It was dusk when I emerged. I crossed the busy High Street and made my way into the Locarno ballroom. To buy a dance ticket was quite out of the question – they cost three-and-sixpence – but a fourpenny balcony ticket was within my budget.

Inside, it was warm and alive, as always. I bought a coffee and, grabbing a ringside seat, rested my chin on the edge of the balcony and absorbed the scene below. Couples were locked closely together, hardly moving. Life could be good for some, I thought, and my inadequacy weighed doubly on me.

After an hour or so, I decided to buy another coffee. I was hungry too. Funny, I thought, how the ordinary feelings came so naturally in spite of final-exit intentions. But on examining the remaining cash, I found I had just enough for the tram-ride home. And, of course I had to preserve that last shilling. I rubbed it jealously between my thumb and forefinger: the little friend who would make good my escape.

It came up to midnight and the last waltz. Somehow, now that the day was coming to an end, I realised I didn't want the music to stop. If the music didn't stop then, the dance would go on and I could, well, hang on just a little bit longer.

Out in the cold night air again, I stood forlornly in the tram queue. It clattered in, and I moved down to the front of the car near the driver. Sitting there, watching the window displays of the shops flitting by, I suddenly caught the reflection of the girl sitting in the seat immediately adjacent to mine. She was staring at me. I stared back – all in the reflection – and this went on, stop after stop, without let-up. It was as though we were mesmerised.

When I got off, she got off. When I turned round the corner, she turned with me. There was something about the sound of her high heels click-clacking on that wet pavement that excited me, a sensation I hadn't felt for a long, long time. I stopped and she caught up. She took my hand, and without a single word passing between us, she came up the dark, rickety stairs to my attic room.

Once inside she took off her raincoat. A slim, wispy thing, she was, yet embodying a strange pale sexuality. She looked at me with her grey, deep-set eyes. 'Give me the shilling you're saving,' she said simply.

Without hesitation I did what she asked, and moving over to the stove, she inserted the shilling. She began to make a pot of tea, then let the flame run naked to heat the cold, damp room.

After tea and a cigarette, she took my hand and led me across the room. The rain now was coming down hard but we were oblivious to the rattling of the sash windows.

Much later in the dark, with laughter in her voice, she said: 'You see, just like that old song, for the King's shilling I've made a man out of you. And wasn't what we did more – productive – than what you had in mind?'

Leaning on my elbows in the dark, I looked into the hollows of her eyes. 'What makes you so damned intuitive?' I asked her . . . 'You are real, aren't you?'

She took a moment or two to answer. 'The last time I saw the look you had in your eyes, it was my father, just before he . . . just after my mother left him for a man half her age . . .'

When I woke up the following morning, she'd gone. And then I realised I hadn't even got her name. I dressed quickly. I wanted to go into work and face the music. I owed it to the girl. To rejoin the human race was the least I could do.

And then while shaving I suddenly realised there was something missing. No trams. That was it. No trams.

And then I remembered the piece in the papers recently about the trams coming off, to be replaced by the trolley-buses. So they'd run the last tram. Yet what a difference a day made. Yesterday, that alone would have been enough to push me over the edge. But today, well . . .

Twenty-five years on, still remembering, I still ask: were you real, girl-without-a-name, on that very last tram to Tooting?

Death Trap

JONATHAN CLARK

'Beer, Mr Kerwin?' asked the white-coated West Indian barman, when the crew-cut young man walked into the Parakeet Bar.

Johnny Kerwin nodded.

'Mr Mallory ready?'

Aldo shook his head as he put the glass of beer in front of Kerwin. 'He ain't going no shark fishing. Fell down the hotel stairs last night.'

'Drunk?'

'Sure was.'

An attractive blonde nearby said. 'You should make your clients pay in advance, Johnny.'

He sipped his beer. 'You know me?'

'Everyone knows Johnny Kerwin,' said Aldo. 'Makes a living with an old boat and likes pretty girls. Sometimes he goes diving in the Caribbean for Spanish treasure. But he ain't lucky yet.'

'I'm Melissa Cade,' said the girl.

'Barnaby Cade's niece, that's right. Staying with him in that ramshackle bungalow over at Turtle Cay.'

She had a handbag that matched her dress. Out of it she took a dull-metal coin. 'Uncle Barnaby says it's a piece of eight. You're a scuba man. How'd you like to dive for a lot more like it?'

Outside in the hot, morning sunlight Kerwin said, 'So you found this coin on the beach at Turtle Cay?'

'There was a big storm a few nights ago. I walked down to the beach for my morning swim and found half a dozen scattered on the sand. Uncle Barnaby figured that the storm had disturbed some old galleon lying at the bottom in the bay.'

'I see.' Kerwin steered her around a pile of rope on the jetty to the battered cabin-cruiser with *Pescado* painted on her stern. 'She's not much,' he grinned, 'but she's the best friend I've got . . .'

A few minutes later there was only the blue of the sea in front of them and the blue of the sky above as they headed out to sea, Kerwin at the wheel, Melissa beside him.

'Uncle Barnaby,' she murmured, 'isn't so bad.'

'He always struck me as a bitter kind of recluse.'

'That's a fair estimate,' the girl agreed. 'But he had a bad war. He was a Major doing demolition work. After the war he found it difficult to settle down so he headed out here and made a home for himself. My father – his brother – built up the family firm and went on to make a fortune.'

'I've heard of Cade Electronics,' Kerwin said. 'That's your old man, eh?'

'Old is right,' Melissa sighed. 'Not so much in years as in health. Uncle Barnaby came to England because Dad's been sick for some time now. He learned I was going to university in a few months so he suggested this holiday first.'

Barnaby Cade was waiting for them on the crude plank jetty at Turtle Cay. He was tall, gaunt and balding – and as brown as a teak table.

'Not my idea – having you around, Kerwin,' he snapped. 'But Melissa seems to have got this bug about underwater treasure and you were the only one I could think of on the spur of the moment.'

It was well past midday when Kerwin and the girl took the cabin-cruiser out into the bay and let down the anchor. Kerwin got out his scuba gear, stripped down to trunks and buckled up. He picked up a spear-gun and flipped back over the side.

Kerwin searched, even though he knew he wouldn't find anything. When he came up at last, Melissa said, 'I've got hot coffee. Find anything?'

He shook his head.

'Never mind. Drink this.'

Kerwin drank and kept his eyes on the bungalow ashore. He saw the glint of the sun on glass. Binoculars. So Barnaby Cade had them under observation.

His mouth came down on her lips.

'Let's go below,' he said.

Kerwin didn't unstrap the webbing of his aqualung in his cabin. Melissa looked up at him puzzled. 'I . . . er . . . want to keep an eye ashore,' he said.

'You think Uncle Barnaby's going to come out with a shotgun?'

'Like Aldo says, Melissa. I like girls. Your uncle knows that.'

Melissa lay on the bunk and closed her eyes.

'You know something, Johnny Kerwin? You've got a reputation that's totally undeserved.'

When he glanced at her, she'd rolled over and appeared to have fallen asleep . . .

There was one hell of a racket to awaken her, Johnny Kerwin was hauling a spluttering and indignant Barnaby Cade aboard.

'What goes on?' she demanded.

'Ask him,' Kerwin snapped. 'Ask him what he was doing planting a phosphorus bomb to the keel to send us both up in a sheet of flame.'

'Ridiculous!' burst out Cade. But he was drawn and ashen beneath his deep tan.

'You told me he was in demolition work during the war, Melissa,' Kerwin said harshly. 'And what he planned was your demolition. You know he inherits the Cade millions – as your father's only brother?'

'Only if I . . .' Melissa's voice tailed off, her eyes wide with shock.

'Your father's far more ill than you thought,' Kerwin went on. 'That's why he sent for his brother. Everyone knows my boat's not the most seaworthy tub around, Melissa. If there was an investigation, Barnaby Cade would come out in the clear. It was much better than involving you in a swimming fatality – as, no doubt, he originally intended.'

'Poppycock!' snapped the retired Major. 'Melissa, my dear,

you're not going to let yourself be influenced by a young – young thug like this, are you? I mean, you're my own flesh and blood . . .'

His voice tailed off under her shocked stare.

Kerwin gave a thin smile.

'You banked on her being influenced by me, Cade. You banked on the pair of us being much too occupied to bother about anyone sabotaging the boat!'

Cade said nothing.

Melissa turned to Kerwin.

'Why, Johnny? Why are you so sure? Why did you wait for it to happen?'

'That piece of eight you showed me – the whole lot in fact – were fakes,' he told her. 'Your uncle planted them to get you and me together. Genuine pieces of eight were die-stamped. The ones I saw were cast in a mould!'

The Treasure of the Ancient Mariner

PETER PETERSON

'You'll have to mind the shop tomorrow afternoon, Tom. I'm going to a sale.'

I wasn't going to let old Saunders get away with that. 'Nothing doing. Saturday's my day off.'

'Not interested in overtime? You'll get paid for it.'

'I've something better to do with my Saturdays.'

Old Saunders gave me a nasty look. 'It's up to you. I won't force you.'

I gave *him* his nasty look back. Force me? He'd best not try that. He'd have a hard time finding someone else to work the hours I did, for the money. As for overtime . . .

The something better I had to do with my Saturdays was to go treasure-hunting. Six months in a secondhand bookshop had taught me there were still treasures to be found. I spent my Saturdays scouring undeveloped Britain, looking for booksellers who didn't know their business.

On this particular Saturday I was delving in deepest Dorset. Round about half-past twelve, just as I was getting ready to find a pub, I noticed a title on a top shelf: *Cooke's Voyage*. Odd, thought I, since when was Captain Cook spelt with an 'e'? I reached up, took it down.

It was by another old sea dog: Captain Edward Cooke of Bristol, who had set off in 1708 on a voyage round the world.

The pages were dog-eared, the binding was falling apart, some vandal had been scribbling in the margins: it was not a good copy. But I fancied it. Early voyages are always worth money. I skimmed through it, thinking it was a pity about those scribbled notes, I remember.

They were unexpected, some of them. Sort of poetic. Not the kind of thing you or I would scrawl in a book. They'd been written, to judge by the style, about 1800. By whom? I wondered.

Suddenly one of them seemed to jump right out of the page.

'*God's creatures of the great calm.*' Where had I seen that before? The penny dropped. Coleridge: 'The Ancient Mariner'.

Half a second after that, I felt as though I had a coronary. I knew the handwriting too, I'd seen it in the British Museum, in a letter of Coleridge's. What I had all but dropped from a trembling hand must be Coleridge's own copy of his source book for 'The Ancient Mariner'. Worth thousands!

I took a deep breath, strolled casually over to the counter, put the book down, and said in a voice carefully controlled: 'How much are you asking for this?'

The old chap behind the counter looked me up and down. 'You a scout?'

'Just an amateur. A beginner.'

'A beginner, eh? Well, you've got an eye. I'll say that for you.'

I didn't like the sound of this. I was beginning to wonder if I was the only one to know Coleridge's hand when he saw it.

I acted innocent. 'Is it rare, then?'

'Yes. It's a scarce book, that is.'

This sounded better. 'It's a poor copy,' I said. 'Foxed. Binding scuffed. Pages loose.'

He hesitated, obviously wondering how much of a sucker I was. I tried not to hold my breath. After a pause that seemed longer to me than the Two Minutes' Silence, he finally made his mind up.

'I won't be hard on you. Don't believe in discouraging beginners. You can have it for two hundred.'

I gasped. 'Two hundred? *Two hundred pounds?*'

'That's right. Would have been three hundred if it wasn't all scribbled over.'

I clutched the counter. These ups and downs – afraid he knew what he'd got, and now finding he didn't had upset my heart rhythm.

I hadn't got two hundred pounds. Far from it. And I didn't dare tell him to hold the book for me. That would have made him take a closer look for sure.

I used the old formula. 'I'll think it over.'

Thinking it over, of course, was what I had been doing at great speed ever since he named his price. I wasn't worrying about the book; I had no doubts about that. What was worrying me was that two hundred pounds.

Money like that I just didn't have, and where would I raise it without saying what I wanted it for? As far as I could see, there was only one answer. I'd have to work for it, earn it in a hurry, before some other browser with a nose came sniffing round.

I looked at my watch. If I skipped lunch I could just make it back to London in time to mind the shop after all. I turned and ran.

From then on my life was sheer Puritan. I gave up beer, cigarettes, girls. The sound of overtime was music in my ears. Saturdays, lunch hours, late-night openings: old Saunders only had to name it. And what few spare minutes I had I spent rooting through bookshops, not looking now for treasure, but for odds and ends I could pass on for a pound or two quick profit. Work, eat, sleep: that was my life. Plus thinking about what I was doing it all for, and dreaming of what I would do when I got it. Never a dull moment.

At the end of three months, I broke the bad news to old Saunders.

'I'm leaving at the end of the month. Setting up on my own.'

'How come? Win the pools?'

'Sort of.'

I held Edward Cooke out to him. 'Take a look at that. Cost me two hundred.'

He arched those bushy eyebrows of his. 'And where did you get two hundred?'

185

'Here and there,' I said. 'Saved it.'

He gave a grunt, the nearest thing to a laugh I'd ever heard out of him. 'So that's why you've been working like a slave lately?'

He opened the book. I watched him wondering how long it would take him to see what he was handling.

Unexpectedly, he smiled. 'I've seen this before. Forty years ago, when I was first thinking of setting up on my own, like you. It fooled me, too.'

'*Fooled you?*'

'Those notes. They're a fake. The Coleridge Forger, we used to call him.'

I never thought of doubting him. I could see from his face he was telling nothing but the truth. He handed me back my book. I took it, wishing I'd never set eyes on it.

'And I thought I'd found a treasure.'

He looked at me in a way he'd never done before.

'You have.'

I stared at him, wondering what in the world he meant.

'I've been watching you,' he said. 'I always thought you had it in you. But you used to be like all the others: you didn't know what work meant – what it could do for you. Now you do. That's the treasure you found.'

More Than One Way to Kill a Cad . . .

TONY STEED

She seemed such a sweet old dear. As I gulped down the last of her hot tea I almost wished we were about to do something clean and honest and decent. Like an armed raid on Dr Barnardo's. You see, she didn't really have rats in her attic, and never would have – not until me and Knuckles got up there, anyway. What she *did* have up there – according to the grapevine – was a fortune in ready cash . . .

I emptied a handful of crumbs into an onyx ashtray and motioned Knuckles to pick up the traps. Her ladyship got the message and rose gracefully to her feet.

'It's a long climb to the top – such a *huge* house!' she apologised. 'The upper part of the building is somewhat dusty – I no longer employ servants . . .'

I grinned inwardly at this last bit of information and we followed the old girl up a succession of wide, marbled stairways. On the top landing a ladder stretched up to the attic. Knuckles clambered up this and slid back the heavy steel bolts on the trap door.

Her ladyship smiled. 'Sir Percy, my late husband, was convinced that a burglar might be tempted to – ah – *drop in* on us . . .' she explained.

I nodded. One way and another, Sir Percy seemed to have had a thing about burglars.

With its thick stone walls, solid oak woodwork and barred windows the place was like a fortress. I shot up the ladder and lowered the trap door behind me. Knuckles lit a couple of candles, brushed the cobwebs from the corner of a tea chest and sank down heavily.

'Supposing it's not in 'ere,' he demanded, jerking a thumb over his shoulder at the jumble of lockers and boxes.

'It's here all right!' I assured him confidently. 'Couple of months ago the old girl was rushed to the hospital for an emergency op. As she came round from the gas she murmured "It's in attic!" over and over again – *It's in the attic!*'

I groped my way across to a hardboard partition and beckoned him to fetch over a candle.

'Some sort of office . . .' I guessed. 'A retreat. Somewhere the late Sir Percy could gloat over his relics in privacy. Collected bones by the looks of it – bones and fossils . . .'

'Funny old geezer!' Knuckles said. 'How did he die?'

I knew the answer to that, too. I do my homework.

'He got involved with another woman – big scandal. Ended up getting lost on a climbing expedition!' I snatched a cassette-player from his fingers and pushed him away. 'The money's not in here – we split up and turn the attic inside-out . . .'

We grafted hard for a full hour without finding anything. You could have hidden a double-decker bus in that darned attic, I can tell you. Every chest, case and biscuit tin had to be pulled apart, every loose floorboard investigated. I was just thinking that Madam might have got suspicious and phoned the law when I heard this yell from Knuckles. And right then his voice didn't sound like the tinkling of a cash register. I stumbled across to find him arched over a heap of rags in the corner.

'It's a *body*, isn't it?' he said accusingly, brushing cold sweat from his eyes. Something in his expression told me that he suddenly wanted to be a long way away. Somewhere nice and hospitable – like the moon.

'Sir Percy? Yeah, that figures,' I replied, trying hard to keep

my cool. 'Her ladyship knew he was giving her the run-around –
and that's a pretty good motive!'

'You mean she *croaked* him?'

'Why not? But not up here – no signs of a struggle . . .' I lit a
cigarette and studied him thoughtfully. 'It adds up, doesn't it?
She arranged for him to get lost – permanently. A climbing
expedition . . . up to his own attic!'

'Oh, Gawd 'elp us . . .' Knuckles breathed. Suddenly his tone
hardened. 'You berk! She said it was in the attic, didn't she? Not
the money – the perishing body!'

I backed away a fraction, fully expecting him to lash out at me.
But he didn't. He glared at me a moment, then thumped his way
over to the trap door.

'You flaming great berk!' he shouted, and slammed the door
shut after him. A couple of minutes later I heard the sound of his
van as it tore down the drive, and I relaxed.

The great thing about being a pro, I thought, is that you've
learned to improvise. Like they say, as one door closes another
one opens – and life, to a good pro, is a series of open doors. The
trouble with Knuckles – and millions like him – was that they
never stopped to think.

To someone like me, a body in the attic was worth money in
the bank. Whichever way you looked at it, Her ladyship had been
a very naughty girl. Concealing bodies in lofts wasn't exactly
croquet, after all. It was big trouble.

But I must admit I spent a long time trying to figure out how
Sir Percy died. Contrary to what I'd told Knuckles, I didn't really
suspect the old girl of killing him.

You see, she couldn't have croaked him in the attic – she'd
obviously never been up there. And if she'd croaked him in the
house – how had she got his body up the ladder?

At the end of my fourth cigarette I gave up. It didn't seem, to
matter. I was just trying to fix a suitable figure for blackmail
when I heard the sound of Her ladyship's laughter. It terminated
abruptly as she rammed home the bolts on the trap door . . .

The Source of the World

H. E. BATES

There was a day when he went with Humph up the far reaches of the brook, beyond places he had never seen before, almost, he fancied, into another country, to find the source of the world.

That was what Humph said it was called and Humph was his friend.

'Rivers go down into the sea,' Humph said. 'They've got to. It's all downhill. But they come from somewhere. Somewhere a long way away. A long way up, in mountains. That's called the source of the world.'

Humph wore big spectacles. They were so big and so thick and so strong that he called them his bicycle-lamps. They magnified. Sometimes Humph let you wear them for a few minutes. When he did you understood why the world appeared so vastly different through Humph's eyes from what it did through your own. It was like looking at the world through two big glass marbles. Everything was round and fat and pot-bellied and shining and wide; rather like Humph himself was.

'We're men,' Humph said. 'We'll be gone days and days. We'll have to go in marches.'

He had been to the brook, he supposed, at least about a thousand times. There were eight fields he knew through which it flowed: a little field covered with golden sheets of dandelion in May, then a field where he had once found a wild duck's nest among a clump of sloes, then the field where you could drink from a spring that came from a high bank and was the purest, clearest water in the world.

Then a field he called the watercress field because the marshy places were dark with cresses, and another he called the pussy willow field, because the brook came down under golden arches of flower at Easter-time. Then the crab-blossom field. Then a field with a pool, under hawthorn trees, that was something the shape of a long black harp, and where he had seen the biggest fish of his life, a pike, lying like a dark green sword on the top of the water.

And last of all the field where he used to cut arrows for his bow: a field like a jungle, full of spears of reed waving pale green ribbons of leaf in summer and shaggy feathers of flower, like the head-dresses of African warriors, when autumn came.

Beyond that he had never been. It could not be far beyond that, Humph said, before they found the source of the world.

'Let's make camp,' Humph said in the fourth of the fields.

That was one of the fields he liked best. He loved it not only because there was something friendly and good about the marshy places, dark with cresses but because, in the brook itself, the water ran very bright and shallow over stones as green as parsley, and where sometimes, if you were lucky, you could lie and watch schools of fish, roach, he thought they were, quivering and flickering against the current in the sun.

They saw shoals of fish that day. At first he didn't think they were very big fish, no bigger at any rate than he had ever seen before. Then Humph said he could borrow his bike-lamps, and when he put them on he saw that the fish were really as wide and flat as plaice, the fish his mother bought from the shop where smoky kippers hung on lines, looking just like shoes that had been run over by steamrollers and varnished gold.

'By Golly,' Humph kept saying. 'By Golly. By Golly.'

His eyes looked funny without the spectacles. Squeezed up and short-sighted and pale, and not properly dressed somehow.

'We got to catch some,' Humph said. 'That'll be our food. You have to tickle them underneath,' he said. 'That's how to get them.'

They lay on their bellies, hanging over the bank. He could see the red fins of the fish winking in the dazzling water. Everything, through Humph's spectacles, was strange and marvellous and magnified.

'Underneath?' Humph said. He stretched out his fat soft hand. He had forgotten about his spectacles and started making bubbling noises of excitement.

'Golly, Golly,' he kept saying; and then suddenly he was slipping, slowly and fatly, down the bank and then, slowly and fatly, into the water.

'That's because I hadn't got my glasses. That's because I hadn't got my glasses. Where are my glasses? Give me my glasses.'

At first he laughed because Humph looked so queer and soft and undressed without his bike-lamps. Then he thought Humph would start crying, and all of a sudden he felt sorry for him and gave him back the glasses. In the end he always felt sorry for Humph. Nobody else did. Everybody teased Humph because he was fat and soft and couldn't see. At the same time everybody said how clever Humph was and what books he read and what a lot he knew.

Somehow he trusted Humph. Somehow all his faith in Humph was restored the moment he put his bike-lamps on.

As they went on it was hot in the little valley. It was August and there was a thundery breath among the brown-silver, turning heads of reed. He and Humph got thirsty and knelt down by the spring and cupped their hands and drank the cold, fresh, spurting water.

'Not too much,' Humph said. 'You don't have to drink too much when you climb mountains. It gives you belly-ache.'

That was an example of the sort of clever things Humph knew.

And then suddenly, from the crest of the field, above the reeds, they saw in the distance a marvellous thing. At least Humph saw it first, and then he did too. 'Mountains!' Humph said. 'Mountains!'

Humph began dancing up and down so that the fleshy part of his face, under his white ears, waggled up and down like a hen's gills.

'Mountains! Mountains! Look how blue they are. Mountains!'

At first he knew quite well that the great dark blue colander domed above the fields in the east was a cloud; he thought he saw it grow larger and higher, thunder-wise, even as he stared at it. Then Humph said.

'Here, you have the bike-lamps. Look at it through the bike-lamps.'

When he put on the bike-lamps the cloud seemed to go much farther away and was blurred. It changed and was softer. The shape of it was not so much like a colander as a shock of wheat in a field. It really looked in some way like a big, lead-coloured, brooding mountain.

'I told you, I told you,' Humph said. 'I told you there'd be mountains.'

'Can you see it without your specs?'

'No.' Humph said. 'But I know it's there.'

He gave Humph his spectacles back. The big blobs of glass danced fatly in that way that always made him feel sorry for him. And then because he did not want to hurt Humph by saying that the mountain was only a cloud he began pretending to believe that it was a mountain. He actually wanted it to be a mountain. He wanted it to be there as much as Humph did.

'Come on,' Humph said. 'We've got to start marching. We've got to get there before night-time.'

Then they were in strange country. They climbed the last of the fences in the fields he knew. They were far from home and he was aware, on the new, high ground, of a sense of exultation. They were explorers, men in a strange land, alone and excited, brave and seeking something.

All the time it seemed to grow hotter. Part of the distances of wheat and barley and grass were shrouded in the day-time duskiness of thunder. On others a queer white light lay stark and brilliant, so that the fields of barley were a mass of flat, still flame.

Then, many fields farther on, they were out on a road. He was disappointed about that. His illusion that they were men in some uncivilised place vanished suddenly. Then from the mountainous mass of cloud across the cornfields there came the first stunning bark of thunder. He saw the cloud actually lift itself like a column of unfurling purple smoke in the sky. He knew that at any moment it would rain from across these sultry burning fields, but Humph thought differently.

'That's the gods,' he said. 'They always talk on mountains. You have to give them offerings. If you don't they growl like that.'

'We ought to get shelter.'

'Not under a tree though,' Humph said. 'Else we'll be struck.'

He had a terrible fear of being struck. He saw a yellow snake of lightening wriggle all the way down the darkening cloud. Another bark of thunder came from a whole pack of dogs charging overhead. He felt a hot fat spot of rain on his face and at the same time a voice shouted.

'Here! You better git in here along o'me if you don't want to git drownded.'

Then they were sitting under the big umbrella of a sloe-hedge with a man. He was a man in a thousand. One of his eyes had a queer solid glassy look, like a marble, and it did not move when the other did. By his side was a sickle, with a white whetstone, and a labourer's straw bag. He was drinking something golden-tawny from a bottle. On a doorstep of bread he had a piece of red cheese as thick as a book, and on top of the cheese, an onion as large as a turnip. He cut at all this with a horn-handle shut-knife. Every time he put the knife to his mouth he turned it over at the last moment, and then sucked in bread and cheese and onion with a great smacking slithering sound.

'Here it comes,' he said. 'Send it down, David.'

He had a sack on his shoulders. His trousers were tied below the knees with string. His boots had great steel tips on the heels and all over the soles.

Rain came hissing down in solid summer sheets and he said, 'here, you git underneath this here sack along o' me. You won't hurt then. There's room a-new for the three on us under here.'

The storm strode across the land in unaccountably swift black strides. The road, hot from noon, steamed under the rain. Sun was already shining on the distances where the mountains had been, and presently the man said, 'it'll be over in two shakes. Where do you boys come from?'

They told him.

'Well, that ain't far. You ain't got far to go.'

That was disappointing. Humph had said once that he reckoned they had come at least twelve miles, reckoning four miles to the brook and half a mile for every field; and most of the time, especially when the mountain was in view, it seemed like that.

But what happened next was not disappointing.

'That's a rare pair of specs you got there, boy,' he said. 'One o' these days I'm goin' to git myself a pair like that.'

'You can try them on if you like,' Humph said.

He took off the spectacles and huffed on them and polished them on his coat sleeve.

'Very like ain't my size,' the man said.

'You try them. Humph lets everybody try them.'

The man put on the spectacles. They were much too small for him. They always looked so large on Humph, but now they looked no bigger than glassy pennies. But with them perched on his nose the man looked very funny and Humph and himself laughed at the way he stared down through the thick white lenses.

'No,' he said, 'they ain't much good to me.'

He took the spectacles off and gave them back to Humph.

'You see,' he said, 'I ain't only got but this 'ere one eye.'

'No?' they said.

'No,' he said.

All of a sudden he did a remarkable thing.

'There,' he said.

In the palm of his hand lay an eyeball.

'You mean you can take your eye out?' Humph said.

'This 'ere one I can,' he said. 'Take it out of a morning and wash it. And take it out of a night when I go to bed.'

Where the eye had been was only a red, bloodshot slit. In his hand the glass eye looked exactly like a wet bull's eye that you had sucked a few times and taken out of your mouth to see if the colour had changed.

'Out she comes,' he said, 'and in she goes again.'

In the flash of a second the eye was back in its socket, glassily staring at the slackening rain.

'Doesn't it hurt when you take it out?'

'No.'

'Did it hurt when you lost it?'

'Like pepper and salt it did.'

'How did you lose it?'

195

'Shot,' the man said. 'Shot out.'

'In a battle?'

'In a battle,' he said. 'Spion Kop.'

'Where's Spion Kop?'

'Africa,' he said. 'It's a sort of mountain.'

He thought that that was a wonderful thing, and he felt he had to ask a question.

'Does everything look different with only one eye?' he said. 'It looks different when you put Humph's glasses on.'

'Well, very like it does,' he said. 'Only I can't recollect now what it looked like wi' two.'

'I wouldn't like to have only one eye.'

'You wouldn't?' he said. 'Well, I'll tell you summat.'

'What?'

'You only got one eye to see with,' he said, 'but then you only got one eye to tune with. When you got summat to cry about you only want half the quantity o' tears.'

Both he and Humph thought that was very funny.

'And that's a very useful thing,' he said, 'when you're a-ettin' onions.'

They thought that was very funny, too. By that time the rain had stopped altogether. The road was steaming in brilliant sunshine. All the grasses of the roadside and the leaves of the hedgerows and the ears of corn were dancing with beads of water.

'If you step out sharp,' the man said, 'you'll git home be dinnertime. So long.'

'So long,' they said.

As they walked home all the fields of wheat and barley dried in the sunshine until they were fiery and brilliant again under rain. The cloud that Humph had said was a mountain had rolled away and the sky was pure with summer.

That was a wonderful day; he never forgot that day. To find a man with only one eye to cry with was a marvellous thing.

Better even than finding the source of the world.

What You Might Call the Stare of the Dog

MARJORIE FISHER

You've just missed him, I'm afraid. He's disappeared upstairs to 'take his face off' as one of his waggish girlfriends once perceptively described the ritual. Go on up if you want – it is all good clean fun and a hoot to watch if you like that sort of thing.

First come the keys, coins and lighter which he carefully places top left of the dresser, next to the action-replay photo of him breasting the tape after some marathon run against the Sussex Martlets. Then it's his wallet, pen and cigarette case which go on the right-hand side. Lastly, his various bits of macho jewellery which he plonks dead centre.

There's the ring he picked up in Tel Aviv and which he bashes on the table if waiters don't bow and scrape on cue; the weighty medallion that nestles in the chest-fur and which unsuspecting women ask to see after the third goblet of Hennessy XO; and, most vulgar of the lot, his ID bracelet that some besotted lady foisted on him in L.A.

And while you're up there, don't miss the clothes bit. He takes the suit off oh, so gingerly, so's not to ruff the creases and then it's straight onto the hangers. Shirts and other dirty disposables get the straight-back-to-the-wicket treatment, zap into the laundry-basket. He rarely misses. All in all, a thoroughly house-trained chap, my master.

But don't get me wrong: he's not as bad as I make him out to be. He feeds me punctually and well, takes me jogging most mornings. In return I try to behave myself in company, make an effort to get on with his friends and snarl dutifully at the postman, cleaning lady and any passing debt-collectors. All in all, a faithful hound – if I say so myself.

No, it's his attitude to women that sets my canines on edge and you can tell him I said so. Let me explain; he's your average, good-looking human in a well-paid job and with the standard accessories: a car that goes vroom, all his own teeth (pearly, to boot), nice hands, a sense of humour and his own pad with hi-fi in one corner and low fidelity in the other.

So why my moan? It's because he seems to regard every pretty face that comes along as a challenge to prove himself. It doesn't matter who he's with at the time or how fat his address book bulges. New lady on the scene: got to have her.

And what happens if, as is most often the case (dammit) he gets his way? Zilch – he loses interest and, if he hasn't already, he's off in hot pursuit of some other unsuspecting lass. Not that they mind either. I've seen them lap it up even when they know he's shooting one of the great corny lines of our time.

Seriously though, it's the nice ones I worry about: Kay, who always says hello to me and insisted I came along on any of their country outings; Gillian, who cooked and always brought her weeding gloves because she knew how much he wanted the garden to look smart. And his latest, the lovely Teresa from across the park who's got a job that keeps her just as busy as him but who still makes time to meet him for lunch mid-week.

She, he leads a right merry dance and it's not right. Come to think of it, who was it organised the meeting in the first place? Right – it was thanks to me bounding across to check the lovely Sheba that they even said hello. Grrr. Let's have credit where it's due, for Pluto's sake.

As I say, he's struck gold with Teresa and I'm not going to crouch silent as he plays silly games with her. Tonight, for instance, as they nuzzled by the door and he asked her to phone him as soon as she got back. Why should she? Supposing she didn't. Supposing he's up there now clogging the room with Gauloise fumes and confidently waiting for her to call and she makes him sweat it out? That would dent the old ego, somewhat, eh? No bad thing at all. But hush! Methinks I hear young master pacing the carpet now and if I'm not mistaken, the dulcet tones of the lovely Kate Bush have given way to muttered oaths. Perhaps she forgot his number, hmmm?

Achtung – he's coming down the stairs and in an evil mood, if I'm not mistaken. Going to call *her*, is he? That's an admission of defeat. No – he's stopped halfway . . . impatient breathing . . . a muttered oath. Changed his mind, I think. Yep, there he goes back to his room. Tee hee and serves him right.

Well, I might as well turn in myself, so if you'll excuse me I'll – gosh, fancy that. The receiver appears to have been dislodged from its cradle. I must have bumped into it accidently. How careless of me.

Love that had to Wait

W. J. ELSHAM

He locked the car and walked to the other side to help her out. She swung out of the passenger seat and stood up beside him. He had an instantaneous snapshot of her, and, for the hundredth time marvelled.

The ordinary acceptances of feminity were there, the lithe physical grace, that wonderful set of head and shoulders, the long, blonde hair framing a face that had been sculpted by happy angels. Yet the appearance was only the frame for something else, an innerness. At times he glimpsed it and it caught his breath.

Without a word they started up the long, grassy slope that was the beginning of the ascent to the Tor. She glanced obliquely at him. Only the very rich could wear old clothes like that; and wearing them, making them look as they did on him. No merit, she thought. And no blame. Just the prerogative of aristocracy, the end result of twenty generations of authority and unquestioned acceptance.

The midsummer breeze pulled at her light, cotton skirt, stretching it diagonally across her thighs as she walked. He glanced at her and discovered something for the first time in his twenty-six years. There were feelings for which there are no words. How long had he known her? Incredibly, seven days – and in that time he had never been alone with her. It came to him that he had never yet touched her, not even her hand.

She swung her shoulder-bag to the other side and quite deliberately put her hand in his. God, he thought, she actually knows what I'm thinking. Sensation mounted in him, familiar, male, pleasurable. Yet different. Not primary, imperious, as he'd always thought it had to be; but secondary and subservient. Discovery Number Two: there was an octave beyond sex, an area where things were resolved, unified.

They walked on, the path getting steeper. 'Well,' she said. 'Did I pass the test with your mother?'

'You were perfect. You were yourself.'

'That's not what I asked you.'

He temporised. 'Was it an ordeal?'

'One doesn't have much practice with servants in a bed-sitter.'

Before he could reply, she said: 'Your mother is no ordinary person. She has . . . what used to be called – wisdom. Tell me, why was she so insistent that you show me the Tor?'

'She probably wanted me to tell you the story of the Tor.'

The minutest pressure on his hand. 'Hadn't you better tell me then?'

'It was in the days of the witch hunts. There was a girl in Brunsdyke – that's the village on the other side of the Tor – a very beautiful girl, by all accounts. The legends say she had repulsed a local called Bundy – a ruffian. There are still Bundys in Brunsdyke. They haven't changed much. Well, this Bundy in a fit of jealous rage denounced the girl as a witch. Maybe the villagers didn't entirely believe it but it's hard for us to imagine the fear of witchcraft that people had four or five hundred years ago.

'Anyway, the girl was really in love with the young lord of the manor. An ancestor of mine. There's a portrait of him at the Hall, if you're interested. Their situation – considering the class barriers of the time – was simply impossible. But they were quite hopelessly in love: and at the height of the witch fever they had an assignation. Up here, on the Tor. Beyond the belt of trees – we're coming to them now – there is a little grassy hollow, at the very top. It's a sheltered, pleasant place. They went there. They were . . . they were going to make love. Then the mob broke through.'

He felt her hand withdraw and the transflux exchange between them that had been so perfect was cut off instantly.

She said, 'Go on.'

'It really is a horrible story. They seized the man, but of course didn't harm him, considering who he was. But his very presence seemed to prove the witchcraft claim. Manor lord and peasant . . . she could only have bewitched him.

'Few witches were burnt in England, they were usually hanged or drowned. But there were some burnings. There was one here. Notice this path. The trees seem to lean across the path from both directions. The legend says the trees leaned over to try and close the path against the mob – and they've leaned inwards ever since.'

'What happened to her?'

'They tied her to a stake and they built a fire. One man, the blacksmith, gathered wet leaves and piled them near her. The merciful sometimes did this. The smoke produced unconsciousness before . . .'

'Go on.'

'Even as the smoke reached her, she tried to turn to see her lover as he was dragged away. Then, according to legend, she called out something very strange. She cried, "Wait for me." The ruffian Bundy then got a burning branch and threw it against her side. The story says she screamed once, horribly, and died.

'The story also says that the birds have never sung in the wood since that day and the trees have always blocked the path to the summit.'

They were through the scrub wood now and the atmosphere changed instantly. In the little green hollow at the Tor's peak there was a stillness that was almost supernatural. He'd been there many times before but had never felt the peace so strongly.

'What did she mean by her last words? Do you know?'

'It's just a story. I don't know.'

She stopped, turned and faced him. 'I think you do.' After a moment she went on. 'When I phoned your mother from London to say I'd be on the second train, she said you'd already left to collect me. I left a message. Did she give it to you?'

His voice fell to the merest whisper. 'Yes, word for word. It said "Wait for me." Oh God.' He buried his face in his hands.

'And you didn't understand? You haven't understood . . . all along?'

'Yes, I knew. But I didn't *know* I knew . . . I've been putting it out of my mind.'

She said, 'You are very young.'

Then with a gesture that was wholly without guile, utterly innocent, she eased her blouse out of her skirt, pulled it over her head and stood naked before him. She pointed to a little area of scar tissue on her side like a birthmark, just under one breast. She walked towards him and touched his face with a terrible gentleness. Then she pulled him down to her on the grass.

From the belt of trees it seemed as though all the birds in England had combined in a dawn chorus. And high above them a lark suddenly began to sing.

Unaccustomed Sheila

KATE GRENVILLE

Authority always made her feel guilty. The sight of a uniform brought the blood to her cheeks. In fact, the men behind the wooden counters at Heathrow didn't wear uniforms, but she swapped her bag from one hand to the other and wiped her suddenly sweaty palms.

She watched enviously as those in front of her, with quiet pride, showed their British passports. Her own passport suddenly seemed much too new to be genuine, and much too blank inside. She wished it had something official inside, with coats of arms and smudged, important-looking ink.

However, she decided not to worry. After all, here she was at last, in London. Here, she'd surely find men who didn't look blank every time she used a long word, men who knew who Scarlatti was, men who'd laugh at her jokes. No more beer-guts, and huge thighs bursting out of tight shorts, and gigantic feet in thongs.

In front of her in the queue was a thin, sensitive-looking man with a violin case. She edged closer. His face was intelligent and he glanced around with interest, listening to the Americans in front with a slight smile. She caught snatches of their conversation. 'Last year we went to Paris, France . . .' 'Europe's so authentic, doncha think?' She met the violinist's eye for a moment and they smiled, sharing a joke.

He was almost at the counter where the official was stamping the passports. She pressed forward in the queue, suddenly anxious to get through as soon after him as possible. Perhaps if she caught up with him (accidentally, of course), she could make some remark about the Americans, they could ride into London together . . . and who knows what might happen? She could drop some remark about Paganini perhaps, or even slip in that she loved accompanying the violin on the piano. He looked just the sort she had come to London to meet.

Suddenly he had left the counter and had joined the throngs of people beyond the barrier. She would have to hurry. She ruthlessly queue-jumped until she was next to approach the desk.

'Next!'

Now, she was standing in front of the official, handing him her passport. He glanced at the photo, then at her, then back at the photo. He seemed suspicious. Would there be problems after all?

The violinist had almost disappeared. He was slipping away with every moment that this infuriating man flipped through her passport and scrutinised the details.

'How long do you intend to stay in the UK?'

'Oh, about six months.'

Hurry, hurry, she silently urged him as he looked again at the photo. He was young, with blond hair and a heavy moustache. His expression was hard to read and his eyes were very clean, very blue, uncomfortably direct.

'Have you enough money to support yourself or are you intending to work?'

She felt her attention snap back from the violinist and focus on the questions. He was trying to trick her. She knew she wasn't allowed to work.

'Oh no, I plan to live off my savings . . .'

He stared hard at her and she felt herself blushing, felt her eyes slide sideways, felt guilt written all over her face. She could see he was going to be difficult . . .

'What sort of work did you do in Australia?'

'Um, administrative. To do with the arts. Music.'

She felt herself stumbling over the words.

'You are interested in music?'

He stared at her expressionlessly. She began to stammer.

'Yes, um, of course, yes . . .'

'Classical music?'

What were all these questions about? Didn't he believe her?

'Yes, all classical.'

'Chamber music, symphonies, *Lieder* . . . ?'

He was definitely testing her. He didn't believe she knew the first thing about music.

'Mainly chamber music. And choral works.'

'Ah. Bach or Britten?'

This was like some bizarre verbal ping-pong. She willed herself to keep her eyes on his and not get shifty-eyed. Any moment he'd probably ask her to hum the Mozart Requiem.

'And who is your favourite modern choral composer?'

No doubt about it, this was a test. She'd almost forgotten about the violinist, halfway to London by now probably, and was only eager to prove herself innocent.

'Oh, Britten, probably.'

He nodded noncommittally.

'Okay. Would you just take a seat over there, please?'

Stunned, she sat down. The worst had happened – she was going to be questioned, doubted, deported perhaps. So much for meeting Mr Right in England.

Magically, the queue cleared and the official came over and sat down beside her.

'Sorry to keep you.'

'That's okay.'

Go along with him if he wants to play it nicely. 'The thing is,' he said, 'I get off duty now and I just wondered if I could give you a lift into town.'

She stared in amazement, seeing him no longer as officialdom, but a young man of her own age, quite good-looking.

'It's taking advantage of my position a bit, I know, but it gets so boring, when someone interesting comes through I like to get to know them if I can. I'm crazy about music. Especially Britten.'

Room with a View . . .

Coming into London, past all those hundreds of huge buildings, street after street of them, Sandy had wondered why people said it was hard to find a place to live here. But day after day went by and none of the friends-of-friends knew of a room to let. She started answering ads in the paper.

She quickly learned the lingo. 'Garden flat' was a polite euphemism for basement. 'Handy to bus' meant nowhere near the Tube. 'Chelsea' meant the end of Fulham. And so on.

She saw an astonishing collection of rooms. Suicidal bed-sitters, up three flights of stairs that smelt overwhelmingly of the landlord's cats. Chintzy frilly bedrooms with too many kinds of wallpaper and a little old lady who opened the door and launched straight into an endless tale about her sister and didn't stop till Sandy had finally smiled her way out.

There were flats run by stony women who quizzed her on her attitude to housework. Flats run by genteel spinster secretaries who quizzed her on her sex life. Flats owned by ageing bachelors with a twitch at one corner of their mouth who confessed they'd never known a woman at close quarters, so to speak, and wanted to find out what it was like. Twitch, twitch.

So the flat in Maida Vale sounded just the ticket. 'O/R, artistic female, 20s, wanted for mxd. ft.'

Her friendly, reliable, solvent smile was fixed into place before the door opened. The young man who stood there smiled back – a friendly-looking type, although too short and bony to be attractive.

'Hi, I'm Ian.'

'Hi, I'm Sandy.'

It's a bit like a job interview, she thought, following him up the stairs. Hoping you give the right answers.

'This is my room,' he said, ushering her into a bedroom. 'The one for rent's upstairs. I'll show it to you in a minute.'

There was another girl in the room, sitting on the edge of a chair with her handbag on her lap. Obviously another contender.

'This is Anna, she's come about the room too.' He smiled. 'Sit down, tell me about yourself.'

'Well, I'm Australian.'

She saw Anna relax slightly. She thinks that's eliminated me straight away. She hurried on, smiling reassuringly at Ian. 'But of course I'm planning to stay at least a year. I'll be working on and off, so there won't be any problem about money.'

'Yes . . . have you got a job?'

'No.'

She gave him a beaming smile. Her competitive instinct was aroused by Anna's smile.

'Good. What kind of thing do you like doing? Pictures, concerts?'

'Yes, both. I like getting out a fair bit.' She glanced at Anna. She looked a pretty introverted girl. 'I'm a pretty sociable type.'

He smiled again. 'Excellent.'

'Could I see the room?'

'Oh, certainly.'

He smiled again in that unreadable way. The room was wonderful. If necessary she'd quietly throttle Anna for this room. It was lived-in, with no signs that it was about to be vacated.

'When will it be free?'

'Well, next week, or maybe the week after.'

He stared out of the window, speaking vaguely. Her heart sank. She was suddenly convinced he'd already promised the room to Anna.

'Jan, that's the girl who's in here now – she's a bit disorganised.'

Ah, she thought, so maybe his vagueness doesn't mean anything? Maybe it's okay after all? Have I still got a chance?

Suddenly he put his arms around her and whirled her around in a brief waltz. 'See, you can even dance in here.'

She smiled back, startled but pleased.

'You like dancing?'

'Yes, very much.'

'That's great. Well . . . I think that's about all I can say at the moment . . . but I'll be in touch.'

He glanced around secretively. 'Just between you and me, I think you might be the one.'

She stared at him, hardly believing what she heard. 'That's brilliant.'

So it was okay! So much for Anna, sitting down there so smugly.

The doorbell rang. 'Well,' she said, 'I'd better go now, but you've got my phone number, haven't you?'

'I have indeed.'

He smiled and put his hand on her arm for a moment. 'I'll be in touch, Sandy.'

She got her coat from his room and said goodbye to Anna with a momentary pang of guilt, quickly squashed. After all, it was her or me.

On her way out she passed Ian on the stairs, leading up yet another artistic young lady. He winked broadly and Sandy bounced to the front door feeling on air. As she opened the door it was opened from the outside, and she and the girl who'd just used her key looked at each other. This must be Jan, she thought. On impulse she said: 'Hello, you're Jan?'

'Yes . . .'

'I've just been to see your room, it's wonderful. Could I just ask when you might be moving out?' Jan's face puckered in bewilderment.

'Moving out? I'm not moving out, I own this flat . . .' Her face suddenly cleared. 'Oh, Ian's up to his tricks again.'

She looked at Sandy with pity. 'He did this once before. He always says it's a much better way of meeting women than a lonely-hearts' ad. Last time he got enough phone numbers to keep him going for a year.'

Sandy Plays a Waiting Game

Sandy was right on time – she checked her watch – it was exactly twelve noon. Robin was late. There was only a girl sitting on the bench where they'd agreed to meet.

Robin's ad in the magazine had been interestingly short. None of the usual modest claims about being sensitive, intelligent, warm and caring, just two lines: 'Friends demented by my odd hours made necessary by my profession of musician. Any other takers?' This had a confident and straightforward sound she liked – and if he was a musician he couldn't be all bad.

Five past twelve. Her answer had also been short. She'd explained she was Australian, not working and therefore free at odd hours, and that her passion in life was music. She'd explained that she wasn't on the phone, so he'd have to write and give her his phone number if he wanted to meet her.

The reply had sounded good. Resisting the impulse to check her watch yet again, she read it through in her mind: 'Dear Sandy, I spent a year in Australia and liked it very much, and a list of my favourite composers would just about match yours, so let's get together. I'm not on the phone either, unfortunately, but can I suggest meeting at noon on 25 August, on the bench outside the French pub in Dean Street? Drop me a line to confirm.'

And today was 25 August wasn't it? And it was noon? She checked her watch again – in fact it was nearly twelve-fifteen. And this was the French pub in Dean Street? Had she made some sort of ghastly mistake? She had a moment's mad impulse to turn to the girl beside her and ask her if today was 25 August and if this was really the French pub in Dean Street, and was it really noon and fifteen minutes?

Give him till half-past – after all, what with the Tube and the buses always late . . .

His letter had been typed, a pity as she believed you could tell a lot about people from their handwriting. However, the signature had been large and bold – Robin, in bright blue ink, confident but not theatrical. Robin. The name brought forth visions of the kind of Englishman she'd fantasised about in Australia – a bit Evelyn Waugh and Cambridge, maybe a tiny bit effete, but she'd had enough of tough bruisers called Bruce and Mervyn.

Had he had second thoughts? Had he reread her letter and found it gauche, colonial, curt? Or just met someone else? Had another answer arrived from his ad that he liked better? She'd written the postcard by hand – had he taken one look at her sprawling, untidy writing and decided not to turn up?

She shifted on the bench and resolutely turned her thoughts elsewhere. Paranoia gets us nowhere. Give him till half-past. Perhaps, she thought, glancing along the street, this is him coming now, this man in the blue duffel coat with tightly curled brown hair like Benjamin Britten's. He walked down the street quickly, carrying a plastic bag from a record shop . . . she sat up straighter, suddenly sure that *this* was Robin and aware that her heart was beating faster.

He was quite good-looking, and his mouth looked as if it did a lot of smiling. As he approached the bench she suddenly realised that he wouldn't know which of the two girls sitting there was Sandy. Should she stand up? Smile? Otherwise he'd have to stand there and say, er, is one of you Sandy? And it wouldn't be a very stylish start.

She settled back against the bench. As she did so she saw the other girl glance at her watch – so she was also waiting for someone. She didn't want to look like a sad sack when Robin came along, so on a quick impulse she said, 'Is it really twenty past twelve, or is my watch fast?'

The other girl looked at her and smiled ruefully. 'No, it's really twenty past twelve, I'm afraid.'

They smiled at each other.

'You're waiting for someone too?' asked Sandy.

'Yes . . .' the other girl sighed. 'It's women who are supposed to be late all the time, isn't it? But it's always the other way around for me.'

'But they know we'll wait for them don't they?' Sandy said.

'Yes. Although I'm not going to give him much longer.'

'No, me neither,' agreed Sandy.

She glanced up the street again. The man with the Benjamin Britten hair was coming back, she saw with a sudden quickening of interest. It must be him, after all – he'd been too shy to stop the first time, was daunted by two women on the bench instead of one.

She sat forward on the seat and smiled slightly as he approached. He glanced at her, smiled slightly, shook his head and walked on. Was it Robin saying, no, you don't look like my sort? Or just someone saying a polite 'No' to a proposition from a lady of Dean Street.

Sandy stared at his retreating back, feeling annoyed now. She glanced quickly at her watch. Very nearly half-past. Damn him, she'd had enough. A girl has her pride you know.

'Well, I think I'm giving up.'

The other girl had taken the words out of her mouth, standing up. 'I'm going to get myself a drink, and if he comes now, it's just too bad.'

Sandy stood up too. 'I agree. It's thirsty work being stood up. Care to join me?'

They went inside and Sandy bought.

'Well, cheers . . . um . . . What's your name, anyway? I'm Sandy.'

The other girl spluttered suddenly into her drink. Then she grinned from ear to ear.

'Well, pleased to meet you, Sandy. I'm Robin.'

Step Inside, Young Stranger . . .

N. TREGENNA

It was nearly dawn. Someone was lurking in the shadows.

Now the somebody lumbered out of his hiding place and the heavy door in its Gothic setting yielded to his touch. The shadowy figure entered and saw a man sitting at a desk.

'Come in,' said the man at the desk. 'I didn't think I'd have any more callers this night.'

Dominic felt uneasy. The man at the desk was more than he'd bargained for; surprisingly well-built, sitting there behind the massive table.

'What's this place?' he asked, insolently now, his courage coming back.

'I'm sorry,' Cartwright smiled. 'I thought everyone knew. This is the vestry of my church, and I'm keeping a twenty-four-hour vigil. I began yesterday morning at sunrise.'

The lad was eyeing the table where lay piles of notes and silver coins. 'Some racket,' he sneered.

'Hardly. I'm sitting here to receive contributions. Some people think churches run themselves, but it costs a great deal to keep them going.'

'Okay, I'll take your word for it,' the other broke in. 'Isn't it marvellous? What sort of mugs give you all this?'

'All kinds. Sometimes I'm able to help them with their problems. Look what happened this morning, for instance. You turned up.'

'Boy, have I got problems?' Dominic rose and limped across to the table, where he stood looking down at the man in the chair. 'What would you say if I pulled a gun on you and just picked up the takings?'

'I'd say you had a pipe or some object in your pocket and were pointing it at me, hoping I'd think it was a gun. Come, you can do better than that.'

'Then what if you gave me the lot, pretended I'd held you up? Nobody would know.'

'Gave it to you? Why should you imagine a pipsqueak like you had any right to other people's money?'

For answer, Dominic made a sudden lunge, but as he stretched out his hands to grab the notes he felt his arms gripped. Apparently effortlessly Cartwright held him. Cartwright's voice was gentle. 'Rest a bit, that's right. What's to be done about you?'

'I'll be off now.' The boy's voice was weary. He made to go.

'Is your leg very painful?'

'How did you know?'

'I guessed. Was it an accident?'

'Yes. They say I'll get used to it, but . . .'

'The new leg chafes, doesn't it?'

'It was a car crash. It was my fault entirely. I didn't know my leg had gone; I kept feeling for it, later on – in fact I still do, isn't that strange?'

'I've heard it can be like that.'

'I couldn't believe it at first there'd always be a part of me missing. You can't imagine it, of course.'

'Maybe not,' said Cartwright.

'Anyway, I was in trouble up to my neck. There was no insurance. I was ages in hospital. Then I was given a suspended sentence. I told my parents I wanted to think it out for myself. It hasn't worked, of course. I've missed seeing my probation officer, and I'm on my beam ends. When I saw all that money . . .'

'I'm glad you came here,' Cartwright said. 'Very glad, for I think I can help. I can't make any promises, but there's this place run by friends of mine. There's more to it than just patching up bodies and souls. It's an experiment in communal living, really. I'm sure they'll make room for you. That's all, no preaching, no do-gooding.'

He wrote a short letter. Then he took from his wallet two five-pound notes. 'That'll cover your expenses.'

'Just like that? No receipt?'

'Just like that. It's up to you. If you decide to go, take this letter. I'll be in touch with them.'

The boy gulped.

'Go on,' Cartwright urged, 'the sooner you're on your way, the better. Don't thank me, I'm only the instrument.'

Dominic smiled, lurched across the room and was gone. Cartwright sighed. The first glimmer of dawn was filtering through. He was beginning to feel chilly.

He heard his wife's light footsteps on the path before she came in, hurrying as always. Shivering in the draught from the half-open door, he glided out from behind the table.

'There's something I must confess, Margaret. I've had to dip into the Fund.'

'Oh, no!' His wife was exasperated. 'Not again?'

'For a young chap who needed the money more than I did. Electrically driven chairs can wait. I don't think he could wait much longer.'

She smiled at him, and put her hand on the back of the wheel-chair, after she had adjusted the lap-rug. Strange how he could still feel his nonexistent legs when she did that.

'I've often wondered why you keep your other cups and things in the study, but you will have these paraplegic ones out here,' she said, as they passed the shelf.

'Perhaps they're the ones I'm proudest of.'

He patted her hand, and together they went up the path to their breakfast.

Fugitive on The Tobacco Trail

MARTIN CONLAN

It was time to go. His suitcase was already packed. Outside, a thin raw wind raked the desolate promenade . . . he could not have left during the season.

In the candyfloss gaiety of streets thronged with summer-bronzed visitors, his disappearance would have been suspicious, investigated. So Parish had waited, holed up in the sparse anonymity of a cheap hotel room. That was in August.

Winter annihilated autumn in scuds of icy rain; sunglasses no longer glinted on the pier. He waited, alone with his fear. Rain splattered the esplanade. Spiteful gusts from the sea drummed like hail on the cupola of the bandstand. It was there that they had first met. She could have been no older than eighteen.

A few blocks away, in the lounge bar of the Grand Hotel, two men sat over drinks. Upstairs, in their rooms, two suitcases were packed.

MacGregor stared moodily out of the window at the churning sea.

'Seems as if our bird has flown.'

'HQ *will* be pleased. Nearly four months and no arrest.'

It gave O'Neill a wry amusement to taunt his superior. MacGregor had come up the hard way. A product of the orphanage, he had risen from foot-slogging cop to detective inspector.

'What else do they expect? This is a needle-in-a-haystack case. Unless you get that essential bit of luck, you draw a blank.'

'You think he's still here, don't you?'

MacGregor nodded and finished his drink. 'Before we leave, O'Neill, we'll just take one last look around.'

In his room beneath the rafters, Parish sat beside his suitcase. The bowl of the pipe had grown cold in the cup of his hand. He wondered whether he should go to the newsagent on the corner for more tobacco. It was the only shop that stocked the brand he liked.

When the two men left the Grand, the rain had stopped. By the time they reached the cliff top, a stinging wind was blowing in from the sea. It flapped the skirts of their raincoats.

Parish, too, heard the wind. It edged his nerves. He tried to relight his pipe. He longed for the old briar he had lost that summer night. He was not to know that at this very moment a man in a raincoat had found it up there on the windy cliff by an accidental scuff of his foot.

'Been here some time. Still got tobacco in it.'

No wonder it wasn't noticed; same colour as the bracken.

'Doesn't mean a thing,' O'Neill said sullenly.

'No, but according to the forensic lab report there were tobacco shreds on her clothes,' MacGregor sniffed the bowl. 'Very faint, but unmistakable, I'd know it anywhere; takes me back to my youth. I didn't know that brand still existed. Let's see if we can find some, O'Neill.'

They walked down the cliff road, passed the dripping bandstand, into the empty town.

Up in his room, Parish could have heard the splash of their boots in the puddled streets. Through the haze of pipe smoke he saw her face, smiling in the dusk. How willingly he had walked with her to the cliff. Guilelessly without thought of touching her, because in this gay summer town his heart ached for the company of youth.

A bell tinkled in the newsagent's shop on the corner. From behind a shabby curtain an elderly man appeared, myopic, mouse-grey and shuffling.

'Have you a tin of Bouldon's Fine Cut?' MacGregor asked.

The shopkeeper fluttered, like a dusty moth among the stale news of unsold papers, the rows of jars of boiled sweets.

'There's not much call, sir.' He was hesitant, reluctant to sell. 'I save the odd tin for a customer at the guesthouse across the road.'

'Does he smoke a briar?'

Behind the steel-rimmed spectacles the small rodent eyes dilated in surprise.

'Yes, he does, sir. He lost his favourite one. Very cut he was too. You get attached to an old pipe. That was in August.'

'You have a good memory.'

The shopkeeper looked sadly at the unsold newspapers. 'I remember it well. It was the morning after that terrible murder when Mr Parish came in to buy a new one.'

Parish was smoking it now with little pleasure. It was not like the briar she had knocked from his hand that night up on the cliff. Sparks from the bowl had fallen on her clothes.

'See what your filthy old pipe has done to my dress!'

The impact was sickening; the stream of invective from a child's mouth. 'Well, do I have to scream my bloody head off, or are you going to give me twenty quid?'

He had the stunned realisation that it was all a put-up job, planned with the infinite cunning of an immature mind. The nightmare horror of his predicament, up there above the innocent August sands. The contorted adolescent face thrust defiantly close to his.

In a delirium of panic he had seized the slim shoulders, shaking her desperately to still her spurious cries for help. It was not until he released her that he realised, in the coming dark, they had blundered so near to the edge; not until she stumbled and fell and her scream diminished into space.

They were crossing the street; the two men, hastening, splashing puddles.

Parish remembered the summer dark, groping with frantic fingers for the fallen pipe. Thank God they never found it!

Boots scraped on the stone steps. Parish heard the front doorbell jangling through the house, muffled voices in the hall, the housekeeper's slippered feet on the stairs. The knock.

'Mr Parish, are you in? Two gentlemen to see you.'

MacGregor smelt the fragrance of good tobacco as the house-keeper pushed open the door. It took him back to the days of his youth. He was standing on the orphanage steps. The principal, pipe in hand, was saying goodbye. 'Time to go now, MacGregor. Good luck. I'm confident you'll make a splendid policeman.'

'Goodbye, Mr Parish,' he had said, gripping the principal's hand.

MacGregor walked quietly into the room and shook the old man gently by the shoulder.

'It's time to go now, Mr Parish.'

Gun-man Meets the Sleeping Beauty

LARRY TALBOT

Once upon a time there was a Capo Mafiosi who had a beautiful daughter and when she was eighteen her daddy, the Capo, gave her a birthday party. So he invited all the Family heads to a modest affair with three or four thousand guests.

There were ten Family heads, all Mafia Dons, around the country and they all had to be invited but one of them had been in hiding for months because the FBI had turned awkward. So, nine Dons only got invited and they gave the daughter birthday gifts like a bulletproof ball gown and the State of Florida.

They were all standing around drinking Chianti when the door opened and two men with guns walked in, followed by a little old guy in a black silk suit. 'So,' he says, 'you not invite Luigi.'

'Now look, Luigi,' says the proud Daddy Don. 'We all thought you wouldn't show because the heat was on.'

'And Luigi gotta pretty good idea who finger him inna first place,' says the old man and the Daddy Don goes white.

'Not me, Luigi,' he says and steps forward with his hand outstretched, but the bodyguards move in between the two men.

'So all right,' says Don Luigi. 'I tell you what. Alla time nothing happen to Luigi, okay. But if the law catches up then there's a contract on you and your wife and daughter.'

So after a bit the heat dies down or maybe Luigi makes an arrangement with the FBI. Then one day the daughter's birthday comes around again.

Some of her daddy's mob come calling with presents and one says, 'I hear Don Luigi got himself blown up with a bomb that someone accidentally wired to his car.'

Daddy Don turns white and ends the party. He shuts up the house and calls in Charley Thorn and his three brothers as defence experts.

So there they are: Papa and Momma and the beautiful Princess all shut up in the big castle, unable to go out because Luigi's relatives have such long memories. Since the only thing the daughter can do is watch TV she gets the name of the Sleeping Beauty. But one day she turns off the TV and starts writing.

'What you a-doing, Cara?' says Daddy Don.

'I'm learning to be a writer, Daddy,' she tells him.

A while later Charley Thorn is doing the morning inspection when all the lights go out. The family are having breakfast and Daddy is asking someone to pass the toast when a voice says, 'You don't want to get shot on a full stomach.'

They turn around and find themselves looking into tommy-gun muzzles. Momma is a little used to this kind of deal but the daughter slides out of her chair in a dead faint.

'Listen,' say the Don, 'whatever you're getting paid for this, I'll double it.'

'No,' says one of the killers. 'A contract's a contract. There is something you can do, though. We want you to call off Charley and the boys so we can get away. Professional courtesy.'

It just so happens that coming down the highway at this time is a large car driven by a fellow named Ferdie Prince. He's a very good-looking boy and because of this people call him Handsome Prince. In the car with him are several colleagues of his carrying assorted armaments and when they get to the Daddy Don's place they go barrelling in.

Inside, the boss hit-man is saying, 'Tell you what. You set it up so we get clear after we shoot you and we let the kid go. Otherwise she becomes the Sleeping Beauty for real.'

'All right,' says Daddy Don and reaches for the phone. Just

then Handsome Prince kicks in the door and there's a lot of confusion and guns start going off.

When the smoke clears there are a number of bodies littering the place, but they all belong to the hit-men. Daughter is still lying on the floor where she has fallen in a faint. Handsome Prince picks her up and says, 'She's a real cute kid, too,' and he leans over and gives her a big kiss. Her eyelids flutter.

'What – what happened?' she says.

Her daddy says, 'This gentleman and his friends have saved us.'

He turns to Handsome Prince. 'My boy,' he says, 'we owe you a lot.'

'You owe a lot more than you think,' says Handsome Prince. 'We are from Internal Revenue and you are all under arrest.'

He takes a letter from his pocket and says to Beautiful Daughter, 'We came here because of this anonymous letter which, by coincidence, has your monogram on it. If you turn State's evidence you'll be in the clear, especially if I look after you and the money which I'm sure we'll find lying about.'

You'd be amazed how happily they lived ever after.

Jeeves Cracks the Great Pearl Robbery

P. G. WODEHOUSE

———

Thanks to the inimitable Jeeves, Bertie Wooster has managed to break his engagement to Honoria Glossop ('one of those dashed strenuous brainy girls'). With Jeeves, Bertie has fled to the Riviera to escape the wrath of Aunt Agatha who was set on the match.

At Rolville, Bertie meets a charming girl, Aline, and her brother Sydney, a clergyman. Bertie is wearing a scarlet cummerbund which Aline thinks is charming. Jeeves thinks it is deplorable and sulks.

Otherwise all is gaiety and mirth till Jeeves drops his bombshell. Aunt Agatha has followed them to Rolville!

At that moment there is a knock on the door . . .

I'm bound to say it was a shock. My heart stood still and I bit my tongue. 'Come in,' I bleated.

But it wasn't Aunt Agatha after all. It was Aline Hemmingway, looking rather rattled, and her brother, looking like a sheep with a secret sorrow.

'Oh, Mr Wooster!' said the girl, in a sort of gasping way. 'Poor Sydney – it was my fault – I ought never to have let him go there alone.'

At this point the brother, who had been standing by wrapped

in the silence, gave a little cough, like a sheep caught in the mist on a mountain-top.

'The fact is, Mr Wooster,' he said, 'I have been gambling at the casino.'

'Oh!' I said. 'Did you click?'

'If you mean was I successful, I must answer in the negative. I left the casino and returned to the hotel. There I encountered one of my parishioners, a Colonel Musgrave, who chanced to be holiday-making over here – I er – induced him to cash me a cheque for one hundred pounds.'

'Well, that was all to the good, what?' I said, hoping to induce the poor egg to look on the bright side.

'On the contrary, Mr Wooster, I burn with shame as I make the confession, but I went back to the casino and lost the entire sum.'

'I say!' I said. 'You *are* having a night out!'

'And,' concluded the chappie, 'the most lamentable feature of the whole affair is that I have no funds to meet the cheque.'

I'm free to confess that I gazed at him with no little interest and admiration. Never in my life before had I encountered a curate so genuinely all to the mustard.

'Colonel Musgrave,' he went on, gulping somewhat, 'is not a man who would be likely to overlook the matter. He is a hard man. He will expose me to my vic-ah.'

'Mr Wooster,' the girl burst out, 'won't you, won't you help us? We must have the money to get back that cheque from Colonel Musgrave before nine o'clock – he leaves on the nine-twenty. Mr Wooster, will you lend it to us, and take these as security?'

And, before I knew what she was doing, she had produced a case and opened it.

'My pearls,' she said. 'I don't know what they are worth – they were a present from my poor father – but I know they must be worth ever so much more than the amount we want.'

Dashed embarrassing. Made me feel like a pawnbroker. 'No, I say, really,' I protested. 'There's no need for any security, you know. Only too glad the money'll come in useful.'

And I fished it out and pushed it across. The brother shook his head.

224

'Mr Wooster,' he said, 'we cannot permit this.'

'What Sydney means,' said the girl, 'is that you mustn't risk lending all this money without security. If you will just give me a receipt, as a matter of form . . .'

'Oh, well.'

I wrote out a receipt and handed it over, feeling more or less of an ass.

The girl took the piece of paper, grabbed the money and slipped it to brother Sydney, and then, before I knew what was happening, she had darted at me, kissed me, and legged it from the room.

I don't know when I've been so rattled. The whole thing was so dashed sudden and unexpected. Through a sort of mist I could see that Jeeves had appeared and was helping the brother on with his coat; and then the brother came up to me and grasped my hand.

'I can't thank you sufficiently, Mr Wooster!'

'Oh, right-ho!'

'You have saved my good name. "He that filches from me my good name robs me of that which not enriches him and makes me poor indeed." I thank you from the bottom of my heart. Goodnight, Mr Wooster.'

'Your brandy-and-soda, sir,' said Jeeves, as the door shut.

'Rather a sad affair, Jeeves.'

'It is not my place to criticise your actions, sir, but I will venture to say that I think you behaved a little rashly. These fashionable French watering places are notoriously infested by dishonest characters.'

'Now look here, Jeeves,' I said, 'I can stand a lot, but when it comes to your casting asp-whatever-the-word-is on the sweetest girl in the world and a bird in Holy Orders . . .'

'When I was in the employment of Lord Frederick Ranelagh, his lordship was very neatly swindled by a criminal known, I believe, by the sobriquet of Soapy Sid, who scraped acquaintance with us in Monte Carlo with the assistance of a female accomplice.'

'I don't want to butt in on your reminiscences, Jeeves,' I said coldly, 'but you're talking through your hat. How can there have been anything fishy about this business? They've left me the pearls.

Haven't they?' I picked up the case and opened it. 'Oh, Great Scot!'

The bally thing was empty!

'Oh, my Lord!' I said, staring, 'don't tell me there's been dirty work at the crossroads after all!'

'Precisely, sir. It was in exactly the same manner that Lord Frederick was swindled. Soapy Sid substituted a duplicate case and went off with the jewels, the money, and the receipt. On the strength of the receipt he subsequently demanded from his lordship the return of the pearls, and his lordship, not being able to produce them was obliged to pay a heavy sum in compensation.'

I felt as if the bottom had dropped out of things with a jerk.

I mean to say, Aline Hemmingway, you know. What I mean is, if love hadn't actually awakened in my heart there's no doubt it was having a jolly good stab at it.

'By Jove, Jeeves, do you think that parson was Soapy Sid?'

'Yes, sir. I recognised him directly he came into the room.' I stared at the blighter.

'You recognised him?'

'Yes, sir.'

'Then, dash it all,' I said, deeply moved. 'I think you might have told me.'

'I thought it would save disturbance and unpleasantness if I merely abstracted the case from the man's pocket as I assisted him with his coat, sir. Here it is.'

He laid another case on the table beside the dud one, and, by Jove, you couldn't tell them apart. I opened it, and there were the good old pearls, merry and bright. I gazed feebly at the man.

'Jeeves,' I said, 'you're an absolute genius!'

'Yes, sir.'

Relief was surging over me in great chunks. 'It looks to me as though you have saved the old home. I mean, even a chappie endowed with the immortal rind of dear old Sid is hardly likely to have the nerve to come back and retrieve these little chaps.'

'I should imagine not, sir.'

'Well, then – oh, I say, you don't think they are just paste or anything like that?'

'No, sir. These are genuine pearls, and extremely valuable.'

226

'Well then, dash it, I'm on velvet.'

'Hardly that, sir. I think that you will have to restore the pearls to their rightful owner.'

'But who is the rightful owner?'

'Mrs Gregson, sir.'

'What? Aunt Agatha?'

'It was all over the hotel an hour ago that Mrs Gregson's pearls had been abstracted, sir.'

The situation was beginning to unfold before me. 'I'll go and give them back to her, eh? It'll put me one up, what?'

'If I might make the suggestion sir. I think it would strengthen your position if you were to affect to discover the pearls in Mrs Gregson's suite – say, in a bureau drawer . . .'

Long before I reached Aunt Agatha's lair I could tell that the hunt was up. Divers chappies in hotel uniform and not a few chambermaids of sorts were hanging about. Among those present I noticed a chambermaid in hysterics, and a whiskered cove who looked like a bandit, as no doubt he was, being the proprietor of the hotel.

Aunt Agatha waved me away. No welcoming smile for Bertram.

'Oh, don't bother me now,' she snapped. 'I've lost my pearls. They have been stolen.'

Here Wilfred the Whisker-King, who seemed to have been taking a rest between rounds, stepped into the ring again and began to talk rapidly in French. Cut to the quick he seemed. The chambermaid whooped in the corner.

'Sure you've looked everywhere?' I asked. 'I've often lost a collar-stud and . . .'

'Do try not to be so maddening, Bertie! I have enough to bear without your imbecilities. Oh, be quiet! Be quiet!' she shouted.

And such was the magnetism of what Jeeves called her forceful personality that Wilfred subsided as though he had run into a wall. The chambermaid continued to go strong.

'I say,' I said, 'I think there's something the matter with this girl. Isn't she crying or something?'

'She stole my pearls! I am convinced of it.'

This started the whisker-specialist off again, and I left them at it and wandered off on a tour round the room. I slipped the pearls out of the case and decanted them into a drawer. By the time I'd done this Aunt Agatha had reached the frozen *grande dame* stage and was putting the Last of the Bandits through it in the voice she usually reserves for snubbing waiters.

'I say,' I said, 'don't want to interrupt you and all that sort of thing, but aren't these the little chaps?'

I pulled them out of the drawer and held them up.

I don't know when I've had a more juicy moment. It was one of those occasions about which I shall prattle to my grandchildren – if I ever have any. Aunt Agatha simply deflated before my eyes. It reminded me of when I once saw some intrepid aeronauts letting the gas out of a balloon.

'Where – where – where?' she gurgled.

'In this drawer. They'd slid under some paper.'

I dug out my entire stock of manly courage, breathed a short prayer, and let her have it right in the thorax.

'I must say, Aunt Agatha, dash it,' I said crisply. 'I think you have been a little hasty, what? I mean to say, giving this poor man here so much anxiety and worry.'

'Yes, yes,' chipped in the poor man.

'And this unfortunate girl. You've accused her of pinching the things on absolutely no evidence. I think she would be jolly well advised to bring an action for – whatever it is.'

'*Mais oui, mais oui, c'est trop fort!*' shouted the Bandit Chief. And the chambermaid looked up enquiringly, as if the sun was breaking the clouds.

'I shall recompense her,' said Aunt Agatha, feebly.

'Yes, by damn! It's too bad!' cried the whiskered marvel. 'You careless old woman! You give my hotel bad names. Tomorrow you leave the hotel.' And more to the same effect, all good, ripe stuff. And presently, having said his say, he withdrew, taking the chambermaid with him, the latter with a crisp tenner clutched in a vice-like grip.

I turned to Aunt Agatha, whose demeanour was now rather like that of one who, picking daisies on the railway, has just caught the down-express in the small of the back.

'There was something you wished to speak to me about?' I said.

'No, no. Go away, Bertie. I wish to be alone.'

'Oh, right-ho!' I said. 'Right-ho! right-ho!' And back to the good old suite.

'Ten o'clock, a clear night and all's well, Jeeves,' I said, breezing in.

'I am gratified to hear it, sir.'

'If twenty quid would be any use to you Jeeves . . . ?'

'I am much obliged, sir.'

There was a pause. And then – well, it was a wrench, but I did it. I unstripped the cummerbund and handed it over.

'Do you wish me to press this, sir?'

I gave the thing one last longing look. It had been very dear to me.

'No,' I said, 'take it away; give it to the deserving poor. I shall never wear it again.'

'Thank you very much, sir,' said Jeeves.

How Ubaldo Cleaned Up at Sloppy Joe's

DOUGLAS RAILTON

'Son of my soul,' Ubaldo's mother said, 'in my opinion, it's long past time you brought home a wife . . .'

Ubaldo was having his supper. The Spanish province of Murcia is not noted for fine fare, and the black-eyed peas and cornmeal bread dipped in rancid olive oil hardly looked tempting. Ubaldo had just given his observation on this. To be exact, he had said that, in future, he would dine with the pig.

'A strong, healthy, obedient wife,' his mother continued, 'handy with a pan and a needle.'

'And who do you suggest?' Ubaldo wanted to know, half interested.

His mother shrugged. 'Does it matter? They all look alike . . . Now in my day, a girl tried to be different from the others in some way.'

She went to an old press in one corner of the kitchen, unscrewed a piece of fancy moulding and took out of a cavity two five-hundred-peseta notes.

'Here,' she said. 'Take this.'

Ubaldo grinned. 'I often wondered where you kept it, Mother.'

'Never mind that,' she said. 'Get the first bus to the city in the morning; and come back with a wife.'

Though Ubaldo was past forty, he had never been to the city before. The height of the buildings, the speed of the traffic, the criss-cross complex of boulevards all made him so nervous he nearly turned tail and got back in the bus to go home again. Then he thought of his mother's scorn. She'd tell all her cronies in the village. He'd never live it down.

So Ubaldo began to follow the streets, his ploughman's walk and coarse black country clothes making him conspicuous among the crowds of well-dressed shoppers. To avoid them, he turned into the poorer thoroughfares and towards midday found himself in what is probably the meanest district in the city which is the Barrio Ruzafa.

Ubaldo was tired and hot and very thirsty. His feet in his new shoes were painfully blistered. He longed for a friendly word from someone, even a nod. And with this thought clearly in his mind he entered an establishment anxious to make its way in the world as Sloppy Joe's North American Bar.

'Sooner or later, a wife is bound to turn up,' Ubaldo assured himself as he ordered a big pitcher of ice-cold beer. He took the pitcher and a pewter pot into a corner where he could see what was going on and, at the same time, not be in anyone's way.

To tell the truth, nothing much ever did go on in Sloppy Joe's. The afternoon slowly wore itself out. Ubaldo sipped his beer contentedly. A dog snored at his feet. Shadows on the uncarpeted plank floor became longer. Dust settled. Traffic noise dulled, and the quiet within Sloppy Joe's contained a hint of infinity.

Ubaldo was thinking of his village, of the strip of famished ground he sharecropped. Such thoughts gave him pleasure. He began to hum, softly, and to knock out the timing with his knuckles on the table-top.

The emotion imprisoned in Ubaldo's soft humming at last made an escape in words, the words of the flamenco-singer's art, and each word was dark and mysterious, carried on a harsh, wailing sob, rising and falling but controlled, pure, noble, true.

Across the room, two narrow-waisted gypsies began a complicated counterpoint with the hard, dry clap of their palms. A dwarf, with one eye like a big hailstone, seated himself beside Ubaldo, babying a battered guitar on his knees. For a few seconds the dwarf only listened, his head rocking with small nods, then he aimed a wedge-shaped thumbnail and with the unexpected suddenness of lightning struck a black thunder of chords, a silver rain of arpeggios.

Ubaldo's head went back, his eyes shut tight. He held a clenched fist at his ear, as if it contained the secret source of his inspiration. A vein knotted and thickened at his temple; sweat off his forehead seeped into his closed eyes and trickled over his purpling face.

He sang of the high sierra and the red earth, the green alfalfa grass withered in the long smouldering-yellow days of summer, the watercourses that dried up and stock barren and without milk, of the white mule ploughing the stony ground and the landlord who raised the rents every year.

He sang of the vine cut by a jealous neighbour, and of the winds, of mountain cats and buzzards and sheep frozen to the ground in winter.

He sang of his cruel and beautiful world, seriously and with respect, honourably and exactly, while the gipsy hand-clapping and the sombre guitar copied his mood, echoed his memories, decorated them with dazzling variations.

Unnoticed, Sloppy Joe's packed to the doors. The waiter was run off his feet serving orders. His brother-in-law came in to help him. Then the brother-in-law's second cousin. They had to send out for extra liquor. The whole district was congregating in the bar. There had never been anything like it. The *juerga*, as it is called, went on for three hours.

'Now we pass the hat round,' the dwarf whispered out of the side of his mouth.

Ubaldo's share was five thousand pesetas. He fastened the notes into the money-belt stitched inside his pants. I'd better go for my bus, he thought.

He got on at the depot and presently the bus was rumbling through the lamplit streets and out beyond the environs of the city. Across the aisle, a woman's face seemed familiar. He looked again. Finally, unable to hold in his curiosity, he said: 'It's Ramona Aguero, isn't it? Your father had the paraffin and candle-store, am I not right? We used to go to school together, but you went to the city to look for a husband and that's the last we heard of you . . .

'I suppose you know your father died last week? Too bad . . . we all liked him. He was highly thought of. Presumably you are going to take over the vending of paraffin and candles? It's quite a tidy business, I should think, although with the electricity coming to the village it may be the future for candles is not too bright, if I may be permitted a small joke . . .'

The bus rolled on . . .

Before the journey was half over, Ubaldo had bought Ramona's shop. And by its end, Ramona had agreed the practical wisdom, at the same time, of becoming Ubaldo's wife . . .

'Go to the city,' Ubaldo's mother had said, 'and bring back a wife' – as though it was a simple, straightforward matter.

His mother had been quite right. It was perfectly simple. You took the bus to the big city and you came back with a wife.

Lucky Thirteen

WILLIAM GLYNNE-JONES

Old Boyo stood on the river bank and smiled as he stuffed into his capacious coat pocket the four trout he had caught that morning.

Earlier he had been disturbed by the thought that today was Friday, the thirteenth. This awesome number signified to Boyo what it conveyed to so many humans, lawful or unlawful – bad luck.

Now, however, his doubts and fears were gone. As he neared Meadow Pool he saw something move beneath the surface.

'Whew!' he gasped. 'What a beauty!'

At the bottom of the pool he saw the salmon.

'Two quid a pound – that's what I'll pay you for a fresh salmon, Boyo,' Tom Burges, the landlord of the Blue Boar, had promised.

Boyo chuckled. All that money – just for pulling a salmon out of the pool! The prospect amused him and, drawing his coat about him, he hurried homewards.

Boyo tossed the limp trout on to the kitchen table. From a drawer in the battered oak dresser he took a long strand of fine, steel wire. He was about to leave his lonely cottage when suddenly his eyes fell on a grease-stained calendar on the wall. He swallowed hard. 'Remember, Boyo, it's the thirteenth! . . . Rubbish! Why should I be frightened of a number?'

The old poacher hastened back to the pool, planning the capture of the big fish.

'How's things goin' Boyo?'

Startled, Boyo looked across the river. Limping along on the opposite bank was his rival, Jacky Simpson. Good job it wasn't the water-bailiff!

'Any luck?' called Jacky.

'Had a couple o' small ones in the stream.'

'Anything in Meadow Pool?'

Boyo hesitated. 'N-no,' he lied. 'Nothing in the pool . . . nothing. Water's too low.'

That lame Jacky Simpson – he was everywhere, watching like a stoat – the old fool! And he was jealous, too.

Boyo waved half-heartedly to his rival and proceeded on his mission.

'In a bit of a rush isn't he, considering there's nothing in the pool?' thought Jacky. 'Today's Friday, and Friday's my lucky day. Wasn't it such a day I caught that whopper of a salmon?' His eyes narrowed. He quickened his pace and limped in the direction his rival had gone.

Boyo reached the pool and, kneeling cautiously on the frayed trunk, he dragged himself along it, his eyes straining into the shadowy waters.

He gripped the tree trunk between his knees, fumbled in his bag and drew out the wire coil. Deftly he fashioned one end into a noose and lowered it into the water, manoeuvring it until it hung directly behind the salmon's tail. Then, with a sharp, strong pull of the wrists, he drew the noose over the tail and along the gleaming body.

The big fish wriggled and turned, lashing and flaying with its powerful tail in an effort to break free. It darted towards the bank – but Boyo held on. He pulled steadily on the wire, inch by inch, until the salmon was not more than a few feet from the side. Then concentrating all his energy he gave a tremendous upward tug.

The salmon hurtled through the air above him. Boyo heard the heavy thud as it hit the bank behind him. He scrambled from the withered tree trunk. The salmon slipped from his embrace, its tail flicking convulsively.

Boyo rose slowly to his feet. 'A twenty-pounder,' he breathed. 'Might be all of twenty-five . . .

'Twenty at two pounds . . . that's forty quid!'

Boyo grinned, and slapped his thighs. He was more than satisfied. He'd caught a twenty-pound salmon and earned forty quid in two hours. He reached for the bag inside his coat and unrolled it on the grass. Dragging his heavy catch by the tail, he forced it awkwardly into the bag.

Suddenly, he heard the rustling of leaves and the tread of footsteps at the far end of the pool. A strange fear seized him – a sort of terror. The footsteps drew nearer, but the figure approaching was hidden from view behind the thick screen of trees and bushes.

Agitatedly, he gripped the heavy canvas bag and strove to lift it over his shoulder.

'Hey there! Drop that bag!'

The voice, deep and commanding, echoed loudly in the silence. Boyo felt a faint, cold tremor sweep through his veins. He saw in his mind's eye the calendar and the fateful number thirteen. He had a vision of a stern-faced magistrate scowling at him from the bench.

'Boyo Jenkins, this is not the first occasion that you have been brought before me. This poaching must be stopped. I have found that a fine is no deterrent, so I sentence you to . . .'

Terrified, Boyo threw down the bag and ran headlong across the fields, not even deigning to look back. Jacky Simpson stepped smiling from the shelter of a bramble bush and loped towards the canvas bag. The salmon, still alive, had slithered to the grass, its tail flicking, its mouth agape.

Jacky's eyes glinted with hate and suspicion. He glared balefully across the fields at the distant figure of his old rival.

'Nothing in the pool, eh? No – nothing for you, Boyo, but something for me. One thing you didn't know, my fine friend. Today's Friday, an' Friday's my lucky day, see?'

Jacky stooped over the salmon. 'Now, my pretty one,' he cooed, 'you come along with me.'

All at once a heavy hand descended on his shoulder.

'So that's your game, eh?' he heard a gruff voice say. 'Caught you red-handed. And Friday's your lucky day, eh?'

Speechless, Jacky looked up into the scowling face of the water-bailiff.

The Thick Brown Door

PETER KNIVETON

He hated that thick brown door. On this side was a full free life of women, drink, fast cars. Of the hunt and conquest, of parties and music. Beyond that door lay fear; raw, nerve-shattering fear. But the life he led was impossible without opening the door and becoming immersed in a sordid world of hate, greed and politics.

The nerve on the left of his scalp twitched and the nervous tic spread down to his left eye. He took a deep breath, wiped his palms on the side of his trousers and, turning the doorknob, walked through into a hell of his own making. Sir Simon Foster-Udell was to receive his next assignment.

Ten minutes later he stood on the pavement outside the house looking for a taxi. It was three o'clock on a London December afternoon and a bitter wind hastened the steps of Christmas shoppers. Their laden arms weighting the effort in red faces and panting white breath, resembling goods engines which in fact they were.

Simon gave up the task of flagging for a cab and bent into the icy blast that was Russia's contribution to an English winter. He made for a convenient club, in order to down several examples of the Scottish use of peat water and barley. A flickering fire cast reflections on mahogany, leather and glass. The old man smiled. 'Nice to see you again, Sir Simon.'

'Hello Stuart, a thumping great Red Hackle please.'

'Of course, sir, right away.'

Simon stood, back to the fire. A tall man over six foot, but lean. Well dressed, dark complexion, black-haired, southern European-looking, but in fact a Scot. His face marked by heavy scars on the left side from temple to chin, the result of racing a Jaguar beyond its road-holding capabilities.

To the world a fun-loving rich baronet, attractive to women to whom his dangerous good looks hinted at a devilry that few could resist. To the man behind the thick brown door Foster-Udell was a calculating, merciless individual. Unable to live on his income from a trust fund set up by his knowing father, forced to eke out a wasteful existence between allowance cheques by undertaking various assignments. The man behind the thick brown door despised Foster-Udell.

Simon swore each mission would be his last. The past four years had played havoc with his nerves. His assessments, at times faulty, had caused unnecessary complications. Reactions that in the past compared with the finest racing drivers, had dulled. He was aware of these facts, aware of the sanctuary he found in the golden liquid of his homeland. Aware that without Nembutal his nights would be a dark extension of day.

He remembered the expression on the face of the man behind the thick brown door. 'Damn him, what gave him the right to prejudge me, a bloody executive, just passing on messages for the people who made the decisions, but lacked the stomach to deal directly with me. A bloody parasite, office at ten, home at five, what the hell did he know of life other than a train timetable, the local rose show, what grade of carpet he was entitled to, and what brand made the best tea.'

Simon stared into his whisky glass, the colour of gold, a material thing that is responsible for more grief than enough. He thought of his orders again; they were brief and concise, he would commence the operation in London at nine-thirty the following morning. It was vital that Simon retained the initiative from beginning to end of the whole operation. He would be in a state of siege at times, but sheer concentration and professionalism would bring him through.

Just after nine the following morning Simon moved slowly towards the huge building, jogged along by the crowds. At the entrance stood a security guard, but the metal identification disc he had been given got Simon through this first screening and he made his way to the first floor where his contact would be waiting. It would be on this floor that the action had been planned.

His contact was ready. 'Good, you are on time.' The contact looked at Simon. 'How do you feel?'

'I'm ready,' replied Simon.

'Come and check the equipment.' He led Simon to a small room.

Simon quickly changed. He realised the clothes made a big difference, and he would be accepted mainly because of that fact. His face was of secondary consideration, although he did manage to hide the scars on his face.

'Weapons?' Simon asked.

'Behind the partition, follow me.'

The people they passed were unaware of anything unusual. Simon was keyed up, intensifying each action. He tried to relax, concentrating on behaving perfectly in his new character. The area that Simon would use put him in full view of the public. At least Simon would have them coming towards him, unsuspecting at first, giving time for Simon quickly to assess the opposition and to decide in which way to deal with the troublemakers.

'I must leave you now.' The contact looked at his watch. 'Everything you need is in the containers.' Simon could see the containers behind him. He took from the left one a Luger-type automatic, and checked the weight and action; it was fully loaded. He also needed a quick-firing weapon and found what he was looking for: an Uzi model machine-pistol. Both weapons were black and treated so that the light would not glint off them. No serial numbers, probably Japanese. But what the hell Simon thought, so long as they did the job, and he had no doubt they would. They had before.

There was no hesitation in his movements now, he knew instinctively what he required. Simon checked his watch again, it was almost zero hour. At any minute they would come towards him.

His pulse rate was up, but now the job was about to start the adrenalin was pumping into his bloodstream.

'Let them come.' He muttered again, 'Let them come.' He tucked the automatic into his wide belt and laid the machine-pistol within easy reach.

Simon saw the doors open, a moment of panic swept him when he saw how many, he fought off his nerves, he was a professional: he could handle them, he had done so before. They were not aware of him as yet and he took a brief moment to check the main trouble. All sizes, standard humans, he thought.

He had been spotted! They turned towards him, their faces changed, hard and cruel, greed in their eyes. 'Oh God,' he said. A howl had gone up and they were almost on him. The sweat poured down Simon's face and his mouth went dry, he fumbled for the guns, the howling became distinct.

'Father Christmas,' the children yelled, and with a shudder Simon pulled the left-hand present container to him.

How he hated the man behind the thick brown door.